UNDER A BLACKBERRY MOON

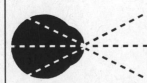

This Large Print Book carries the
Seal of Approval of N.A.V.H.

Under a Blackberry Moon

Serena B. Miller

THORNDIKE PRESS
A part of Gale, Cengage Learning

GALE
CENGAGE Learning·

Farmington Hills, Mich • San Francisco • New York • Waterville, Maine
Meriden, Conn • Mason, Ohio • Chicago

GALE
CENGAGE Learning®

Thorndike Press® Large Print Christian Romance.
The text of this Large Print edition is unabridged.
Other aspects of the book may vary from the original edition.
Set in 16 pt. Plantin.

LIBRARY OF CONGRESS CATALOGING-IN-PUBLICATION DATA

Miller, Serena, 1950–
    Under a blackberry moon / by Serena B. Miller. — Large print edition.
        pages ; cm. — (Thorndike Press large print Christian romance)
    ISBN-13: 978-1-4104-6646-4 (hardcover)
    ISBN-10: 1-4104-6646-9 (hardcover)
    1. Ojibwa women—Fiction. 2. Wilderness survival—Fiction. 3. Wilderness areas—Michigan—Fiction. 4. Upper Peninsula (Mich.)—Fiction. 5. Large type books. I. Title.
    PS3613.I55295U55 2014
    813'.6—dc23   2013047707

Published in 2014 by arrangement with Revell Books, a division of Baker Publishing Group

Printed in Mexico
1 2 3 4 5 6 7 18 17 16 15 14

"I will never leave you nor forsake you."

Joshua 1:5 NIV

1

Bay City, Michigan
May 15, 1868

"Whose squaw are you, girl?"

The hand gripping her upper arm belonged to a man with bad teeth and foul breath. Moon Song did not know him, but the sidewalks of Bay City were thick with men right now. Young ones. Old ones. Broken ones. Mean ones.

With the spring river drive still going on, "river rats" and "shanty boys" were flowing into town along with the giant pine logs they had herded down the many rivers draining the Saginaw Valley. In fact, the bay was so full of logs right now it bore no resemblance to a body of water. It looked more like a giant, undulating wooden floor.

"Answer me!" The man gave her a slight shake.

Moon Song was glad she had secreted a sharp knife in the side of her right moccasin boot before walking downtown. Her new friend, Delia, had suggested she do so. Delia was a former prostitute, an old woman who had quit the brothel business and was now Robert Foster's business partner. She knew a great deal about survival. Moon Song paid attention when she spoke.

"Lots of shanty boys prowling the streets," Delia had told her. "Most aren't bad men, but with a winter's worth of pay in their pockets and too much liquor in their bellies, they're on the lookout for any woman they can find. A good sharp knife helps a woman keep control of her . . . options."

Fortunately, Delia told her, they tended to leave those women they deemed "decent" or "respectable" alone, choosing to pour much of their winter's pay into the coffers of the Catacombs, a huge warren of a building that was a city block square, where hundreds of "indecent" women plied their trade. Delia had told her to stay as far away from that building as she could, and she had.

"Who do you belong to?" The man shoved his face close to hers. He had one weepy eye, and his foul breath made her wrinkle her nose. The diseased eye was disgusting.

"Answer me. Are you someone's woman?" He let go of her and fingered one of her braids. "Or are you free for the taking?"

She was grateful that she had left her baby with Katie. Without the little one strapped to her back, she was free to fight if necessary. She hoped it would not be necessary.

"Leave alone, please," she said in a reasonable voice.

"You back-talking me, girl?" The man's voice lowered a notch and became deadly.

There were plenty of people on the wooden sidewalks of Bay City, and it was broad daylight. Still, she disliked attracting attention to herself unless it was necessary. Even though she was living in a white town, if she was quiet and kept her head down, people usually left her alone whenever she went on errands.

"What you got there, Daddy?" A younger man who resembled the man with the bad teeth walked over to investigate.

"A pretty little Indian girl nobody seems to be claiming."

He grabbed the back of her neck and squeezed. A threat.

"Leave alone, please." This time she enunciated a little more carefully. Her English was getting better every day.

The son stood in front of her. "What's your name?"

"My name?" In spite of the older man's

11

hand at her neck, she drew herself up to her full height. "Moon Song!"

In her village, each child was given a unique name by the village elders. There were no other Moon Songs. It was her name and hers alone.

The moon had been full the night she was born in her mother's tent. The elders heard her grandmother, Fallen Arrow, singing a soothing song to her new little granddaughter minutes after her birth, and that had been the root of her lovely name.

She was Moon Song, and she came from the wise Chippewa. Her grandfather had once been a great warrior and chief. She was not a possession. She was not a purchase. She was not a toy. She was definitely not one of the low women so hungry for alcohol that she would do anything for a few minutes of drink-induced oblivion.

The shaft of her knife was hidden by the long, full, white-woman skirt she wore, but it was there, and easily reachable. This white-woman skirt was a handy thing with its deep pockets and ability to conceal.

"So what are you doing downtown, little Miss Moon Song?" It was the son who now stroked one of her long braids. "You working for someone?"

She wished these men would let her pass

so that she could go back to her errand. She had looked forward to purchasing some small beads today. Her baby was eight moons old this week and would enjoy playing with the bright pattern she had devised to decorate the new little moccasins she had made for him.

"I work Robert Foster camp. I cook."

She waited for recognition to dawn and for the men to leave her alone. Robert was greatly respected in this town. Maybe the two men would leave her alone if they knew she was associated with him.

"I never liked Foster much." The son grabbed a handful of her hair and jerked her back against the outside wall of the store where she had been planning to do her shopping. "He makes all the other lumber camp operators look bad. Me included. It would serve him right to take his girl."

Strangely enough, the sidewalk was full of people hurrying by on various errands, but no one was coming to her defense.

She knew the sad truth. If she had been a "respectable" white woman, not only would people intervene, but there was a good chance that the men would be thrown in jail. The fact that she was Indian made her fair game, which was why she carried a knife in her boot. She lifted her right foot and reached for it. Ready to do battle, she gave voice to a loud war cry.

Before she could grasp the knife, the older man grabbed both of her arms and pinned them against the small of her back.

"Unless I miss my guess" — he chuckled as she struggled against his vicelike grip — "this little lady has something in her boot she was planning to gut one of us with."

The son reached down, slipped the knife from her boot, and held the tip beneath her chin.

"Daddy's lived with squaws before. We know all your little tricks."

A small knot of townspeople had begun to gather. None of them moved to help her. She scanned their faces for an ally. Most of them, even the women, appeared only mildly curious.

"Maybe you could soften her up with a pouch of beads," one of the men offered. There was a ripple of laughter.

What the man did not know was that there was a second knife that smart Delia had insisted she hide in a secret pocket of her billowing skirt. A thin knife that Delia called a "stiletto" was within easy reach, if she could free one of her hands long enough to access it.

"I not fight," she lied. "Let go. I go with you."

"What do you think we are?" the son sneered. "Stupid?"

Old Stink Breath was standing directly behind her. This was a mistake on his part. She was young and strong and could kick like a mule. With both of his hands holding hers, his crotch was woefully unprotected. It would not be difficult to back-kick against the man's oh-so-vulnerable spot. If she could make him lose his grip, it would take her less than a second to grab the small stiletto.

She willed herself to relax her body, hanging her head, allowing her shoulders to droop as though giving up. This was hard, because she was ready to fight. Pretending to give up was difficult when every muscle was coiled and ready to spring into action.

"You win. I go." She allowed her voice to rise as though with hope. "You have whiskey?"

He gave a grunt of satisfaction and relaxed his grip. She could almost feel him grinning at the spectators as he savored his victory over her. "These squaws are all alike."

No they weren't.

At that moment, she kicked backward with all her might and felt a satisfying give in the man's soft underparts. He cried out and doubled over, holding himself with both hands, and as the full effect of her kick hit him, he began to retch. His son, seeing the vomit splashing on the sidewalk, let out a curse and took several steps backward to put plenty of distance between himself and the vile stuff.

She should have run back to Delia's at that point and gotten clean away, but her blood was boiling with anger, and not one drop of caution remained in her body. All she felt was a wild exultation as she whipped out Delia's stiletto and raised it above her head, grasping the shaft with both hands.

Isaac Ross, who was known to his logging friends as Skypilot — their nickname for anyone who had ever been a preacher — was thoroughly enjoying a day of lounging on the front porch of Mrs. Wilcox's boardinghouse. It had been a month since he'd come into town with the rest of Foster's lumbering crew, and it had been a glorious month. Robert and Katie had offered to let him stay with them for the summer, but that house of theirs was all crowded up with their three children, Robert's sister and brother-in-law, and Moon Song.

Just because he'd gotten hurt trying to

save Robert's little girl from a falling tree did not, in Skypilot's opinion, obligate Robert to shelter him beneath his roof all summer long. He loved Robert and Katie's combined family, but the peace and quiet of having a boardinghouse room all to himself was a luxury for which he was willing to spend his hard-earned money.

Most of the shanty boys, when the logging was finished each spring, felt compelled to engage in a wild spree the minute they came roaring into town. Their pockets heavy with their winter's pay, and their heads empty of any thought except spending it all in a few glorious days, were a great enticement to various enterprising individuals.

The woodsmen were lucky if, at the end of their spree, all they ended up with was a vicious hangover or a busted head from fights with other shanty boys over various injustices, imagined or not. Many were "rolled" by the pretty ladies who worked out of the Catacombs, after being drugged by knockout drops that were thoughtfully provided to the girls by saloon keepers who got a cut of whatever was found in the men's pockets. Some of the men were not only robbed but dumped unconscious into the waters of Lake Huron. Sometimes they survived. Sometimes they did not. No one in town seemed concerned one way or the other.

Bay City was not known for law and order, especially when it came to the anonymous shanty boys who infested their town once a year like hungry locusts.

It had taken self-discipline to keep from going the same route. He well understood the hunger that sent men barreling into town ready to drink it dry, but Skypilot had managed to avoid all of that. A long-standing personal temperance pledge had kept him out of the saloons, as well as the brothels and gambling houses.

His own coming-out-of-the-woods spree had not involved liquor or painted women, but there were other pleasures in Bay City upon which to splurge, and he had enjoyed every one. First had been the purchase of new, ready-made clothing from the skin outward. These he had paid to have delivered to the bathhouse, where a long, hot soak in a deep porcelain tub had sluiced the smoke, sawdust, sweat, and lice from his body. While he soaked, a barber cut his hair and shaved off his itchy beard, leaving about a pound of hair mounded on the floor behind him.

When he finally rose from the soapy water, he toweled off, donned his fresh set of clothing — which was not crawling with vermin — and felt reborn. With stylishly short, wet brown hair parted in the middle and the scent of bay rum splashed upon his bare face, he had then sought out a boarding-house with the reputation for the cleanest sheets and the fewest bedbugs in town. After securing a private room, he had set out to walk around Bay City and see the sights. A small theatre group set up in a tent outside town had given him several hours of plea-sure. There were plans afoot to build a lend-ing library next year — which would be a remarkable thing — but for now, a new mercantile store had been added since he'd last spent time in the city. In it, he had found a corner devoted to reading material they had for sale, which to him was like discovering buried treasure.

Newspapers from faraway cities, albeit some a few months old, beckoned to him with news of the world. He bought stacks of them. He also bought four brand-new *Police Gazettes* as well as a red-colored volume entitled *The Celebrated Jumping Frog of Calaveras County,* a collection of stories by a new author calling himself Mark Twain.

This afternoon, he found himself settled on the boardinghouse porch with a glass of sweet, iced lemonade at his elbow. He shook open a fresh newspaper and settled down for a nice, long afternoon of doing absolutely nothing.

The paper rustled in his hands when a high-pitched, undulating war cry split the air, making chills run up and down his spine. He dropped his paper and saw a dark-haired Indian woman in a voluminous blue skirt struggling to extricate herself from two men. Skypilot leaped over the banister and ran. That woman was Moon Song, the woman who had stumbled into their camp this past fall with a starving newborn baby in her arms. Moon Song was his friend, and from what he could see, she was getting ready to plunge a long, narrow knife into the back of some man's neck.

Moon Song felt a strong, muscular arm grab her around the waist, lift her off her feet, and grab the hand that held the stiletto.

"Not a good idea, little one," Skypilot said.

"Stink Breath deserve to die!" Thwarted, she fought back against the man who was holding her.

"Nope," Skypilot said calmly. "He might deserve to die, but I'm not going to let you do this. Now stop squirming and behave yourself."

The impulse to kill the vile old man was so great that her feet kicked against the man holding her, but he did not give in. Perhaps it was because her kicks were not quite as strong as they had been. She didn't really want to hurt Skypilot.

"Where did you get this?" He twisted the stiletto out of her hand and held it up to inspect it closer.

"Delia." She could feel her heart rate begin to slow. She stopped struggling, and when she did, Skypilot sat her back down on her feet and let loose of her. She nodded at the older man, who was looking pale and shaky from the kick she'd given him. "That bad man needs to go away."

"No doubt." He smiled down at her, and she felt herself calmed just by his presence. He was one of those rare men who never got upset and never lost his temper. Even more importantly, he had always been kind to her. "But not now, and not by you."

"That is my boot knife." She pointed at the son. "He take it from me."

"Give it here." Skypilot reached out his hand, palm up. "You know it's rude to steal a lady's knife."

Skypilot was so much bigger than the father and son duo that the son handed it over to him without a fight, but couldn't resist a parting shot.

"That squaw ain't no lady, she's an animal." The son spat on the sidewalk. "She's nothing but a rabid dog that oughta be put out of its misery."

This was more than even the easygoing Skypilot wanted to hear. He grabbed a handful of the man's hair and practically lifted him up off the ground by it. "Apologize to the lady."

"She ain't no —"

Skypilot lifted him three inches higher and gave him a shake. "Apologize to the lady."

The man mumbled an unrepentant apology, and Skypilot dropped him. "I guess that will have to do." He handed the knife back to her. "Here you go. Just don't go waving it around again." She slipped it into her boot. The crowd, sensing the entertainment was over, wandered off.

Skypilot gave a low whistle as he watched the son help his father limp down the street. "I surely hope you never get that mad at me."

2

"She had a boot knife?" Robert closed the door of his office. "And stiletto?"

"She did." Skypilot laid the stiletto in the middle of Robert's scarred mahogany desk. "And she had full intentions of using it."

Robert collapsed into a chair. "Where did she get them?"

"Evidently Delia has been coaching her in the womanly art of self-protection." He walked over to the window and drew aside a lace curtain.

Good. Moon Song was sitting quietly outside on the garden bench where he'd deposited her while he had a talk with Robert. He had asked her to stay there until they sorted this out, but he had no idea if she would actually comply. Moon Song had a mind of her own, and he could rarely read it.

"As long as self-protection is *all* Delia is coaching her in!" Robert exclaimed. "When

I took Delia on as a business partner, I was basing my choice on her business sense and her ability to read men. The old woman seemed so broken and desperate to get out of the brothel business, I took a gamble. I just hope we don't all live to regret it."

"I suppose her having enough savings to purchase a big part of next year's timber tract didn't hurt?" Skypilot pointed out.

"You got me there." Robert laughed. "But besides that, I trust her. She's a tough old bird and she's definitely lived a hard life, but I think she's honest. Still . . ." He fingered the pearl-handled stiletto. "When I asked her to give Moon Song a few chores and errands to keep her busy and out from under Katie's feet, I didn't expect her to start tutoring Moon Song in the proper use of an instrument like this. Where did Delia get her hands on such an object, anyway? This doesn't look like anything I ever saw here in Bay City."

Skypilot dropped the lace curtain and turned to face Robert. "Delia told Moon Song that a 'gentleman admirer' from New Orleans gave it to her."

"Of course." Robert tossed the stiletto onto his desk. "That little lethal instrument will be going back to Delia, of course. I don't want Moon Song carrying it. A knife

24

like that is only good for one thing, and it isn't peeling an apple."

"The fact remains that Moon Song did nothing to bring this on herself." Skypilot felt himself yet again growing angry at the thought of the indignity that had been forced upon his young friend. "All the girl was doing was shopping in broad daylight for some little beads for her baby's moccasins. If that old coot had done to her what he intended, not a thing would've happened to him. He knew that."

"Well, thank God you showed up when you did."

"That's exactly what I have been doing," Skypilot said. "Thanking God."

Robert shoved his chair away from his desk and stood. "What am I supposed to do with the girl? Katie loves her and doesn't want her to leave, but you know what it's like here in Bay City. The loggers come in from the woods and they only want the lumberman's three Bs."

"Beer, battle, and bawds." Skypilot grimaced. "I wish I had a nickel for every time I've heard a lumberman say that."

"Exactly." Robert began to pace. "Because she's Indian, some of them are going to see her as fair game unless there's a man standing beside her with a gun in his hand."

"You can't keep her locked up here in the house," Skypilot said. "She loves to explore. I've seen her going in and out of these stores, buying little things for herself and the baby. I don't think it's possible for her to stay out of the sight of scum like the man who accosted her today."

The door to the office opened. It was Katie, the beautiful redhead who had taken over Robert's kitchen as well as his heart. Watching their courtship during the dark days of winter had been as entertaining to the men as watching a play. She and Moon Song had become fast friends.

"What are the two of you talking about? And why is Moon Song sitting on the garden bench looking like she's being punished for something?"

Right behind Katie was Robert's sister, Sarah, a tall, thin woman who wore her black hair skinned back into a tight bun and seldom smiled. Most people who knew Sarah had been surprised when she finally found a husband who could put up with her prickly personality, but the butcher she'd married seemed to be content.

It surprised him that Sarah did not have a problem with Moon Song. They were an unlikely pair to be friends, but he thought that Sarah's tolerance might have something to do with Moon Song's eight-month-old son. Sarah acted like a different, softer woman whenever she held that baby in her arms, as she was doing right now.

Robert put his hands in his pockets and leaned against his desk. "Moon Song pulled a knife on a man today."

Katie gasped.

Sarah sniffed and hitched the baby a little higher on her hip. "I'm sure he deserved it."

"He probably did," Robert said. "But Moon Song would've hung if she'd killed him."

"Even for protecting herself?" Katie asked.

"In this town?" Sarah scoffed. "Most likely."

"I don't know what we're going to do about her," Robert said. "Skypilot won't always be around to get her out of situations like that."

"No, but I can be." Katie's voice filled with determination. "I just won't let her go out of this house without me beside her from now on."

"And how long can you keep that up, sweetheart?" Robert asked. "And how long is she going to allow it without thinking that you've become her jailor?"

"I don't know." Katie's lower lip trembled.

"I just don't want anything bad to happen to her."

"What do you think we ought to do?" Robert asked.

"Maybe we need to talk to the sheriff?" Katie suggested.

"The sheriff?" Sarah's voice dripped contempt. "Nearly every law official in town takes bribes. In case you haven't noticed, this town you've brought your children to, Robert, is not the most law-abiding place."

"This is where the lumber is. It's how I make my living now. I'm doing the best I can, Sarah."

Skypilot had heard this argument flare up between the brother and sister before. He wondered why they even bothered to go into it anymore.

"You know," Robert mused, "Moon Song is as smart as a whip. I can't believe how quickly she picked up English this winter. She speaks it nearly as well as a white person now. Do you suppose we could get her into one of those schools for Indians they're starting to set up? The ones where they teach them a vocation?"

"She's a twenty-year-old widow with a child," Skypilot said. "I doubt she wants to go to some white man's school."

"Well, I don't know the answer," Robert

said. "The girl is obviously in danger if she stays in town. The only thing I know is to watch her very carefully and never leave her alone."

Moon Song heard every word as she sat outside on a small bench where Skypilot had admonished her to stay.

They were talking about her as though she were a half-wild animal they had brought in out of the woods that might bite if they did not watch her carefully. She had defended herself. Stink Breath was the one who had done wrong, not Moon Song.

Robert, Sarah, Katie, and even her friend Skypilot were speaking about her as though her future was theirs to determine. A government school indeed!

Did they think she had no home? No people? Just because she had been half-starved and weak from childbirth when she came to them did not mean she was helpless. It had taken every ounce of strength and willpower she possessed to carry her new baby toward the distant haze of the lumber camp's chimney smoke.

Most women could not have done it. Even most Chippewa women could not have done it, but *she* was not just any woman. She was the granddaughter of Standing

Bear and Fallen Arrow. There was a fire inside of her.

Now these pale friends were discussing the chore of having to take turns watching her?

Had they not been kind to her these past months, she would have slipped away from the house with her infant son and not said a word. She had been carefully trained by Fallen Arrow in many things, including how to walk away without leaving a trace.

They *had* been kind, however, and even though she was angry at them right now, it would be impolite to leave without a word. They were her friends, and in their own way they were trying to take care of her.

Skypilot was surprised when Moon Song entered Robert's office.

There was a ruddy blush upon her cheekbones, her dark eyes were snapping, and her head was held high. She was still wearing that full blue skirt that had once belonged to Katie, along with the loose pink and white calico blouse she had taken a fancy to and kept belted at the waist.

She also wore those moccasin boots she'd found at one of the mercantiles that kept a small supply of Indian articles for sale. He'd been with her at the time. She'd explained that they were not the kind her people made, but she had seemed delighted with them anyway. Today, he understood why. They gave her a good place to hide a weapon.

"Don't worry," she said simply. "I go away now. Far away." Then she lifted her baby from Sarah's arms, turned on her heel, and headed toward the door without another word.

Go away? What was she talking about?

"Moon Song!" Sarah cried. "Where are you going?"

"Home." The girl looked straight at Sky-pilot with eyes filled with hurt. "I not walk streets of Bay City again."

Those eyes were like daggers to his heart. He had let her down somehow.

"Now, Moon Song," Robert soothed. "You said that your people live far up north. You aren't going to just start walking up there, and you are certainly not going alone with your child."

"I know ancient trails. I walk them here." She drew herself up. "Moon Song is not crippled animal white friends must care for."

"You're not a burden, Moon Song," Katie said. "We love you. We're worried about your safety and the baby's. You walked those trails back when your husband was still with you, before you had a child to carry. Things are different."

"I go now." She turned to leave again.

"Robert, do something!" Sarah pleaded. "She can't just leave like this with the baby. Not alone."

"Moon Song, stop!" Robert said. "I'm sorry, but what you're proposing to do is dangerous in the extreme. I can't allow you to do this."

Skypilot knew her better than all the others. Even though she'd shared a cabin with Katie, it was he who had spent so many hours alone with her as she'd cared for him after his accident. He saw the hurt pride in her eyes. It was obvious now that she had overheard what they had been saying. How that must have sounded to her ears! He felt ashamed that he'd been part of it.

Yes, her presence was a problem — only because they loved her and wanted to protect her. But to her it had sounded as though she were nothing more than a bothersome houseguest.

"Where exactly do your people live?" Skypilot asked. It occurred to him that he'd spent many hours with her and had never thought to ask. Probably because he had been too busy trying to teach her how to read the white man's alphabet.

Her eyes lit up with pleasure. *"Ocīkaeqsyah-Kaeqcekam!"*

Skypilot, Robert, and Sarah looked at each other. None of them had any idea what she had just said.

She saw their puzzlement. "Lake Superior," she translated. "Very beautiful. Near *Wēsk&omacrhsek."*

"Wisconsin," Robert said. "That's one word I recognize."

"Ayasha and I go now." Moon Song turned once again to leave.

Ayasha. That was the temporary name she had given her son. Ayasha meant "Little One" in Chippewa, she had explained to him. She said that an elder of her tribe would choose the permanent name of her baby. She had refused to give her Little One a name, and had resisted the efforts of the members of the lumber camp to give him a name as well, although there had been plenty who had tried.

If she walked into the wilderness with Ayasha, there was an excellent chance that none of them would ever see him or Moon Song again. Moon Song and that baby had become precious to him over the months they'd spent in the close confines of the camp. The idea of them simply walking away was not acceptable.

"At least let us help provision you better and let me find someone to help take you, Moon Song," Robert said. "I could buy you a ticket on one of the steamships. There is absolutely no need for you to try to walk through hundreds of miles of wilderness. That's crazy."

"Crazy?" Moon Song cocked one eyebrow. "No. Staying here is 'crazy.' "

"He didn't mean it that way," Katie placated. "It's just that we love you so much and we can't bear to see you just walk away like this. Not alone. Let Robert buy you a boat ticket and hire someone to help . . ."

"I'll go with her," Skypilot said.

"You?" Robert's voice held hope that this situation could be resolved so quickly. "Do you mean it?"

"If we take a steamship, it will only take a few days at most. I should be able to get her safely to her people and come back within a couple of weeks."

"Are you sure you want to do this?" Robert asked.

"Why not? I don't have anything else I need to do. Besides, I wouldn't mind seeing a different part of the country for a day or two. It should be interesting."

3

Moon Song stood on the shore of Bay City and watched the congested boat traffic, trying to get used to the idea of getting onto one of those gigantic vessels. It would be like getting swallowed by a giant animal and it frightened her more than she wanted to admit.

There was a bit of everything on the water today. In addition to the logs bobbing inside their corrals, there were working steamboats, sailing ships, ornate paddle wheelers, and smaller vessels down to a one-man rowboat. Far to one side was a sight that made her sad — a lone birch bark canoe, beautifully made. The woman who had made that canoe — and among her people it was almost always the woman who built the canoes — had been a true artist. One of her people had probably brought it here.

There had been a time when that canoe and others like it would have been the only things skimming silently through the water on these sparkling lakes. Now the bay was filled with steamships belching smoke, a calliope playing tinny music on one of the paddle wheelers, and the sound of workers yelling over one another.

She'd heard the steamship stories as she'd walked about town. Too many had their wooden decks catch fire from sparks from the smokestacks. Some had blown up while racing with other ships. Some had simply wrecked or torn apart in heavy waves.

No, it was better to walk the few hundred miles home. It had taken her and her husband less than one moon to make the trip.

Skypilot seemed to think it foolish to even consider such a thing. Since he was so determined to accompany her, and since she did not want to inconvenience him any more than necessary, she had agreed, even though she didn't like the idea.

"Are you looking forward to our trip tomorrow?" Skypilot asked.

"On big gray boat?" She pointed at the steamship upon which she had been told they had rooms. "No."

"I am." She could tell that Skypilot was completely at ease as he gazed out over the water. "They say that in good weather, those things can travel up to twenty miles per hour, and I can't wait to see what that feels like."

"Why go so fast?"

"I don't know." He shrugged. "I guess just because we can. There are lots of things happening these days, Moon Song. Inventions I've been reading about in the newspapers that I would never have dreamed of a few years ago. Things are changing fast. A person has to hurry to keep up."

Moon Song thought that the people she saw hurrying along the wooden sidewalks of Bay City needed to slow down, but she kept quiet. That was their problem. Not hers.

"I go back now, to Katie's house," she said. "Sarah said she help pack."

"Sure thing," Skypilot said. "I'll walk you there."

As they left the bay, Moon Song glanced back over her shoulder at the giant hulk of the steamboat. It did not give her a good feeling. She wished she had simply started walking north with Ayasha when she first decided to leave, before anyone else could get involved. The ship looked like a monster to her, but she would walk onto it because Skypilot was her friend and she did not want to disappoint him.

■ ■ ■ ■

"The postman brought something for you, Isaac." Mrs. Wilcox, the woman who owned Skypilot's boardinghouse, nodded toward a letter lying on the corner of a square worktable where she was busily kneading bread.

"For me?" That was odd. He got one letter a month from his brother back east, and he wrote one per month in reply. That was it. He had received his brother's monthly letter only yesterday.

"From the handwriting, it looks like it might be from a lady friend." Mrs. Wilcox was middle-aged and genial in her nosiness about her guests. She meant no harm, but their lives were her principal form of entertainment.

He didn't have any "lady friends" and hadn't since his former fiancée had broken their engagement.

The envelope was of heavy, lilac-colored stationery. He had seen this stationery before. It also had a generous sprinkling of flour upon it.

"Sorry about the flour," Mrs. Wilcox said. "Sometimes things get a little out of hand when I'm making bread."

He knew it would make her day if he sat

down and read the letter out loud to her, but this was a letter he needed to read in private.

"I'll see you at supper, ma'am," he said.

"Oh." She was visibly disappointed. "All right, then."

As soon as he got to his room, he kicked the door shut, locked it, and sat on his bed. The letter was from Penelope. The palms of his hands were beginning to sweat, and he wiped them off on his pants leg. It surprised him that after all this time, the mere sight of her handwriting could cause this kind of physical reaction.

"Father, give me wisdom," he asked aloud. "Whatever this letter might hold, please give me wisdom."

He glanced at the envelope again and realized that there was something peculiar about it. Instead of her customary black India ink, Penelope had used pokeberry juice to write it.

In spite of the way his former fiancée had treated him, this small observation made his heart ache. The South had been hit hard by the privations of war. Evidently, although Penelope still possessed a few scraps of luxurious stationery, she had been forced to use homemade ink to pen her words upon it.

He slit open the envelope, drew out the rich paper, and began to read.

Dear Isaac,

I found out only last week that it might be possible to contact you through the Bay City post office. The word came through many convoluted sources, so I have no idea if this will reach you. I shall pray that it does.

First of all, I want to apologize for the shoddy way I treated you. You need to know that I have spent many sleepless and tearful nights because of it.

My loyalties were greatly divided between my father's needs and your ideology. It seemed to me at the time that it would be remarkably easy for one to espouse the cessation of slavery from one's pulpit when one does not have to run a plantation. My father's health was deteriorating. If he had freed his slaves like you seemed to think everyone in the South should do, his fields would have been overrun with weeds, no crops would have been planted, and we would have been penniless within the year. I begged you not to give that sermon, and was furious with you for having gone against my counsel.

All that is beside the point now. The slaves are gone — at least most of those who are able-bodied have gone. The elderly, infirm, and weak are now ours alone to care for. Because we are Christian people — in spite of what you seemed to think back then — we do the best we can with severely limited resources.

You would not recognize our plantation now. My father passed away at the height of the war. There are only a handful of us living here. I managed to plant twenty acres of cotton this spring. Yes, I said I helped plant — with my own hands — twenty acres of cotton. It will give us a little to live on.

You would not recognize me now, either. I've not had a new dress in six years. My hands are the hands of a workman instead of a lady of leisure. I have looked back to the years before the war, when we were young together, and wished I could have handled things differently. I truly did love you.

I still do.

I have told you the situation we are in here. If you were to come home now, there are those who would probably avoid you on the street, but you would be most welcome, so very welcome, to call upon me at my home. I still have one dress that is not too shabby to receive guests in. I would enjoy donning it, on the occasion of your visit, and we could see if there was any chance we could let bygones be bygones and begin again.

Your much humbled former fiancée,
Penelope

P.S. There are many of those among your former congregation who, like me, regret the circumstances under which you left. They remember the many fine sermons you preached and the many kindnesses you performed. I believe there might be a chance you would be welcomed back into your old pulpit if you were to come home. I have heard you have been working in a lumber camp. Forgive me for saying this, but it seems a great waste of your talents and training.

The letter drifted from his fingers onto the faded cabbage roses of Mrs. Wilcox's carpet. He stood and walked over to the window. The harbor was visible from there, and he could see the ships vying for position, including the one he would be boarding tomorrow morning. He had actually been looking forward to taking that voyage and seeing some new countryside until a few minutes ago. Now, it felt as though Penelope had taken Moon Song's stiletto and plunged it straight into his heart.

"I know this is best for you and the child, but I will miss you and the baby," Sarah said to Moon Song. "I never had an Indian friend before."

"Chippewa."

"Excuse me?"

"My people are Chippewa."

"Chippewa?" Sarah looked confused. "I thought someone said you were Menominee."

"My mother-in-law Menominee. We live with her people many moons."

"I thought your husband was a French-Canadian trapper."

Moon Song nodded. "He also French-Canadian trapper, like his father."

Sarah frowned. "Then you're telling me that your husband was a half-breed? He had a Menominee mother and French-Canadian father?"

Moon Song winced at the sound of contempt in the older woman's voice, a woman she had considered a friend. "Yes. He a half-breed."

And this — she did not say to the older woman — was the very reason she seldom mentioned her husband's connection to the Menominee. The only thing worse than an Indian, in some white people's eyes, was a half-breed. French-Canadian trappers were somewhat respectable. Half-breeds were not. Moon Song had long ago become weary of trying to figure out why.

"Oh, all that doesn't matter." Sarah dismissed her explanation with a wave of her hand. "An Indian is an Indian in my book."

Sarah's rudeness was so incomprehensible, Moon Song did not try to further explain the difference between the various tribes and native nations to Robert's sister. It was obvious that the woman was no longer interested.

"The thing that is important," Sarah said brightly, "is that you and Ayasha will get to go home."

"Yes." That was something on which she and Sarah agreed. Home. The word sounded sweet to her, even in English.

"Is there anything else you'll need?" Sarah asked.

Moon Song took stock. Even though she had been so angry yesterday that she had been ready to head off with nothing but her baby and his cradle board, packing the right supplies for her journey was important. After the steamship docked, there would be a long trek through the wilderness. She needed to be prepared.

Ayasha was still nursing, so feeding him would not be a problem. Feeding herself might be. Sarah's kitchen did not afford the rich pemmican she would prefer for the overland trip she would make after the boat docked at Copper Harbor. That combination of dried meat pounded to a powder, mixed with venison fat, flavored with dried berries, and mixed with powdered wild rice was so nutritious and satisfying that she had spent much of her young life helping her grandmother prepare it.

Unfortunately, pemmican was complicated to make and there was no time to prepare it now. Living in the lumber camp where food had been plentiful had lulled her into a regrettable unpreparedness.

Still, she had all the skills she would need to forage for food as she went along. The Michigan forests and swamps in the spring were a very different thing than the barrenness she had faced in October when she'd made her way to the lumber camp. She was young, strong, and well versed in her people's woodcraft. There were a hundred ways to fill her belly, and in so doing, fill Ayasha's.

She could feed herself, but keeping Skypilot full could become a burden if he insisted on accompanying her all the way to her people. She'd watched that man put away towering stacks of Katie's flapjacks at the logging camp. She hoped he wouldn't expect to stay with her people long if he did insist on accompanying her all the way back to her grandmother's wigwam. The Chippewa were a hospitable and peaceable people. It was not unheard of for them to sacrifice too much of their own food supply in order to feed guests. Unfortunately, in the early spring, their winter supply of food would already be depleted. They would be on short rations until summer came and the earth began to give generously of its abundance.

She knew that Skypilot was good with an axe and good at reading a book. He had been *very* good at running the day he had saved Robert's small daughter from a falling tree, but she had no idea if he had any other skills. Her guess was that he did not. At least, she had never heard him boast of any, and most men she knew liked to boast. At least the braves in her tribe did. Of course, their boasts were a great deal more empty these days since moving to the reservation.

"I hope you're doing the right thing," Katie said. "I would never forgive myself if anything happened to you."

Forgive herself? Moon Song wondered about this statement. Once Skypilot left her, if she did get hurt or meet with an accident, she doubted Katie would ever hear about it.

The death of a great chief was one thing. Word would go out even among the whites. The death of a squaw and fatherless baby? It would barely make a ripple. There were only a few people to whom it would matter — her grandmother and maybe some members of her tribe.

Right now, apart from the lack of pemmican, her biggest concern was gathering enough soft, absorbent moss to get Ayasha through the next few days upon the steamship. White women used cloth on their babies' bottoms and then laboriously cleaned that cloth. In the lumber camp, Katie had pressed something she called diapers upon her. To make Katie happy, Moon Song had gone along with it since it was winter and moss was hard to find, but in all other seasons it seemed such a waste of time. White people could be so impractical.

For instance, she did not understand why white mothers found it necessary to keep their infants covered with clothes once the weather was warm. Allowing a baby or toddler to play naked outdoors meant no diapers to wash. A baby secured upon a cradle board, wrapped in leather and surrounded by absorbent moss, was so much easier. The soiled moss had to be removed only a couple times a day, and the child washed and allowed to play for hours in camp to strengthen its little body. The whole process would only take minutes out of her walking time versus hours of scrubbing and drying diaper cloths. She marveled at the fact that white women didn't use such a method.

She had little to pack for herself. A few articles of clothing and the money Robert had been gracious enough to give her for her work in camp. A comb she had purchased. A few sweets she kept in her room. That had been her greatest luxury in Bay City, the purchase of penny candy. None of it, in her opinion, was quite as delicious as the cones of maple sugar her tribe made every year for the children, but it was still very good. And so many colors and tastes! Yes, she would miss the counters of candy.

She decided she would spend the rest of

the afternoon finding and bundling the proper moss. One couldn't always depend on finding a ready supply. No doubt Sarah would insist on coming with her. The woman seemed to think she had to watch her all the time since the incident with Stink Breath.

4

As Skypilot packed the few items he would need for his journey, he felt no excitement about the trip. None at all. Thanks to Penelope's letter, he had not slept well. Memories of Richmond and the life he had once lived plagued him on and off all night.

He could see the harbor from his window. The bay was peaceful. The sky was a brilliant blue. It had been warmer than usual, and the ice had broken up on the lake two weeks earlier than expected. There was a carnival atmosphere down at the docks because of the early arrival and departure of the steamboats taking supplies from Detroit to the far-flung settlements farther north.

He should have been raring to go, but not after that letter. He felt like he needed to rescue her, much like he'd once rescued slaves who had run from men like her father.

Could he become a successful farmer? He

didn't know. Would he want to preach for that church again? Probably not. Some wounds went too deep.

Could he spend the rest of his life with Penelope?

Ah, that was the real question. The woman who had penned that letter? Maybe. The woman who had put her nose in the air and flounced out without a backward glance while he was standing in the pulpit trying to reason his congregation out of a terrible war? No.

He had loved her once, though, and hated to think of her sitting there at her elegant spinet desk, writing this letter, hoping it would reach him. Wondering what he would say. She would have to wonder awhile longer, however. The boat would be leaving soon, and he could not pen a letter in such a short time. Especially when he had no idea what to say.

The *Belle Fortune* was one of the smaller steamships, and as Skypilot and Moon Song boarded, he tried to push his concerns about Penelope's letter aside. They were having fine spring weather, and he was determined to enjoy the trip.

This was the first time he had ridden on one of these ships, and the mechanics fascinated him. He intended to get Moon Song and little Ayasha safely tucked away in their room and then roam around and see if he could figure out how the thing worked.

In the beginning, steamships had the reputation of being unsafe, but he had not heard of an explosion, wreck, or fire for at least a year now. Hopefully, the wrinkles had been ironed out and all would be well from this point on.

The captain was waiting on the deck to greet the passengers. "I'm Captain Fowler." He shook Skypilot's hand. "And you are?"

"My name is Isaac Ross. My employer, Robert Foster, made the arrangements for us."

"Ah yes. He reserved the last two rooms." The captain glanced at Moon Song standing beside him. "And this is, um, your . . ."

"This is my friend Moon Song. I'm accompanying her back to her home on the Keweenaw."

He supposed he could forgive the captain for staring. As usual, Moon Song was an interesting sight in her clash of brightly colored white-women clothes and Indian comfort. At the moment, she was also wearing eight-month-old Ayasha in a cradle board on her back.

"And is this your . . . son, ma'am?" The

captain craned his neck to see around her. Moon Song obligingly turned completely around so he could see her pride and joy.

Like most cradle boards, Ayasha's had a strip of wood that curved around his face for protection. From it, Moon Song always tied interesting small objects with which to entertain her baby. A tiny pair of intricately beaded moccasins dangled from it now. These were new. Yesterday she had seemed worried about getting them finished before the trip. She must have been up half the night sewing those beads on.

It occurred to him that perhaps it was more important to her how she and her baby appeared than he'd realized. He was grateful when the captain took notice.

"What lovely workmanship on these little moccasins," the captain said. "I don't think I've ever seen finer."

Moon Song beamed.

Yes, it mattered to her. It mattered very much. She wanted people on the ship to know that she was a good mother to her son, and she had chosen to work diligently in order to prove it.

"This is little Ayasha," Skypilot said. "Moon Song stayed at our lumber camp last winter after her husband died. I'm accompanying her back to her people."

It was more than he needed to say, but somehow he wanted the captain to know that Moon Song was a respectable woman.

"Welcome to my ship, ma'am," Captain Fowler said. "Dinner will be at six."

Skypilot decided that he liked the captain very much.

He helped Moon Song deposit the few bundles she'd brought with her into her room and get settled for the next two days. He tried to ignore the look of fear he saw in her eyes as she turned toward him after entering the tiny stateroom.

"I cannot breathe. This room is so small."

"Nonsense, Moon Song," he said. "You'll be able to breathe quite well in here."

Her eyes grew wider. "I cannot breathe!"

He gave a sigh. He cared deeply about her, but she was such a child sometimes. He guessed he would have to bring her and the baby along with him as he looked around the ship.

"Come along," he said. "We'll get you some fresh air."

There really wasn't anything "fresh" about it when they came back out on deck. The bay was so filled with boats that the smell of fire and smoke from the belly of all the steamships was all around them.

It was invigorating, though. The crowded

bay, the shouts and calls of various sailors, the creaking of the great wooden sailing ships anchored farther out in the bay. Over all was the perpetual smell of fresh pine. That scent seemed to cling to everything in Bay City, from the sawdust sprinkled in the streets, to the lumber camps situated all around, in the very air that they breathed.

Another couple came on board. The woman was dressed impressively in a gown the color of sunshine that showed off her mane of chestnut-colored hair perfectly. The man wore a military officer's uniform. The woman carried an infant who appeared to be not much older than Ayasha. As she held her infant, the white, lace-edged baby blanket fell gracefully over her left arm.

The woman was not especially beautiful, but she was so exquisitely turned out that it was hard not to stare. He tore his gaze away and looked at Moon Song instead.

That was a mistake. The poor girl certainly suffered by comparison. Her skin wasn't the lovely, pale white that was the fashion, and the clothing she wore seemed all wrong. Moon Song's clothes seemed ill-fitting and rumpled beside this woman's perfectly coiffed, professionally tailored loveliness.

Then, there was that cradle board she insisted on carrying Ayasha around in. If

55

anything made a woman look like a squaw, it was that cradle board. The woman in yellow velvet holding the baby in her arms looked so graceful in comparison.

He saw Moon Song glance at him, then at the woman, then back to him. She must have seen the admiration on his face. He hoped she had not been able to read his thoughts. He would not deliberately hurt Moon Song for the world. In fact, he loved her like a little sister.

Seeing this elegantly dressed woman caused his mind to float back to the letter he continued to carry around in his pocket. Imagine. Penelope had actually humbled herself enough to write and apologize for her actions and invite him back home. He felt an unexpected pang for the gracious culture he had once been part of, one to which Penelope held the key.

He was tired of living in lumber camps, around men whose idea of pleasure was to get drunk and stomp each other senseless. The war was over. Everyone had learned their lesson. Maybe it was time to let bygones be bygones.

The idea of sitting in Penelope's father's library, reading from the man's vast collection of leather-bound volumes, a soft-spoken, grateful wife bringing him coffee, while all around him were rich fields producing food for an impoverished South was a heady one.

He brought his thoughts up short. The plantation would no longer be the graceful oasis it had once seemed. Most of the land was no doubt overgrown with weeds from lack of field hands; the leather-bound volumes were probably musty from neglect; and the soft-spoken wife of his daydream did not exist. Penelope had never been particularly soft-spoken unless she was trying to impress the older women who ruled her social world.

Deep down, he had a nagging suspicion that Penelope was less in love with him than that he was her desperate last chance at a normal life. The war had been so utterly brutal that most of the young, able-bodied men who had once ruled the South were lying now beneath the earth. Left behind were thousands of women longing for homes, husbands, and children. A man who still had his legs, arms, hands, and senses intact was a prize indeed.

There was every chance that Penelope felt nothing more for him than her father would have felt while choosing a prize stallion. She knew he had not fought in the war, so she would be gambling on the chance that he was still healthy and strong. She was also gambling on the chance that his great love for her would pull him back to her if she crooked her little finger.

The problem was — she was not entirely wrong. He had loved her once and deeply. After all that had happened, even he was surprised that the pull to go back to her was so strong.

5

Moon Song saw Skypilot's head pivot toward the woman in the yellow dress the moment he heard her voice. She also saw his approving glance before he tore his eyes away. Skypilot was not the kind of man to gawk at another man's wife, but he was still a man, and the way he'd looked at that woman bothered her. It was a peek into his soul that she did not like. There was a hunger there, and she did not think it was for the woman. There seemed to be something else in his eyes. Something far away that Moon Song could not fathom.

As they stood on the deck with so much movement about them, her eyes caught sight of Delia standing on the shore, waving frantically. Moon Song lifted a hand and waved back. The old woman needn't have bothered to see them off. They had said their good-byes yesterday.

Delia cupped one hand around her mouth

and tried to shout something, but a blast of the steam whistle drowned her out. Moon Song jumped at the blast and clapped both hands over her ears.

That was another reason she was glad to leave this place. Her senses were more acute than most. That gift had saved their lives back in the fall when she had sensed the forest fire coming and awakened the lumber camp in time for everyone to get to the safety of the lake.

There was a negative side to this gift, though. The blast of that whistle made her feel as though someone was physically piercing the inner parts of her ears. It must have had the same effect on Ayasha because he began to wail, and he was a baby who almost never cried.

She pulled the cradle board off her back to comfort him, just as the steamship's whistle let off with another blast. Instinctively, she covered her child's ears and withstood the pain herself.

Skypilot seemed immune to the sound. He was leaning over the deck railing, trying to hear what Delia was shouting at them. She noticed now that Delia was waving a package in the air.

"It looks like Delia brought you something," he said.

Moon Song and Skypilot started working their way toward the gangplank while Delia elbowed her way through the crowd on the shore, trying to get closer to the ship. Delia had dressed for the occasion, wearing what Moon Song thought of as the older woman's war paint. Rouged cheeks, darkened eyes, bright red lips, a bottle-green silk dress that shone in the sun. She even wore a matching hat with a green plume that rose into the air, adding another six inches to her height.

Delia was a parade, even when she was alone.

Moon Song couldn't help but notice the looks that the former brothel owner was getting. Disapproving glances from both men and women. Even Bay City wasn't uncivilized enough to tolerate a woman like Delia out and about in broad daylight. She apparently couldn't have cared less. Delia was on a mission. Moon Song discovered what that mission was the minute they met on the gangplank.

"This just arrived." Delia shoved a bundle at her. "It's for you. I'd been having it made as a surprise, but then you decided to leave so quickly. I think it might be helpful where you're going. I hired a Chippewa woman I know to make it for you."

"What is it?"

"That would spoil the surprise. Don't open it until you're back in your room."

"We need to take this gangplank up, ma'am, we're leaving," a crew member said. "Right now."

There was another steam whistle blast. Moon Song jumped, and Ayasha once again started crying.

"Don't worry." Delia seemed unperturbed. "They're not going to just go off and dump us in the lake."

Moon Song wasn't so sure.

"If there's one thing I've learned through the years . . ." Delia patted Moon Song's cheek. "Listen to me now, child, I'm trying to tell you something important . . . it is that a woman doesn't get anywhere in this world by trying to act like she's something she's not. About the only thing you get from that is sad. Don't you ever apologize for who you are, and don't ever, ever let other people tell you who or what they think you ought to be. Do you hear me?"

Moon Song nodded.

"Good."

Delia blew Skypilot a kiss and took her time sashaying down the gangplank, ignoring the scowls from the bystanders.

Moon Song glanced up at Skypilot and saw that he was grinning as he watched

Delia disembark.

"If the Confederate Army had possessed half the brass of that woman," he said, "they might have won the war."

Moon Song did not get many gifts, and the fact that Delia had brought her one delighted her. What could it be to make Delia go to so much trouble?

"Hold, please." Moon Song thrust the now-quiet baby into Skypilot's arms and inspected the bundle. It appeared to have been wrapped in leather. She untied the leather thong holding it together, and the bundle fell apart in her hands. She gasped when she saw what it was.

Instead of being wrapping, the leather itself was the gift. The light-colored, fringed, beaded doeskin dress with matching leggings was lovely. She held it up to herself and saw that Delia had guessed her size accurately. It was a beautiful piece of clothing. One of the nicest she had ever owned.

She cupped her hands around her mouth and shouted over the railing at Delia. *"Miig-wetch!"* Then she remembered that Delia wouldn't understand what she was saying and switched to English. "Thank you!"

Delia looked back, grinned, and waved.

Then the ship began to back away from the shoreline, and the faces of the people onshore grew smaller and smaller until all she could make out was Delia's bottle-green hat in the distance.

"Look!" She held the garment up for Sky-pilot to see.

"I knew Delia was worried about whether or not it would be finished in time," he said. "It's a nice gift."

"Delia is good woman," Moon Song said. "Very kind."

"I don't know about that," Skypilot said. "From what I've heard, she's not always been good, or kind, but I'm glad she got that gift for you since you like it so much."

"When I walk through woods, this will be good. Briars not tear."

"Yes, I can see how protective this would be." He fingered the soft doeskin. "Maybe I'll have to have me some leather clothing made."

"No." Moon Song looked him up and down. "You take too big deer!"

He laughed. "Was that a joke, Moon Song? Don't worry, I'll not be staying long enough on the Keweenaw to need a buck-skin suit."

As Moon Song carefully folded the clothing, she saw the white woman in the yellow dress glance over at her curiously.

"How fascinating, James," the woman said

64

to her husband. "We are traveling on the same ship as a real Indian woman. You told me there were some of those people still living up here, but I didn't expect to be traveling with one!"

"Don't worry, Isabella, my dear. If the captain allows her into the dining room during our meals, I'll make sure that we're seated at a separate table."

"Oh no. I shan't want that. I wouldn't miss a chance to talk to her for the world. Is her very large husband one of those trappers you've told me about?"

"I doubt he is her husband," James said. "These squaws are not known for their morality. They're different from us, you know. Quite primitive. They've not been taught right from wrong."

The couple was not standing all that far away. Did they not realize that she could hear every word they were saying? The only answer she could think of for their rudeness was that they must think she did not understand their language.

Skypilot had evidently not heard a word. He was still holding Ayasha and had moved to the end of the ship to point out to him the giant moving boards that were going around and around in a circle.

Husband?

Ignoring the rude couple, she watched Skypilot as he held her baby. For such a large man, he was always surprisingly tender with Ayasha. She cared deeply for him, but if there was one thing that she would never consider, it would be a marriage. Skypilot was a good friend, a good man, but their worlds were too far apart.

It was inconceivable to imagine him coming to live with her in one of her people's communal longhouses, or even their own wigwam, and equally inconceivable to imagine going with him to live among his people. In the weeks following his accident, he had sometimes entertained her by telling her stories about his life in Virginia when he was still a preacher.

As her English rapidly improved and they could communicate better, she found that he could be quite humorous as he explained what it was like to be sitting down to formal dinners where there was a special utensil for every dish, or as he described how clumsy he felt standing around at a dance, desperately trying to memorize the intricate steps so that he would not blunder and hurt the delicate women with whom he was expected to dance. He always made a joke out of his own perceived shortcomings in what he referred to as "polite" society.

They had laughed together, and it had helped pass the long winter days as he healed and she waited for the snows to leave so she could go home, but it left her with the indelible impression that she wanted nothing to do with his former life.

A husband? Skypilot? She would love him forever for his many kindnesses, but as a husband? Never.

Even though she had very deliberately moved several steps away, she could still hear snatches of the rude couple's conversation.

"I know I was upset when you first told me you had been given this appointment to Fort Wilkins," the woman in yellow said. "But now I've changed my mind. I believe it is going to be a great adventure."

"You are my brave little woman," James said. "I shall see that you get every comfort that can possibly be found in such an out-of-the-way place. I know there are two other officers' wives living within the stockade now, so you will have at least some entertainment with . . . suitable companions. I believe one of them even had a pianoforte brought up. I was told she livens up the post on many a harsh winter night with her playing."

"I am just grateful that there was enough

room in our trunks to hold my drawing supplies," the woman said. "I believe there might be scenes and artifacts worth recording. I think I might start by sketching out that thing the Indian woman was carrying her papoose in a moment ago."

Moon Song grew tired of listening to them talk about her as though she did not have ears. With all her heart, she longed to get back to the enormous lake that helped sustain her people's life, back to the land where she belonged.

She went to where Skypilot was prattling to Ayasha some nonsense about steam and mechanical things. "I want my baby now. I go to room."

Skypilot seemed surprised. "But I thought you said you couldn't breathe in there."

"I learn." Taking Ayasha in his cradle board, she went straight to her room. One thing she did not intend was to become some curiosity for that yellow-dress woman to draw.

No matter how much Skypilot cajoled, he could not entice Moon Song out of her stateroom for dinner. She seemed determined to remain hidden away for the rest of the journey, and for the life of him, he could not figure out why. She had been fairly out-

68

going in the lumber camp, and she'd seemed to enjoy walking around Bay City during her weeks there. Why she had suddenly become too shy to come out in public, he had no idea.

The moment he got to the dining room, he asked a porter to take a plate of food to her cabin, then he seated himself at a table near the couple he'd met on deck.

"Tell us about your . . . woman," Colonel James Hatchette said, after Skypilot had been served.

"Woman?"

"Perhaps she is your wife," the colonel's lovely wife suggested.

It took Skypilot a moment to figure out what they were talking about.

"Oh, you mean Moon Song. She's not my woman or wife. She's just a friend and a ward of my boss. I'm accompanying her to the Keweenaw Peninsula to find her people."

"So, how does your boss happen to have an Indian ward with a baby?" Colonel Hatchette asked.

It might have been Skypilot's imagination, but he thought he detected a tone of censure in the commander's voice, as though the man was insinuating something about Robert and Moon Song.

"She was widowed and starving with a newborn baby in her arms when she made her way to our lumber camp," Skypilot said. "The camp cook took care of her and the baby."

"Oh, the poor thing!" The colonel's wife, a woman who had been introduced to him as Isabella, seemed genuinely concerned. "How terrible it must have been for her."

"Well, it's over now, and Ayasha is as healthy as a tick on a hound dog these days." He was suddenly grateful that Moon Song had decided to stay in her room. These two made him decidedly uncomfortable. "Will you be stationed at Fort Wilkins long?"

"That is in the hands of the government." The colonel frowned. "The place was shut down for years, then suddenly during the war, someone decided there was a need for fortification on one of the farthest points from the South in the entire United States. I have no idea what the government's plans are, but my plans are to do my duty wherever they send me. I just wish it didn't involve my wife having to live in such an out-of-the-way place. Isabella has been gently reared and is not used to such primitive conditions."

"I'm not a hothouse rose." Isabella seemed

slightly embarrassed by her husband's concern. "I'll be fine. And when we are allowed to go home, I will have all sorts of new and wonderful drawings in my portfolio to show to our friends so that they will know what our life was like up here in the great wilderness they've only read about. I shall be quite a success at dinner parties."

"My wife is an artist," James said. "She studied in Paris the whole time our country was at war. When she came back, I proposed the moment I saw one of her sketches."

"And I accepted," Isabella said, "because he was the first suitor who ever took my drawings seriously."

"But Isabella has better things to occupy her time these days." James Hatchette patted her hand. "I doubt she'll have much time to draw now that she is a mother."

"And where is your baby?" Skypilot inquired. "I only saw him briefly on the deck. He seemed a nice little fellow."

"Oh, our child is back at the room with the wet nurse, of course," James said. "I wanted to preserve Isabella's magnificent figure."

Skypilot inadvertently glanced at Isabella. She had stopped eating and was staring down at her plate, blushing a deep scarlet. James seemed not to see or care, but went blissfully on with his meal and his conversation.

"I looked a long time during Isabella's confinement, trying to find just the right wet nurse," James said. "This girl suits the bill quite nicely. Her child died in infancy, so she isn't divided in her loyalties like some."

"Please, James," Isabella pleaded. "May we please talk about something else?"

"I've embarrassed you." The colonel spoke fondly, as though talking to a favorite child.

"Yes." Her eyes blazed for a moment. "You have. Now can we please talk about something *else*?"

"Excuse me," Skypilot said, scooting his chair back from the table and nodding a quick good-bye to Isabella as he left.

There were a dozen sharp retorts on his tongue, but his mind was so thick with anger over the contemptuous way that the man had spoken about the poor woman caring for the colonel's child, he did not trust himself to speak. He knew if he did not walk away from the table immediately, he would do something he'd regret.

As satisfying as that would be, it would do no good. People like the colonel could not be taught manners with a fist. He doubted that the colonel could be taught anything at all.

He had no appetite now, only a deep need to go to Moon Song's cabin and reassure himself that she and the baby were being treated with respect by the ship's staff.

6

The trip up the coast of the lower peninsula of Michigan was interrupted a few times. Stacks of firewood and coal were purchased to keep the boilers going. There was a short race with another steamboat, during which all passengers stood on the deck and cheered the two crews on.

A Scandinavian family that had been on board since before Bay City got off at Sault Ste. Marie. No one in that family spoke a word of English. All they had were the tickets necessary to take them where they wanted to go. At meals, they had clustered together around one table, speaking their own language. The wife was weary and pregnant. The children were bright-eyed and curious. The father was rugged and determined.

No one saw much of Colonel Hatchette's wife after that first night. She seemed to prefer taking her meals in her cabin. He wondered if she was doing so in order to avoid any chance of being present if her husband had other disastrous conversations at the dinner table. Moon Song, on the other hand, soon tired of being cooped up inside and roamed the boat at will with Ayasha strapped in his cradle board on her back.

Skypilot couldn't help but think how handy a cradle board would have been for the young mothers in his congregation in Virginia, who were constantly trying to do something with one hand while holding a baby in the other. Ayasha's bright eyes took in everything as his mother walked the deck.

The Hatchette baby, whose father insisted he be kept inside the cabin for fear that the fresh air flowing over the lake might harm the child's lungs, was fretful and cried a great deal. Colonel Hatchette grew impatient with the ship's progress, and Skypilot saw him in serious conversation with the captain several times. The captain did not appear to be enjoying the discussion.

There wasn't much in the way of civilization or other ships once they got past Sault Ste. Marie. Instead, there were long stretches along the shore of Lake Superior in which nothing could be seen but the densest of woodland. It was fascinating to him to see that so much true wilderness still existed here.

The acres of trees around Bay City were gone. The white pine had been cut first, then the hardwood as Bay City grew and the inhabitants' need for firewood increased. The lumber camps had to go deeper and deeper into the Saginaw Valley to find stands of white pine. As the lumber disappeared, there was more thievery as unscrupulous loggers cut into other owners' property, and river pirates attempted to make a living off of logs secreted into small, secluded tributaries.

In the Upper Peninsula, however, even in the year 1868, there was still true wilderness. He saw it all through the eyes of a timberman, evaluating board feet and admiring the straight, tall pines that crowded the shores as they passed. There would be several fortunes made here someday.

Even though the word frequently used to describe Michigan's forests was *inexhaustible,* he knew better. His guess was that this sight would someday disappear completely. He'd personally counted the rings on some of the trees he had cut down. Then he had done the math. Most of the trees they were harvesting had been mature at the time Columbus landed.

There was enough of a skilled axe man inside of him that his hands fairly itched for the challenge to take down a few hundred of those trees. He longed for the smell of fresh pine as his axe bit into the tree's flesh, and the shout of "timberrr" echoing through the forest. There was just enough of a poet in him, however, to value the fact that he was getting to see this before it disappeared — this never-ending sea of living green. He understood why some called this coast-to-coast wall of ancient trees inexhaustible, but he had seen firsthand how fast a small group of determined loggers could clear an acre of trees. If one multiplied what Robert Foster's camp could do, by dozens of small, independent camps — that was a great deal of cleared land.

As they steamed closer and closer to their destination, he found it interesting to see a change come over Moon Song. She held her head a little higher and prouder. He had always known her to have a deep sense of personal dignity, but that increased the farther north she got.

"Steamboat stink," she had announced on the second day of travel.

"That's true," he said.

"I will get off soon."

"Me too."

77

"No. You will go back. Remember?"

"I might stay a few days." He was teasing her. He had sensed she didn't want him sticking around once she got to her own territory.

"No need for you to stay."

"I don't know, Moon Song. It's awfully pretty up here. I might just settle down real close to you."

"Enough white people here already," she huffed. "No room for Indians."

He grinned. "Looks like there's plenty of room to me."

"You not yet see Keweenaw." She shook her head sorrowfully. "People dig, dig, dig. All the time."

For a minute, he was puzzled. What kind of people was she talking about? Then he realized that she was referring to the copper and iron mines. He had heard that there were many people trying to wrest fortunes out of the rich mineral deposits in upper Michigan.

Although he was only teasing her, it did bother him a little to see her so dismissive about the fact that they would soon be separating from one another for good. She seemed to be pulling away from the friendship they had enjoyed in the lumber camp. Instead of the eager student who had soaked

78

up everything he had been teaching Katie's younger brother and Robert's two children, she was becoming more and more distracted and withdrawn.

It had been over a year since she had seen her beloved North country. Unconsciously, she stood a little straighter and breathed a little deeper. Because of all she had been through these past few months, she knew she was stronger and smarter than she had been before. Wintering in the lumber camp had given her several gifts. She had learned English. She had learned many new ways of cooking food. She had made a lasting friendship with Katie, Robert, Sarah, and Skypilot.

Tomorrow evening they would be docking at the tip of her beloved Keweenaw Peninsula at Copper Harbor. From there they would sail to Ontonagon near the range of mountains named after the porcupine. Soon, she would be among her people again. It had not pleased her when her husband insisted on traveling so far south, but he had felt the need to see new places. She did not.

Their marriage had not been a success. He had inherited a regrettable taste for alcohol that had forced her to be as watch-

79

ful of him as a hawk. This frequently made him furious with her for thwarting his purchase of liquor. He did not lash out with his fists, like so many husbands, but he did lash out with his tongue. She feared that as his desire for strong drink increased, it would come to blows between them.

After two years of marriage, the only time they truly got along was when he was too far away from civilization to get his hands on the liquid he craved. That was why she had agreed to travel so far with him when she was so far along in her pregnancy. Giving birth alone in the wilderness was far preferable to living with an angry drunk man.

He had been a handsome man, strong and brave when she married him, but it had not taken long to discover his great weakness.

Discovering that his disappearance had been caused by his death had brought a strange combination of grief and relief to her heart. She tried not to spend too much time thinking about it. Mainly, she just wanted to get back to her grandmother's tribe. Her grandmother was a wise woman and would help her figure out the warring emotions of her heart.

After all she'd been through, all she wanted was a chance to sleep in her grandmother's wigwam again, a chance to tell Fallen Arrow the stories that she had been saving up to share with her. With all her heart, she looked forward to the familiar scents and sounds of her small village. Most of all, she looked forward to enjoying the fluency of her own language once again.

She was coming home with a little money and a few presents, intending never to leave again. Robert had told her she could have a job helping Katie in the kitchen next fall if she wanted to come back, but she would not go back to the southern peninsula of Michigan. It was too crowded, and the air smelled too much of wounded and bleeding pine trees.

She sniffed the clean, pure air of the lake the whites called Superior.

It was time to become Moon Song again — the real Moon Song — not the one who had tried briefly and unsuccessfully to fit into Bay City.

She went back to her cabin and laid the cradle board gently on the bunk. It was time to feed and change Ayasha. She untied and unwrapped the leather outer layer and exposed her naked boy baby to the air. He smiled and kicked, happy to be free of the tight bindings. She scooped the soiled moss from around him, lying it on a newspaper to be disposed of later. Then she poured water from the pitcher into the basin, which was exactly like the one Katie had used in her cabin. With a piece of soft flannel, she bathed her baby as he kicked his feet and babbled. She supposed other women had loved their babies as much as she loved hers, but it was hard to imagine any mother loving her child more.

Ayasha was her heart, her breath, and apart from her own longing to see her people, he was one of the main reasons she was making this trip.

It was the right of the elders of her village to give him the name that he would carry into adulthood. Of all the good reasons to go back, obtaining a name for her son was at the top. She could hardly wait to hear what they would choose. He was a handsome, healthy child, with bright eyes, glowing fat cheeks, and a belly laugh that made her laugh aloud with him.

As she rinsed the cloth out in the basin, she wondered what kind of man her son would be. She wanted Ayasha to grow up to be a great brave among her people.

She began to sing softly in her native tongue as she cleansed him. Her heart was so full of love for this child that mere talking words were not enough, and so she made up words and a simple melody with which to soothe her baby. "For your journey. For baby's long journey. Your mother will sing songs to you." She lifted him into her arms and nuzzled his neck. "Your mother will gather sweet Juneberries for you. For your journey. For baby's long journey. She will gather Juneberries from the hills behind Grandmother's lodge."

She wrapped the material of her skirt around his naked body for warmth and nursed him, humming, until he fell asleep, satiated and content in her arms.

With Ayasha asleep, clean, and content, she rinsed out the basin and poured the rest of the water into it. Then she locked the door to her stateroom and, using another soft cloth and sweet-smelling soap Delia had given her a few days ago, she stripped and washed herself thoroughly. She wanted to be completely clean when she slipped into Delia's thoughtful gift.

After washing, she sat cross-legged on her bed and combed the tangles out of her hair. It was thick and heavy and it took a long time each day to work the wooden comb through it until she had a sleek, dark mass that she divided and plaited into two thick braids that fell over her shoulders.

Finally, at last, she could do the thing she

had dreamed of since Delia had marched up the ramp with that light-colored bundle. She pulled the soft doeskin dress over her head and let it slip down over her body. It had sleeves that came to her wrists, and she put the dress up to her nose and breathed in the rich scent of well-cured deer leather. Yes, that was the way clothing should smell.

The hemline was deeply fringed and felt soft against her knees. From the particular kind of expert design work of the carefully dyed quills to the carefully sewn seams, she could see that whoever had made it had done beautiful work. Since it was spring and still cool, leather leggings had been provided. She pulled the leggings on and then laced her moccasin boots up.

This felt right. She had almost forgotten how much she enjoyed the freedom of movement her simple clothes gave her. The dress was soft and pliable enough to allow her to move freely, and yet strong enough to withstand briars and branches she might have to walk through to get to her tribe.

With all her heart, she blessed Delia for having the compassion and foresight to purchase this for her.

Slinging Ayasha's cradle board onto her back, she left her stateroom, truly feeling like herself for the first time since her journey began.

It was very late, and most people were in their cabins asleep. Skypilot was taking advantage of the abandoned deck by taking a quiet stroll while praying for clarity about the Lord's will for his future. Then he saw Moon Song walking toward him, illuminated by the full moonlight, and he lost all thought of the future.

This was not the girl he knew, working around the camp, wearing one of the high-necked flannel nightgowns she had appropriated from Katie in lieu of a dress. Nor was she the Indian girl he'd known back in Bay City. This was someone else entirely — and the sight of her nearly brought him to his knees.

The dress Delia had made for her fit her perfectly. Loose enough to look comfortable, form-fitting enough to allow a man to know she was a woman. The nearly white, pristine doeskin was a perfect and simple contrast to her tanned skin. The bead and quill work was more beautiful on her than the costliest jewelry.

She stood tall and straight, her eyes shining with pride and happiness.

"You look . . . beautiful."

The word *beautiful* felt woefully inadequate, but it was the best he had.

"Delia know I need real clothes," Moon Song said.

Real clothes. He wondered what Moon Song thought the dresses and skirts she'd worn before had been. Obviously not "real." After seeing her like this, he tended to agree.

"The ship will stop soon," she said. "I will go see my people. You go back to Bay City."

He was not an egotistical man, but it bothered him that her voice rose as though hoping he would soon be gone from her life.

"I promised Robert I would see you safely all the way to your people."

"There is no room for you in Grandmother's lodge."

"I wasn't expecting there to be." Actually, that was exactly what he had been expecting. He had assumed that if he kept Moon Song safe by accompanying her back to her people, he would be welcome.

But what was all this talk about a grandmother? Where was her mother? Or her father, for that matter? Suddenly, he wished he'd asked her more about her life. Instead, he'd entertained her with stories about his own.

He should have been more curious. The only Indians he knew besides Moon Song were the men who came out of the woods every spring, hired, because of their great agility and balance, to ride and herd the logs down the rivers and streams.

Moon Song looked at something over his shoulder and then she turned on her heel and strode away without another word.

He realized the reason why the moment he heard Colonel Hatchette's voice directly beside him.

"It appears that your Indian woman is all dressed and ready to go back to her people."

He stiffened. "She is."

"That one is quite a looker." Colonel Hatchette stared after her.

Skypilot remained silent and hoped Hatchette took the hint. He had no intention of discussing Moon Song with this man.

Hatchette suddenly pointed. "We're passing Painted Rocks."

"Painted Rocks?"

"Look at those cliffs. I've been told that minerals leach from the rocks and give them various colors. It looks a little like paint in daylight."

As they steamed past, the full moon illuminated mile after mile of the most amazing rock formations he'd ever seen. He could see only the shadows of the colored striations, but some of the minerals glittered in the moonlight that was reflected in the water. It was eerie and magical, and for the first time in his life, he wished he was a painter so that he could capture this scene and show it to Robert and Katie back home.

He noticed that farther down the deck, that was exactly what Isabella appeared to be doing as she stood at the railing, scribbling furiously on a large pad of paper. She'd glance up at the rocks and then back down at the paper or canvas or whatever it was she was using.

"It looks like your wife is using her talent to capture the view." Skypilot nodded toward Isabella standing there wearing a wine-colored dress that was so dark it nearly blended into the night.

The three of them were the only ones on deck at the moment, unless Moon Song was still wandering about. He couldn't help but think how much the other passengers were missing by being asleep. The captain would be watching, of course, but he had probably seen it all many times before.

"Doesn't my wife look lovely in the moonlight?" the colonel said.

"She is a handsome woman." Skypilot was careful with his answer. This was thin ice. Too much enthusiasm about another man's wife could be considered fighting words, and too little admiration could be considered an insult when the man was so obviously besotted with her. That was the colonel's one saving grace that he had seen so far. He was a man in love with his wife. Then Hatchette opened his mouth and ruined what modicum of respect Skypilot had for him.

"I kept an Indian woman when I was here before."

Skypilot's stomach roiled. Even though he had once been a minister and had heard his share of intimate, sinful confessions, he most definitely did not want to hear this man's.

Then he realized this was not a confession. It was a boast.

"She thought we were married." Hatchette chuckled. "I even have a couple of half-breed children running around Copper Harbor somewhere. Maybe three."

Skypilot was appalled. Compared to this oily snake, the rough-and-tumble shanty boys he worked with looked like chivalrous knights.

"And you feel no remorse?"

The easy conversational tone with which Hatchette had been addressing him disappeared, and a belligerence entered his voice. "Where are you from?"

"Virginia."

"I thought I heard some Southern in your talk." Hatchette gave a contemptuous snort. "Are you telling me there's no part-white children running around those plantations?"

"There are, but none of them are mine. When I do father a child, I have every intention of sticking around and raising it."

"You really are an ignorant fellow, aren't you," the colonel said. "Indian women like having white men. They think it gives them prestige."

"How does your former 'wife' manage to feed your children?"

The colonel shrugged. "She's probably taken up with some other white man by now. That's what they do, you know. That Indian girl you're so fond of? She'll do the same thing when you're finished with her. Find another white man to keep her in beads and geegaws. These primitive women don't have any good Christian morals — unless some missionary gets hold of them — and then it's barely skin-deep."

Skypilot had experienced similar callousness in some plantation owners in the past. It was why he had put his livelihood on the line by preaching against slavery in Richmond, Virginia. Now, as he looked into this man's face, he wondered that there was no

90

outward sign, no indication of the rotten-
ness in this man's soul. No, Hatchette's face
was smooth and untroubled. Even handsome, perhaps, if one did not know him.

Skypilot had never been under the miscon-
ception that he was a sinless man. He had
always tried hard not to judge the weak-
nesses of others. But to be this blatant and
careless about another human being? To
boast of having abandoned a woman and
one's own children? He automatically
stepped away from the man. He didn't even
want to consider himself from the same spe-
cies as Hatchette.

"How can you possibly justify —"

He was never to finish that sentence.

He felt the vibration through his boots. By
the surprised look on Hatchette's face, he
could tell that he felt the vibration too. He
saw Isabella, down the way, lift her head
and look around as though she sensed
something was wrong. Then an explosion
ripped through the air.

7

Moon Song felt the tremor beneath her feet and heard the mounting rumble. She knew there was trouble, but she did not know whether to dive overboard or run for her cabin. In the end, there was time for neither.

She felt her breath leave her chest as she was hurled into the air by what felt like a giant fist. Her lungs barely had time to refill before that same giant unseen hand plunged her beneath water that was as cold as ice. She struggled, thrashing deep in the water, not knowing which way was up and which way was down.

Then, as her senses came flooding back, she became nothing more than one focused thought — to get herself and her baby to the surface of the water as quickly as possible.

The height from which she had been dropped had plunged her several feet into the depths. The water had been smooth, but now, it was rough. Somewhere deep in her mind, she realized that her fear of getting on that boat had been justified. This ship had blown up, and now the pull of it sinking was dragging her down with it.

She fought her way against that pull, struggling her way to the surface with every ounce of strength she had. The moment she broke through, she took one great gasp of air, getting her bearings at the same time, then she plunged her face back into the water until she knew for certain that her baby's face was out of the water. She began to swim, turning her head to the side only about every fourth stroke to gasp in some air, and then plunging her face back into the water. She had to get to shore and quickly. She had to get Ayasha out of the cradle board and the water out of his lungs or he would die.

But it was so far to shore.

Like the other Indian children living beside the great lake, she had learned to swim almost before she could walk. She and the other children, like little glistening otters, had played and cavorted in the water while parents looked on fondly. The waves of the lake had been part of her natural environment. The skills she had learned as a child served her well now as she fought for her life and for the life of her child.

She had thought her bad days were behind her, but what she had endured so far in her life was nothing in comparison to desperately swimming toward shore while wondering if her son — her heart — had drowned.

Skypilot was a strong man, but he was not a strong swimmer. In fact, his mother, a fearful and nervous woman, had not allowed him near the water when he was a child for fear that he would drown. He had always thought the wiser course would have been to make certain that he knew how to swim well — but she had not seen it that way. As an adult, he had intended to learn, someday. That day had never presented itself.

Now, he found himself in water that could very well be several fathoms deep. This knowledge struck great fear in his heart. That fear caused him to thrash around terrified because he knew what an abysmal swimmer he was. The knowledge that he was going to drown made him fight, with no skill whatsoever, even harder.

It was not pretty or graceful, but somehow, while praying constantly in his heart, he managed to kick and stroke and fight and splutter his way to a blessed place where his feet touched the ground.

■ ■ ■ ■

It seemed like weeks had gone by instead of seconds, but at last Moon Song heard the sound she had been longing to hear.

Her baby's angry, wailing cry was the sweetest sound she had ever heard. It had taken a bit of time for him to get his breath enough to howl, but howl he did. Knowing that her baby still breathed renewed her strength. In a few more moments, she had gained a foothold on a narrow, sandy spit of land from which a cliff soared straight up above her head.

She immediately dropped to her knees and pulled the cradle board off her shoulders. Ayasha's face was red and swollen from crying, but he was alive. Quickly, she unstrapped him and gathered him up in her arms. She scooted a few feet to where her back was against the face of the cliff, as far away from the water as she could possibly get, and sat there, rocking back and forth with her baby in her arms.

On his hands and knees, Skypilot dragged himself onto the narrow spit of land where he gagged and retched up water. It felt like he had swallowed half of Lake Superior.

After every drop was gone, he flopped onto his back, exhausted. It was then that he realized there was an oily taste in his mouth that lake water should not have put there. There was also a stinging sensation on his back and shoulders.

He crawled the few feet to the base of that soaring cliff he had been admiring only a few minutes earlier. He leaned his sore back, carefully, against the smooth stone surface and stared unbelieving at the water in front of him. The bright, full moon that had been smiling down upon him earlier now beamed, quite cheerfully, upon the pieces of debris dotting the water.

How could an entire ship simply disappear?

As he slowly regained his senses after his desperate swim to shore, he figured out where the oily taste had come from. There was a slick of oil on top of the water.

He had heard of massive boiler explosions that had ripped through dozens, perhaps hundreds, of steamboats in past years, sinking entire ships within minutes. He knew that hundreds of lives had been lost because of such explosions, but like everyone else on board, he had not thought it could happen to him. He had also assumed that as new inventions were patented and safety inspections increased, the danger had lessened. He had been wrong.

Moon Song and Ayasha had paid the price for his optimism. She had not wanted to board the giant ship. She had wanted to simply walk away into the forest, a journey he had deemed too dangerous. That position seemed ludicrous to him now.

The shock of what had happened washed over him as he stared at the inky-black lake. What was he supposed to do now?

Anything that had been on that boat that could float now bobbed up and down. Some of the flotsam hitting the boulders was not far from his feet. He saw what looked like a length of dark red cloth bobbing against one of the boulders. It took his brain a second to realize that the water-darkened cloth was close to the hue of the dress that Isabella Hatchette had been wearing as she had sketched on her pad.

He sprang to his feet, his own close call forgotten as he waded out, grasped the cloth, and discovered Isabella lying faceup, washed against the cliffs.

He half carried and half dragged her onto the ledge. At Bible college a group of do-gooders had come one weekend, teaching something they called first aid. One lesson dealt with saving someone's life after a drowning. Get the water out of the lungs, he'd been told, but he couldn't remember the exact method he was supposed to use. He thought it involved lying the body facedown over a barrel.

He did not have a barrel, so he did the first thing that occurred to him. He held her by her waist, her head hanging straight down like a half-opened jackknife. When nothing happened, he pounded her hard on the back with his free hand.

Suddenly, he heard a gush of water splashing against the rock upon which he stood. And then he heard a heaving gasp. He stood Isabella back up on her feet and steadied her while she took great gulps of air. Her eyes were glazed with shock.

"My skirt," she gasped. "My petticoats. They weighed me down. I couldn't breathe. I couldn't . . ."

She turned her head and glanced at the lake, taking it all in, the slick of oil, the items floating on top of the water. He heard a quick, deep intake of breath. She held it for one long moment, and then the screaming began.

Moon Song had been too occupied with comforting her baby and comforting herself with his warm little living body pressed against her, to notice if there were survivors. Less than three minutes earlier, she had been fighting for her life. Now, she heard a woman screaming somewhere far down the spit of land. Someone else had survived!

She scrambled to her feet, held Ayasha tight against her chest, and began to run toward the sound of the woman's voice.

Two figures came into view as she got closer. Her heart leaped up to see that Skypilot was alive and trying to deal with Isabella beside him. Moon Song had never seen a woman who would not stop screaming before.

Except for one time. A long time ago. When one of the women in the village was told that her young son had been killed. That had been a bad night for the whole tribe until the woman's husband had threatened to beat her unless she stopped. Even after she stopped, Moon Song had been able to hear her tortured breathing in the tipi next to theirs as the woman tried to control her sobs.

It had been an embarrassment to the husband. Chippewa women did not act that way, but she had been a slave, stolen from the Shawnee tribe farther south. Moon Song did not know if the woman was especially weak or if that was the Shawnee way, but she never forgot it.

"My baby!" Isabella screamed over and over. "My baby! He's gone!"

Moon Song hugged Ayasha even closer to her chest, grateful beyond words that she was not having to choke back her own screams right now.

Skypilot glanced around, and she knew it the instant he saw her. Their eyes met, and his face lit up with pure joy. He left Isabella to her grief and ran to her and Ayasha, gathering them both against his broad chest the moment he reached them.

He had never embraced her before, nor had she ever embraced him. Even though she had cared for him after his accident, she had always been careful. Men could get wrong ideas. Even decent men like Skypilot.

In the lumber camp, she had admired him above all the other men. She saw his kind heart and appreciated his fine mind. She had been told about how he had used his great strength to protect Robert Foster from harm when a Canadian axe man had gone after the lumber camp foreman, and she was proud of him. Most of all, she had secretly loved him — secretly because he had never shown the slightest interest in her as a woman — only as a friend. Because of this, she had carefully protected her heart from caring about him too much.

Now, finally, she welcomed the feel of his strong arms around her. It would have been a terrible thing to be alone tonight.

"You're alive. And the baby is alive. Praise God!" He cupped her face and gazed into her eyes as though making absolutely certain she was all right, and then he ran a hand over the baby's hair. "I thought I'd lost you."

Moon Song's heart swelled with the knowledge that he had been so very concerned about them. She laid a hand against his cheek. "I am not alone."

"No, my friend, you are not alone."

He kept one arm around her, as though he couldn't make himself lose contact with her, as they watched Isabella pace back and forth a few yards from them, crying, wringing her hands, and screaming the name Archibald over and over.

"Archibald?" Moon Song asked quietly.

"Her husband's name is James, so I'm guessing that is the baby's name."

"What happen?"

"The boilers must have exploded. I'm starting to wonder if that steamboat race the captain engaged in could have caused some damage."

"Why us alive?"

"Maybe because we were the only ones

101

on deck. Maybe because of that, we got blown clear while everyone else was asleep in their cabins."

"Hatchette survive?"

"I don't think so, even though I was standing only a few feet away. At least, I've seen no sign of him. No sign of anyone yet."

"There might be no sign. Probably ever."

"What do you mean?"

"Lake is very deep. Very deadly. Not like other lakes. Something in bottom grabs people. Keeps them down."

"You mean like a monster?"

"No. Like . . ." She shook her head, frustrated that she didn't have the ability to communicate what she wanted to say in English. "I have no words."

"Could you be talking about currents?" He made a motion with his hands.

"Yes. Currents. Bad currents."

Isabella appeared to notice Moon Song and Skypilot for the first time. Then she saw that Moon Song was holding a baby. She started laughing and crying, as though with relief, and came at them at a dead run, holding her sodden skirts with both hands.

"I knew he was alive! I just knew it! God would not allow me to suffer so."

Moon Song instinctively clutched Ayasha closer to her as the crazy screaming lady came at them. Isabella's arms were held out, ready to scoop Ayasha into them.

"Ayasha." Moon Song held a hand up as though to keep her away. "Not Archibald."

"Not . . . ?" Isabella peered at the infant curled in Moon Song's arms. "Why, this is just a dirty little Indian baby." She grabbed a handful of Moon Song's hair. "What did you do with Archibald?"

Skypilot pulled her away from Moon Song. "Stop it," he said. "Moon Song had nothing to do with your baby. She had Ayasha strapped to her back when the boat blast happened. I saw them. He was in his cradle board. She can't help it if having her child with her at the time saved him."

A horrified look came over Isabella's face, and she collapsed into her wet skirts, pressed her face against the stones beneath her, and began to sob. Skypilot laid a comforting hand on Isabella's shoulder and tried to say soothing words. Moon Song wondered why he bothered with the soft words. Words could not take away the horror of the truth.

As Skypilot tried to console an inconsolable woman, Moon Song began to take stock of their situation. The full moon helped. It was starting to become clear to her that unless they could find a way past that cliff and off this small sliver of land that graced the edge of it, they were in a terrible situation. She paced the length of the tiny, rocky beach toward the north. Then she paced all the way to the southern end. It was only about ten feet wide and maybe fifty feet long. It stopped abruptly at both ends, with nothing but sheer cliffs as far as she could see. She waded in a few feet at both ends. The water became deep quickly. Too deep to wade.

"What are you doing?" Skypilot asked.

"We trapped," Moon Song said.

"What do you mean, we're trapped?"

"Water get very deep here very fast. We need to swim to better place."

"I'm not a good swimmer. Frankly, it's a wonder I didn't drown out there."

Moon Song called to Isabella. "You swim?"

Isabella ignored her.

Moon Song walked over and shook her by the shoulder.

"You swim?"

Isabella had been crying so hard, her face was practically unrecognizable. "Not very well," she choked out. "Why?"

"Better to swim than climb." Moon Song nodded meaningfully at the moonlight-illuminated cliff face.

Isabella dragged herself to her feet and walked over to where Moon Song stood. Her head went back farther and farther as her eyes measured the soaring mass of the cliff towering above them. "I could never climb up that thing."

"Maybe I could climb it." Skypilot's hands were on his hips as he stared at the cliff. "I'd stand a better chance of climbing it than I would of swimming out of here."

"In boots?" She pointed at his feet. "They slip. You fall. You die."

"I could try it barefoot."

"You ever climb cliff before?" she asked.

"No."

"You ever see cliff like this before?"

"No."

"It best to swim."

"But I can't swim." He glanced out at the lake water and gave an involuntary shiver. "Honest, I really can't."

"Then how?"

"I vote we sit tight and wait for another steamer to come. Word will get back to Bay City that our ship blew up. They'll send help."

"Yes." Isabella seemed to be getting a little sense back into her head, at least enough to participate in a conversation about survival. "Let's wait for a ship to come pick us up."

"Bay City hear about this?" Perhaps white people had new ways of communicating that she did not know. "How?"

"I don't know." Skypilot sounded exasperated.

It was interesting to her that Skypilot's and Isabella's first thoughts were not about how to get out of here. Instead, their first thoughts had been on the chances of being rescued by another white person.

For the first time, she noticed that a portion of Skypilot's right sleeve was burned away. "You hurt."

"It doesn't matter." He glanced down at the sleeve. "I'll live."

That was more than she could say if they didn't get off this bit of land. Ship or no, they could not stay here. A storm could materialize so quickly on this lake, and she could see the watermark on the cliff where the waves would hit in a storm.

She looked up at the cliff and out at the dark water. A conversation she had overheard on the ship the day before greatly concerned her. The captain had told another passenger that there were so few people traveling this far north at this time of year, there would not be another steamship coming along for another two weeks.

Help was not coming. If they didn't get

off this barren strip of rocky, wet land soon,
they would be in deep trouble.

8

He was trying his best to put a good face on the situation, but the fact was, they were in a mess and he did not know what to do about it. He cursed himself for being a lousy swimmer. He cursed himself for having taken them on that ship. Then he stood back and looked up at that cliff face once again. What had seemed beautiful and pleasantly awe-inspiring from a distance looked strange and menacing up close. A lizard might be able to climb up the surface of that sheer rock face, but he was no lizard. Nor was Moon Song.

Isabella had finally cried herself out, and the only sound now was the splashing of the gentle waves against the tiny beach. He had loved listening to the waves while snug in his cozy boardinghouse room in Bay City.

Now, the waves slapping against their beach sounded desolate and carried a menace. The three of them could survive for several days without food. That was not a problem. With plenty of fresh lake water to drink, they would be fine, including Ayasha, who would thrive on his mother's milk alone. But if there was any sort of a storm, they would be washed out into the lake or battered to pieces against the face of these cliffs.

In spite of his brave words to try to calm Moon Song, he knew they did not have the luxury of simply waiting for the passing of another ship. Maybe there would be one in time. Maybe not. They might not starve for several more days, but unless the weather remained fair and calm, or a ship passed soon, or God chose to bring about a miracle, they were doomed.

There had never been a situation in his life in which he could do absolutely nothing. Even when he was drummed out of the Richmond pulpit, he fought back by helping desperate people escape. When he saw a tree was crashing near a spot where Robert's little girl had wandered, he knew he was fast enough to save her, even if it meant giving up his own life in order to do so. Now . . . nothing.

The strength had gone out of him. He was cold and wet. The skin on his back hurt. He had no earthly idea of what to do except wait.

Moon Song seemed to have given up. She simply sat with Ayasha on her lap as she leaned against the cliff face. Isabella appeared to have gone far away from all of this in her mind. She sat staring into space, her eyes apparently seeing nothing. There was nothing he could do for any of them. He didn't even have the ability to start a fire to get them warm.

Many times, he'd heard people use a phrase that had always bothered him. "The only thing left to do is pray," they would say. Like prayer was a last resort. A sort of mystical, lost hope kind of faith. He knew the Bible well enough to know that it didn't teach that prayer was a last resort. It taught that prayer was the first and continuing thing a man should do . . . not the last.

Funny how he seldom remembered that fact until his back was against the wall — like now.

Unfortunately, it was easier to pray with faith and courage when one's teeth were not chattering with cold and one's shoulder was not throbbing. The only thing he could think about was wishing he had one of Mrs. Wilcox's warm comforters to pull about his shoulders. Instead, all they had was each other.

Moon Song must have been having the same thought. She came over and sat down as close to him as possible. He drew her close to him. It helped. He saw Isabella sitting in a heap by herself, shivering.

"You'd better come over here," he said. "It will help a little if we sit close together."

It took her a few seconds to respond, but then she came and sat down beside him on the other side.

"That's a little bit better," Isabella said. "But I'm still so cold. What do we do now?"

"I don't know about you," Skypilot said, "but I'm going to pray."

He rested his head back against the stone, closed his eyes, and began to silently plead. *Father, please. I don't mind dying so much, but these women? This baby? Please spare them. Keep the weather calm. Send a ship to rescue us. Help Isabella stay calm in spite of her great loss. And I wouldn't mind if you made this burn on my shoulders stop hurting a bit.*

He was praying with such fervor, such faith, he allowed himself to crack open one of his eyes, half convinced that he would see a boat on the horizon. But except for the bits of debris floating on top, the lake

111

was as empty as a desert. At least they had been spared one horror. By the grace of God, there had been no bodies washed ashore with them. For the women's sake alone, he hoped Moon Song was right, that Lake Superior never gave up her dead.

Suddenly, Moon Song nudged him and handed him Ayasha.

"I am warmer now. I go."

She headed toward the water.

"No, Moon Song." He scrambled to his feet. "Stop."

She ignored him and waded waist deep out into the cold water.

"What are you doing?" he shouted.

If anything happened to that girl, he would never forgive himself.

"Why you so worry?" Her head disappeared beneath the water, then reappeared as she faced him, several yards out into the lake, treading water. She looked at him impishly, a small smile on her face as she teased, "You afraid?"

Then she dove and was soon out of sight.

After nearly a half hour, he heard from a distance a sound that could only have been described as an Indian war whoop.

The cliff face that she swam beside was even more vertical than the one where she had

left the others. The water was shallower in
some places than others, but it was always
next to a bare cliff. Some of the cliffs were
even higher and more impossible to climb.
Glancing back over her shoulder as she'd
left the place where they had washed ashore,
she saw that their cliff was on a slight, very
slight incline — but an incline that someone
might be able to climb with the help of a
good, strong rope. Unfortunately, they did
not have a rope.

In spite of all the praying she knew Skypilot had been doing, there was no rope
miraculously bobbing around in that lake.
The only things that had survived the explosion were just pieces of this and pieces of
that. Everything metal had sunk, of course.
There had been a couple of body parts she
had to work her way around, but that was
not information she would share with Skypilot and Isabella. Skypilot might think it
their responsibility to have some sort of
burial, and Isabella might start screaming
again. Who knew what white people might
do?

Then she saw something wedged between
two boulders up ahead. She swam over to
investigate and saw that it was a barrel.
Slightly waterlogged but still intact. There
were two words stenciled on top. She was

pretty sure that one word said "sheets," but she could not read the second one. She did not know if this carried some form of sheets of food, or the kind to put upon a bed.

While walking about the ship, she had noticed many barrels and boxes sitting on the deck. When she asked Skypilot why they were there, he said his best guess was that they had run out of storage down below. The mission of the *Belle Fortune* was not just to take on passengers but also to resupply Fort Wilkins after the long winter when no ships had been able to get through the ice. He said it looked as though the government was being generous.

She had laboriously sounded out the labels of contents as he helped her with prompts each time she got stuck on a word. Soda crackers. Mess beef. Mess pork. Soap. Condensed milk. Essence of coffee. Steamed oysters. Yeast. Pepper. Salt. Flour. Sugar. Ammunition. She had learned enough from him over the winter that she could recognize some of the letters and put them together. It had given them some entertainment to read the labels.

If the barrel contained food, it would be a good thing. If it were bedsheets, they could use them to help keep warm. Either way, she would somehow get this barrel back to them once she had finished her explorations, but more important than anything else — more important than food or warmth — was to find a way out of here. This wall of cliffs could not go on forever. Nor could they cling to that spit of land much longer.

She swam for less than a quarter of a mile before fissures began to appear in the face of the cliffs. At long last, she saw a crack big enough for a slender person to work their way through, and it led all the way to the top.

She dragged herself out of the water and sat for a few minutes, getting her strength back, thanking the Creator for her swimming skill, her youth, the extra layer of nourishing fat she had stored beneath her skin from eating so well at Katie's table all winter, and most of all for the fact that she was not a person who was easily afraid.

It took quite awhile to make her way to the top of the cliff as she picked her way over the sharp rocks and boulders, but make it to the top she did, growing warmer and warmer with each step. When finally she was able to look out over the cliff's edge and see the moon glinting off the black waves far below, she knew that she would survive and could help the others survive. Her feeling of exaltation was so great she gave voice to it in one high undulating war whoop, savoring the sound of her own strong voice echoing out over the lake.

He could tell that Moon Song was exhausted when she crawled up out of the lake.

"Here." He handed Isabella the baby and hurried to help the girl.

Moon Song collapsed still half in the water, evidently unable to crawl another inch. He waded in, lifted her in his arms, carried her back over to the rock cliff, and sat down, cradling her in his arms.

The cliff wall still retained a modicum of heat from the sun, and he was grateful for the small bit of warmth it gave. She was so cold and was shivering so badly that her body was absorbing every bit of body heat he possessed. It was a shock to him how small she felt as he cradled her in his arms. The strength of her will had always made her seem larger than she was. It shamed him that she had to do the job that he should have been able to do. Instead, he had sat here helplessly, praying that she would return. Praying that he would not have to watch her baby starve because its mother had bravely tried to save them.

"You almost didn't make it back, did

you?" he said.

She could barely hold her head up. She just nodded, and he clutched her tighter.

"Did you find anything?" He held his breath, hoping that war whoop had meant something.

She looked at him for a long moment, and then she nodded.

"You found a way to get to the top?"

She found her voice. "Yes."

"How far away?" It felt like she had been gone forever.

"Not far, but so cold!"

He could hardly imagine swimming that far even once, let alone twice. How could this slightly built body he held in his arms be that strong? Or was it her great heart alone that had brought her back to them, just as it had once brought her stumbling into their lumber camp?

At that moment, sensing that his mother was near, Ayasha began to whimper. Sky-pilot watched Moon Song visibly will the strength into her limbs to rise and lift her baby from Isabella's arms.

It hurt to see her, wet and cold, hunched over that hungry baby, comforting him by nursing him.

They were all silent. Moon Song was too exhausted to answer the dozens of questions he wanted to ask about what she had found. When Ayasha had finished his meal, she curled her body around the baby and laid down on the ground like she was preparing to sleep.

"Come here." Isabella roused and patted her skirt. "Use me as a pillow. It is one thing I can do to help."

Moon Song did not argue. She scooted over a few feet, then curled up beside Isabella with her head on her lap, both Skypilot and Isabella shielding her and her baby with the warmth of their bodies. She soon fell sound asleep.

"It would be nice to have a fire," Isabella said to him. "We have a little wood washing ashore."

"Neither Moon Song nor I have the skill to make wet wood burn with nothing but our bare hands."

Isabella touched Moon Song's hand. "She feels so cold." She turned in such a way that it freed up some of her bountiful skirt, with which she was able to cover the girl's shoulders. They were all wet, and he knew Isabella's skirt was not very warming, but it was a little better than nothing. He appreciated her gesture of kindness.

He watched as Isabella gently stroked Moon Song's black hair. "She nearly killed herself trying to help us, didn't she?"

"Yes." It was exactly what he had been thinking, but he was not prepared for her next comment.

"My husband was a fool. Were you aware of that?"

That had been his conclusion as well, but it was surprising to hear it come out of Isabella's mouth.

"You don't have to say anything." Isabella continued to stroke Moon Song's hair. "But I know you're probably thinking that I did not know about the native wife and children he abandoned. I heard him boasting to you on deck when I was pretending to be absorbed in my drawing, but I knew before then. I found a letter from one of the officers of Fort Wilkins, telling him of her plight. I checked his accounts when he was not around. I was appalled when I discovered that James did not find it necessary to send her any money. That bothered me even more than the discovery of her existence. And so I sent her some and continued to do so. Had I known what kind of man he was before we married, I would not have married him."

"Why *did* you marry him?" He'd pondered it from the moment he had first spent time with Colonel Hatchette. "It wasn't just

119

because he admired your paintings, was it?"

"It's hard to say. I desperately wanted a home and children. I was older than most when I married. I had begun to fear that I would never be able to attract a man's affections."

Moon Song stirred, and a portion of Isabella's skirt dropped from her shoulders. He watched as Isabella gently covered her again.

"Why not?"

"All well-bred ladies draw, you know. We learn how in finishing school, along with embroidery, singing, playing a pianoforte, and how to set a lovely table. Unfortunately, I was considered quite odd by my friends."

"How so?"

"I learned all those things. I was even adept at them, but I made the mistake of taking the drawing and watercolors entirely too seriously. Suddenly, it was no longer a hobby; it was all I could think about day and night. It became an obsession. The fact that I was good at it only increased my oddity. Ladies are supposed to strive to be competent, never to excel."

There was evidently more to Isabella than he would have guessed. "So what did you do?"

"I begged my father to send me to Paris

for one year. To study. He agreed to do so. Not because he understood my passion, but because he had begun to see me as an embarrassment. In his set, one's daughter was not supposed to draw pictures that, had they been drawn by a man, would have hung in galleries."

"You were that good?" A rock was digging into his hip. He extracted it and flung it into the lake.

"When I came back from Paris, I made a friend, a male friend whom my parents did not know. He, too, was an artist, although not a very good one. He took my drawings and exhibited them under his name. People paid him. He was supposed to give me the money after he took out a small commission."

He was a little surprised. She must have truly been as good as Hatchette had boasted. "And did he?"

She laughed. "Of course not."

In spite of the cold, in spite of the danger, he found himself fascinated with this conversation. He'd never known a true artist before. "What happened?"

"He took every dime and left town and there was not one thing I could do about it. It was a great lesson."

"But why marry James?"

"Like I said, I was getting older. Spending one's time drawing and painting all day long is not the best way to meet men. I suppose I married him simply because he came to my father's house on business and complimented me on a drawing I had hung in the parlor. At the time, he seemed perfectly adequate. I wanted to have children, and since men were not exactly knocking down my door, I said yes to the first one who asked."

"Certainly you could have met someone who would have suited you better."

"You have to understand. There really weren't all that many men to choose from by then. The war took so many." Suddenly, to his consternation, she began to weep again. "And I wanted children."

Her grief was so raw, and there was nothing he could do to help her. Not one thing. There were no words that would comfort a woman who had lost a child. He had learned that years before when he had ministered to a large congregation.

Her comment about the war taking so many men reminded him of Penelope's letter again. Was she like Isabella? Did she see him as her last chance at marriage? All those years without a word from her made that assessment quite likely.

He reached into his breast pocket for the lilac envelope and brought out a fistful of wet, crumpled paper, which he flung as far as he could into the lake.

That soggy paper reminded him that in his back pocket was a small leather Bible. He drew it out now, wondering how badly it had been damaged.

"What's that?" Isabella said.

"My father's Bible. I've carried it with me for so many years and gotten so used to the feel of it, I almost forgot it was there."

He untied the leather string with which he kept it bound and opened it to see if it, too, had dissolved into a mass of wet paper.

To his surprise, it had been tied so tightly, the leather had protected the inner pages from the water, and only the outer edges were soaked. With care, it might be salvageable.

"Is it ruined?"

"No. It's wet, but I think it will be all right once it dries out."

"Under the circumstances, I think a wet Bible might be the least of our problems."

"I agree, but I'm still grateful." He reverently tied the leather string around the Bible and slipped it back into his pocket. In the middle of such tragedy, his heart leaped up at the discovery of this small miracle.

9

It did not take long for Moon Song's strength to return. Long before dawn, she felt recuperated enough to dive back into the frigid waters. The barrel was exactly where she'd left it earlier, wedged between the two boulders. Now that she had rested, she had enough strength to bring it back with her. Even though it was waterlogged, it still had just enough air in it that she was able to half push/half float it back to the slice of land upon which Skypilot and Isabella sat.

Isabella jumped to her feet. "Is it food?"

Skypilot inspected the top of the barrel where the words were written. "No. It says Sheeting Fabric."

"Oh." Isabella sat down again, disappointed. Moon Song didn't blame her. They were all hungry.

"I need help to open," she said.

"I'll try to be careful," Skypilot said.

"Maybe I could use it to float out of here on."

She shook her head. "Too much damage. No fix."

"If you say so." Skypilot lifted the heavy, sodden barrel above his head and brought it crashing down upon a boulder. A barrel full of unbleached cotton fabric came spilling out.

"I suppose it will help keep us warm," he said. "But that's about all."

"No, no." She had already been thinking about what she would do if it held bedsheets instead of food. She lifted one of her braids to show him. "We do this. Long, long time. We make rope."

Using her teeth to start the tear, she began to rip the sheeting material into wide strips. Then she started holding the strips to her nose and drawing them out as far as her arm would reach.

"What in the world are you doing now?" he asked.

"I measure. One yard. Katie show me how."

"It's one yard from your nose to the tip of your finger?"

"Katie say."

"Well, if Katie says it, I'm sure it's true."

She thought sixty-five feet would be

enough rope, and so she measured out enough yardage for each strand, tying on more strips when necessary.

When all the strips were finished and counted, she told Skypilot that they had enough fabric strips to do a four-ply braid. Then she showed both Skypilot and Isabella how to do it, spelling them in turn so that everyone's fingers got a short rest.

After several hours of untangling and braiding, untangling and braiding, even Skypilot with his big hands had become somewhat of an expert. He discovered that it worked better for him to hold the make-shift rope between his knees, braiding outward as Moon Song or Isabella kept the end of the strips untangled.

Dawn broke and it was past noon by the time they had a rope finished and coiled at the base of the cliff.

Unfortunately, it was no longer the clear, calm day they had enjoyed yesterday before the explosion. Thunderclouds blocked the sun, and the lake took on an ominous cast.

Moon Song hurriedly cared for Ayasha before she left. She wished she still had her bundle of dried moss to pack the little fellow in, but all there was to use was the soiled moss from the day before, which had partially dried. The smell was getting bad.

Hopefully, they would be able to find some fresh in an hour or two once they managed to make it to the top of the cliff.

Everything was in readiness. All she had to do was coil the rope around her waist and make that swim one more time, then she would walk to the top of the cliffs, make her way to a spot above them, and hope that they could climb up before the storm broke.

"I have a gift for you before you go," Isabella said.

Moon Song could not see how Isabella could have a gift. They had nothing except the clothes on their backs and this rope.

Isabella pulled an apple from her pocket. "It isn't much, but it might give you enough strength to do what you have to do."

"Your stomach make hungry noise in night," Moon Song said. "Why did you not eat?"

"I saved it for you. Right now you are the most important person here. You're our only hope, Moon Song, unless a ship comes along, and if this storm that's coming is a bad one, no ship is going to save us."

Moon Song was impressed. "This is a thing our people do — sacrifice food for braves who hunt in winter."

"Just eat it, and get us out of here, please," Isabella said. "I don't particularly want to

127

live without my child, but I'd prefer not to spend what life I have left sitting on this pile of rock."

Moon Song devoured the apple, eating well past the part that most people would have thrown away. The sweetness flowed into her mouth, juicy and delicious. She stopped just short of eating the bitter seeds.

"How did you just happen to have an apple in your pocket?" Skypilot asked.

"It's a habit of mine from my Paris days. I'd sometimes get so engrossed in a scene I was drawing that I would forget to eat until I was suddenly ravenous. I've kept an emergency apple in my pocket ever since." She gave a small smile. "I told you that I was a little odd. Remember?"

"Well, I'm grateful," Skypilot said.

Moon Song glanced up at the threatening sky. "Help me wrap, please," she said. "Before storm come."

The rope had weighed about twenty pounds before she'd stepped into the water. Now, saturated with water, she estimated it weighed twice as much. She could not swim out in the clear without fear of sinking. This time, she worked her way around the cliff, resting from time to time by steadying herself with one hand on the rock wall while she kicked in place. Then she'd swim a few more feet. Twice the weight of the rope along with the increasingly large swells in the lake almost took her under.

She knew the waves probably meant the storm was already raging somewhere in the distance. Her position next to the cliff began to be a hazard as the height and strength of the waves increased. She had to fight not to be battered against the rock face.

Time after time she was slung against the cliffs. The force wasn't yet great enough to destroy her, but it began to take on a desperate rhythm. As the wave would go out, she would claw her way, kicking, across the face of the cliff. Then the wave would come crashing back, and she would flatten herself against the cliff face, holding her breath until the wave pulled away. A few more inches, another wave. A few more inches, another wave. She felt like a piece of driftwood being pounded again and again against the rock — except this piece of driftwood was not helpless. It had arms and legs and could effect a little bit of move-ment toward her goal — that blessed fissure in the rock she had discovered last night.

At long last, there was a wave that knocked her, sprawling, onto an extremely narrow, rock-strewn beach where she lay facedown, panting. Then she scrambled up and away from the next wave that she knew would come crashing down over her.

Her leather clothing sagged. The heavy rope dragged at her, but she headed toward the opening in the cliff and began her ascent. The lake was even emptier than it was yesterday. Most of the flotsam had either sunk or been washed away.

Lake Superior could gobble a life or dozens of lives in an instant during a storm, then a few hours after the storm passed, exhibit nothing but crystal-clear water. Much like a person who has done great wrong but is determined to hide it behind a sparkly façade.

She loved this lake and she hated this lake. Right now, as the storm clouds darkened, she hated it. If she couldn't get the people who were depending on her out of there soon, the nightmare she had dreaded would begin as the waves rose and began to wash over the small piece of land.

She held the rope tightly where it was wrapped around her waist, grateful for the good knot that Skypilot had tied. Lumbermen tended to know how to tie good knots.

The moment she got to the top of the cliff, she began to trot toward her goal. It was impossible to run. She had to keep a sharp eye on where the edge was. She was sure that there had been more than one person or animal who had accidentally gone over these dangerous cliffs and been dashed to their deaths.

Finally she spied the tree growing at the top of the cliff where they had been trapped. It was an unusual tree, strangely misshapen and twisted by the wind. She had focused hard on it this morning, wanting to have a landmark.

She caught sight of the tree just as she heard the rumble of distant thunder.

"It is taking too long!" Isabella shouted. "Something has happened to her."

She had to shout because the crashing of the waves had increased and normal conversation was impossible. He and Isabella were as far away from the water as they could get, but even against the cliff, the waves were washing over their ankles. If this turned into a real thunderstorm, he didn't even want to think about how bad it would get.

"She'll make it back to us or die trying!" he yelled.

"That's what I'm afraid of!"

At that moment, something fell against his shoulder. He glanced up and saw the rope he had so laboriously braided lying against the rock face beside him.

Moon Song was peering over the cliff, motioning them to come up. They had discussed the kind of knot she would have to make around the tree, and he had had her practice it until she was proficient.

"She made it!" he told Isabella and pointed upward. "Are you ready?" He had the rope in his hand, ready to tie it around her.

"I don't think so." She stared up at the cliff face.

"Why? If it's going to break, it will be with my greater weight."

"True, but I'm not sure I have the strength to pull myself up. Drawing pictures doesn't exactly make one physically strong. I might need you to be at the other end of that rope to help."

He gave this some thought. She made a good point. "All right, but tie the rope around your waist when I throw it back down — don't depend on your hands being able to grip it."

Moon Song had made a small bundle of the leftover sheet material before she left, which he now tied around his own waist. The nights were going to be cool. They all knew that they could use what little warmth the sturdy material could afford.

Isabella helped secure Ayasha and the cradle board on his back. Thus encumbered, he began his climb.

He felt the rope stretch as he began to work his way up the cliff. He thanked God for the very slight incline that made it possible to gain just a little traction and not have to rely entirely upon his upper body strength. He prayed every step of the way that the rope would hold, that the knot would hold, that Moon Song had tied it the way he'd shown her.

The jerky way he had to make his way up the cliff with the wind buffeting them made the normally happy baby wail with fear. Ayasha's cries melded with the howl of the wind. Skypilot had to use every ounce of strength he had to muscle his way up.

By the time he got to the top, a light rain had begun and the sound of thunder was growing closer. In the far distance, he saw a crackle of lightning.

"We need to go." Moon Song was lying on her belly, peering over the cliff edge. "You think white woman can do this?"

He inspected the rope and the tree around which it was tied, and tested the security of the knot. "I guess we'll see."

He threw the end of the rope as far out as

he could and watched it drop near Isabella. She wrapped it around her waist twice, tied it, then looked up at him and gave it a tug.

Isabella was not a small woman. She was about four inches taller than Moon Song, and even though well proportioned, she was at least 50 pounds heavier. He was guessing he would be pulling a load of about 160 pounds if the woman couldn't help herself.

They watched as she started the difficult climb to the top. It was a false start. She'd barely gone three feet before she dropped to the ground again.

"What is she doing?" Skypilot was appalled. The storm was intensifying.

"Long skirt," Moon Song pointed out. "No good for climbing."

She was right. Isabella took the front of her skirt and tucked the edges into the rope that was wrapped around her. Freed from stepping on the material, she began the ascent again.

He saw immediately that she was as weak as she had feared. She did not have the strength to go hand over hand as he had done. About all she had was enough strength to hold on. He handed Ayasha to Moon Song and began to pull, throwing his weight against hers by leaning backward. It reminded him of a tug-of-war where the opponents are equally matched.

"Pull!" Moon Song was peering over the cliff. "She try to help. Rock very wet now. Her feet slip."

He could feel his arms nearly jerked out of their sockets each time she slipped.

He heard Isabella scream.

"Is she hurt?" he asked.

"No. She scared," Moon Song said. "She slip. It scare her."

"I don't know if I can do this." He grunted with the effort.

Moon Song stopped watching the cliff's edge, propped Ayasha against a tree, and began to put her strength and weight into helping him. She was not a big force, but she was a force, and even her slight body helped. By the time they saw Isabella's face appear above the cliff edge, the storm was intensifying. She crawled onto the floor of the forest that rose around them and lay there, hugging the ground, gasping for breath, while the wind began to whip the lake into a froth. The lightning Skypilot had seen in the distance worked its way closer, and a hard torrent of rain began to pelt them. He saw Ayasha gasp from the shock of the cold rain against his face.

"No time!" Moon Song said. She jerked Isabella to her feet and untied the rope from around her waist. "We go!"

Skypilot couldn't have agreed more. "Absolutely, we go!"

While Moon Song grabbed up Ayasha's cradle board, he gathered the rope into a tight bundle, and he and Isabella followed Moon Song.

Moon Song seemed to know exactly where she was going, and yet where she was leading them didn't make sense to him. They should be headed downhill into the woods, where there would be danger but also at least some semblance of shelter. Instead she was trotting along the edge of the cliffs. Did she not know that it was best to seek low ground during a lightning storm?

"Moon Song!" He pointed. "We should be going that way!"

She waved him off and kept going.

At last they arrived at the place where Moon Song had been headed. She sat down on the ground and began to scoot down a long incline. He could see the waves crashing high against the rocks now. Just then, Moon Song ducked beneath a rock overhang off to the side of the path. The elements had carved out a cave-like hollow in the side of the cliff.

"In here!" she shouted.

She didn't have to tell him and Isabella

twice. They ducked in, panting, and collapsed onto the ground. After he got his breath, he realized that they not only had shelter that a lightning strike would not penetrate, they also had a ringside seat to the most awe-inspiring sight he had ever seen. Lightning flashed, bolt after bolt, putting on a display that rivaled any fireworks show. It was like sitting in a balcony while a great performance went on before their eyes.

Best of all, they were finally in a dry place. In fact, it was so dry, the combination of earth and sand where rain never fell created a soft, dusty surface for them to sit upon. With all his heart, he praised God for the shelter. A few minutes more, and it would have been terrible to be outside.

None of them said a word as they sat there, catching their breath. Then Moon Song began to hum softly and rock her baby while they all watched the lake beat itself into a frenzied foam at the shoreline, as though it were a mad dog turning upon itself.

If a ship didn't come soon, he had no idea what he was going to do with two women, a baby, and no food. But at least they were alive.

10

Moon Song had observed that white people only slept at night. Someone who slept during the day, unless ill or a child or an old person like the camp cook who had worked with Katie, was considered lazy.

She had learned differently from her people, especially her grandfather, a great hunter, who grabbed snatches of sleep when the animals were sleeping, the better to be alert and ready when it was time to hunt. She, too, had trained herself to fall instantly asleep, and to be just as instantly awake.

There was not one thing she could do until the rain stopped. Then she would go see what the pantry of the countryside had in store for them. Thanks to Grandmother, there were few plants for which she did not know the medicinal or edible use. Early spring was not the best time to go foraging, but if one knew where to look, one could almost always find something. And so, reasonably content beneath the sheltering rock, she curled up in the velvety dust and fell sound asleep to the sound of waves crashing on the rocks below.

Visions of stewed squirrel or rabbit, perhaps some roasted fish, accompanied her into the oblivion of sleep.

"How can she do that?" Isabella asked.

"How can she do what?"

"Sleep like that, in the midst of all that is going on."

"I guess she's tired," Skypilot said. "She's worked harder than both of us."

"I know, but she's smiling in her sleep."

"Maybe she's having a pleasant dream."

"Under the circumstances, I would think she should be having nightmares. How are we going to get out of this mess?"

"I wish I knew."

"Do you have any idea how far away we are from a settlement?"

"My best guess is sixty, maybe seventy miles. I heard the captain say that a place called Marquette was the next stop."

"And we're going to walk?"

"Unless you have a better idea."

"What about food?" She had unpinned her hair and was now wringing out the rainwater as though wringing out a washrag.

"How are we going to eat?"

What did he look like, a magician? He said the first thing that came to his mind. "I've heard of people surviving on grubs and worms."

"That's disgusting."

"I agree, unless that's all you have."

"Certainly you can do better than that."

"Me? I have no idea, but I'm hoping that girl over there who is smiling in her sleep knows a thing or two. I suggest we stop talking and let her get her rest so she can be clearheaded when she wakes up. In fact," he said as he lay down on his side, "it might be wise to follow her example. There's nothing we can do right now."

"I won't be able to sleep a wink."

"Suit yourself. I'm worn out."

He closed his eyes and pretended to sleep while she rustled around, trying to get comfortable.

"This is miserable."

"Not as miserable as being in the lake."

He felt sorry for the woman, but there wasn't a thing he could do for her. He fell asleep to the sound of thunder.

Moon Song awakened in the morning to a clear day. Only the drip, drip, drip of water off the lip of their cave-house shelter gave any indication of the deluge they'd endured last night. No one else was stirring — not even Ayasha.

This was good. It gave her time to gather breakfast.

She made her way down the path, making plans. The quickest way to fill everyone up, she thought, would be with fish. It took time to make a rabbit or small game snare, and more time to wait for something to blunder into it. Instead, she found a long, slender stick and made it into a spear by lashing the knife to the end of the stick.

Then the fun came. Oh how she had missed this!

Wading out to her knees, she stood as still as a crane, completely motionless, poised with her makeshift spear in hand. She waited for several minutes, not moving, her eyes roving the shallow water. It was early morning and the lake had calmed. She had grown up beside this lake and knew its moods as well as she knew her own. It was as though it had thrown a tantrum last night, and having used up all its anger was now as placid as a small child sucking on a cone of maple sugar. Hopefully it would be in the mood to give up a fish or two this morning.

If a ship didn't pass soon, she would have

to take them overland, which was a problem because she was not familiar with this part of the lake. She knew much more about the western side. Unfortunately, the western side was becoming overrun with white people.

There were white people like Katie, Robert, Skypilot, and Delia whom she liked and trusted, but she thought the ones who worked over where her people lived were crazy. They sank deep tunnels in the earth, digging out the shiny bright copper that turned green the minute it was exposed to air. Her people had used this metal for years. In some places the metal actually laid exposed on top of the ground, available to anyone who wanted to take the time to shape it into some useful or decorative article. Her people had done this for as long as the oldest grandfather of her tribe could remember and beyond.

The white people, however, had not been satisfied with the chunks they found close to the surface. They dug deeper and deeper, taking out wagonloads of the metal, building huge buildings where it was rumored they had large machines that crushed the rocks so that they could get every last bit of copper out to put on their ships to carry away.

There! She thrust the spear downward, striking as quickly as a rattlesnake, the muscles in her arm coiled tight from the wait. She felt the satisfying crunch as the knife went through a fish, and then she brought it up out of the water, wriggling and fighting. It was nice-sized, a good meal for one hungry person or enough to satisfy at least a little hunger for all of them if this was all she could catch this morning.

She could not stand in the cold water any longer, so she stepped out while she gutted the fish and allowed her legs to warm.

Soon she would be very warm. They all would. She had found a great gift this morning. They were not the first people to use that particular rock shelter. The first thing she'd seen when she'd opened her eyes was something more precious than food. Lying on a small ledge above her head was a piece of flint, left behind by someone else who had taken shelter there at one time. It could have been left there yesterday or a thousand summers ago, but she was grateful. It was possible to make a fire without a flint, but it was time-consuming and nearly impossible after a rain had drenched everything combustible.

She waded into the water again. Even moving shadows could frighten a fish, so she moved slowly, carefully. Then she took up her stance again, ready to spring, hoping the lake would provide more food.

Skypilot awoke with a start. He glanced around, disoriented. His exhaustion was so deep and his sleep had been so profound, it took him a moment to remember why there was a rock ceiling above him, a woman lying in mud-encrusted red velvet nearby, and a baby leaning against the stone wall, blinking solemn coal-black eyes at him.

Then he came to his senses, shook his head, rubbed his eyes, and realized that Moon Song was gone. He duckwalked out from under the rocky overhang and then stood and stretched to his full height. The clouds had disappeared, the rain was gone, the air was fresh, and they had escaped death twice in the past few hours.

His eye was caught by a slender figure standing in the shallows of the lake down below. It was Moon Song, still as a statue, looking down. It struck him as a strange thing for her to be doing until he saw the spear in her hand flash downward and come up with a fish flapping on the other end.

Moon Song had gone fishing?

His mouth began to water at the thought of fried fish. Then he realized he would have to eat them raw, and his stomach recoiled at the thought. He would have to be a lot closer to starving before he could chew raw fish and keep it down.

Still, watching that beautiful girl standing so quietly in the water, every muscle taut and ready to spring, did something to his stomach that had nothing at all to do with food.

It was obvious to him now that he had spent an entire winter underestimating her. He had been kind, but he had never taken her seriously as she stumbled over English words and struggled with white mannerisms.

As he had recuperated from his injuries, she had been a source of entertainment and sometimes a delight as he realized how lightning swift she was to learn, but she'd also seemed innocent and childlike, so much younger than she truly was.

In Bay City, she had seemed awkward and out of place, prowling about the city, wearing white women's clothes with her baby on her back. All who had known her in the camp had loved her, but she had become a worry and sometimes a bit of an embarrassment to him and the Fosters once they came into town.

But here?

Watching her here was like watching a graceful doe melt into the shadows of the forest. The perfection of it tugged at his heart.

She struck again and came up with another fish.

Standing there in the shallows of the lake, poised and natural, dressed in the fashion her people had worn forever, she was in her element, and she took his breath away.

Now he and Isabella were the ones out of place and awkward. Moon Song belonged here. They did not.

Funny how he had never really seen her before. Watching her like this — so intent on her task, framed against the beauty of the lake — was like candy to his eyes.

Ah. Fishing was over now. She had evidently caught as much as she wanted. He watched as she worked over the fish, squatted and rinsed them out, then slipped the knife back into her boot and came walking up the path.

He steeled himself against the miserable thought of chewing raw fish. He'd do it, though. Not only to avoid starvation but to keep from hurting Moon Song's feelings.

"Looks like you've been busy," he said when she entered.

"Fish will taste good." She was obviously

146

well pleased with herself.

"I've never eaten raw fish before," he confessed.

"Raw?" She made a face and shuddered. "Why eat it raw?"

Fascinated, he watched as she placed the fish on a rock and then walked into the shallow rock house. When she came out, she had a piece of rock in her hand and some small bits and pieces of wood that looked like the remains of an old fire. Then she looked around until she saw a large tree, long dead, lying on the ground a few feet away. It had broken when it fell from the heights above them, and the end of it was not only rotten but hollow inside. She pulled her knife out and dug into the heart of that hollow.

"Here." She handed him a couple of handfuls of dry pith that she had dug out. Then she searched until she found a few dead limbs lying about. Carrying the pith, he followed her over to a place near the overhang where she'd put the pieces of dry wood she'd found.

She took the dry, rotten wood from his hands, made a small mound of it, and then began to make sparks fly from the flint stone by striking it with her knife.

"Where did you get that?"

"Inside. On rock shelf."

She ignored him while she concentrated on gently blowing a spark that had fallen on the pith into a small flame. Soon the dry pieces of wood were also afire, and she began to feed some of the damp, dead wood into the flames. Within minutes, she had a good, strong fire going, and Isabella had awakened.

"What's going on?" she asked.

"Moon Song is cooking breakfast for us."

Isabella's eyes opened wide. "Breakfast?"

"Fresh-caught fish."

"How?"

"She speared them."

Moon Song left for a few minutes, then came back with several small green twigs. One was forked and it formed the base for whatever it was she was making. Her fingers flew as she wove those twigs together in a shape that reminded him vaguely of a very small snowshoe. When the twigs were woven together, she laid the fish on it, split-side down, then wove three more twigs over it, securing it to her green-twigged cooking implement.

Holding the fish expertly secured in the woven cooking device over the fire, she roasted the fish first on one side, then turned it over to roast on the other. Soon it had turned flaky, and steam rose from it.

"It is done." She withdrew the three twigs, shook the now-cooked fish out onto a clean flat rock she had brought close to the fire, and handed the warmed "plate" to Skypilot.

"Ladies first." He passed the dish to Isabella, who fell upon the fish like the starving person she was.

Moon Song frowned. "Braves eat first in my tribe."

"It's different for whites," Skypilot said. "The polite thing to do is to allow the women to go first."

"Oh." Quickly, she positioned the second fish on the woven twig cooking device, and held it over the fire.

"I don't believe I've ever eaten without a fork," Isabella mused as she wiped her hands on her skirt. "As a child I was taught that it was rude to eat with my fingers."

"If we make it out of here," Skypilot said, "I promise not to tell anyone."

Isabella smiled as she picked up the last bits and dropped them into her mouth.

"Ingenious," Skypilot said as the second fish started steaming. His mouth began to water as he anticipated the taste of the fresh-caught lake fish. In minutes it was done. Moon Song placed it on the small warming stone. He started to reach for it, then stopped when Moon Song calmly began to eat what she'd cooked.

Ladies first. Of course.

It was hard to wait, but she soon finished, wiped her mouth on her sleeve, and began to prepare his fish. She had obeyed the letter of his law.

"Let cool," she instructed as she placed the fish on the third stone. "Fish hot."

Skypilot snatched a piece off the still-hot rock and flipped it from hand to hand for a few seconds before tossing it into his mouth. It was quite possibly the most delicious thing he'd ever eaten. Being careful of bones, he gobbled up every ounce of the savory food.

The burning hunger in his gut eased, and he relaxed against one of the boulders near the fire, enjoying the warmth. Soon, he saw steam rising from his damp clothes, and he thanked God for the discovery of that piece of flint and the amazing Indian woman who knew how to use it.

Moon Song now rose and carried Ayasha down to the lake, where she rinsed him off, dried him, and wrapped him in one of the pieces of leftover sheets, and then brought him to Skypilot.

"You hold," she said. "I find moss."

Skypilot held the damp baby, who was

now studying him with those dark eyes. What would it feel like to have and then lose a child like this? He could not fathom how Isabella was feeling, and yet she seemed to be a fairly strong woman who was coping the best she could under the circumstances. He just hoped she was strong enough.

11

The only thing they saw all day was a large sailing ship, but it was so far away, it was hardly visible. They yelled and waved, but the chances that it might see them were next to impossible. Isabella hung one of her frilly petticoats over the face of the cliff and anchored it with rocks, hoping it would catch the eye of anyone who might be passing.

They did not allow the fire to go out. It had dried their clothes, cooked a second meal of fish, and given them all heart. There was also the possibility a passing ship might see the smoke from the fire.

He spent a large part of the day carefully trying to dry out the pages of his Bible.

"Good idea." Moon Song nodded her approval. "Paper make good kindling if the fire go out."

"No, Moon Song," he said. "We'll not use the pages of this Bible for starting a fire."

"That will make your God angry?"

He thought about it. She had asked a very good question.

"I suppose it would depend on whether someone was doing it out of desperation or out of contempt for his Word."

"Your Bible looks funny now."

That was certainly true. The drier it got, the more misshapen it became. Where the edges of the pages had gotten wet, they were now ruffled. His Bible was starting to look downright fluffy.

He turned pages, separating them, reading here and there the familiar passages.

"Read to me?" Moon Song asked. "Please? Will make time go fast."

Her request gave him pleasure. While he was recovering from his injury at the lumber camp, he had tried to talk to her about God by telling her Bible stories.

"Yes," Isabella said. "Read something to us. It will make the time go faster."

With two women as his audience, he thought it made sense to go with a story about a woman, and unless a ship appeared on the horizon soon, they definitely had some time to kill.

Moon Song had been so courageous; the story of a brave queen seemed appropriate. He spent the next hour alternately reading

153

from and explaining the book of Esther to her while Isabella looked on with flashes of amusement as Moon Song struggled to understand the story.

"So the two tribes, they do not like each other?" Moon Song asked. "Why did Esther marry the chief if they at war? Why not marry a brave from own tribe?"

"I don't think she had a choice," Skypilot said. "And he wasn't a chief, he was a king."

"She is a slave?"

"Not exactly."

"Then why no choice?"

"Because the king got everything he wanted. Esther was very beautiful, and he wanted her for his queen."

"Moon Song hide plenty good if chief want to marry her and she not want to marry him back!"

"I'm sure you would. Back then it was considered a great honor to be chosen by the king."

"Why she not just go in king's house then? Why they make Esther wait twelve moons?"

"They had to get her ready for him. They prettied her up with special oils and perfume."

"Twelve moons is lot of oil and perfume." Moon Song shook her head at the waste. Then she brightened as though at a happy thought. "Maybe they teach her how to cook. Snare rabbits. Clean fish. So king can eat good?"

"Maybe." Getting through this story was becoming more difficult by the minute.

"I heard once that those ancient queens spent a lot of time bathing in goat milk." Isabella shot him a teasing glance.

"Goat milk?" Moon Song was astonished. "Why goat milk?"

"It was supposed to make their skin soft."

"This passage does not say anything about goat milk," Skypilot said. "Don't make things any more complicated than they already are, Isabella."

Eventually Skypilot worked his way to the crux of the story — Queen Esther's courage in trying to save her people.

"She was very afraid of the king. Her uncle Mordecai, who knew how desperate the danger was, told her that she was her people's only hope, and he thought she might have been made for that moment."

"What did Esther say to that?" Moon Song's eyes were bright with interest.

"She agreed to go to the king, and she said, 'If I perish, I perish.' Those are five of the bravest and most famous words in the Bible."

"So, Esther died?"

"No, the king listened to her, believed her, and her courage saved her people."

Moon Song sighed with pleasure. "She good chief's wife."

He gave up on correcting the word she had used. "She was a very good chief's wife, indeed."

"What do you think, Moon Song?" Skypilot asked. "Stay here and wait or try to walk to Marquette?"

Moon Song glanced at Isabella's stylish high-topped shoes with their two-inch heels that were drying near the fire. She shook her head. "Bad shoes."

"I know." Skypilot inspected one of Isabella's shoes. "How would you feel about taking these heels off, Isabella?"

"Are you considering mutilating the leather shoes that my husband had imported from Italy for me?"

"I'm afraid so."

"If you can take those heels off without the shoes falling apart, I would appreciate it. Those things are miserable to walk in."

Moon Song handed her knife to him, and he worked at sawing the heels off while Moon Song turned the new moss over that she had gathered. He was grateful that the baby would have dry, clean moss for tomorrow. It would certainly make their day more pleasant.

Isabella kept an eye on Ayasha while the infant crawled and toddled in the warm dust of the shelter. He was just beginning to learn how to walk, and Isabella was holding both of his hands right now, helping him stand up.

"You are a strong little fellow, aren't you!" she exclaimed.

The baby gurgled and laughed.

"He's such a fine child," Isabella said. "My son, Archibald, is about the same age. I named him after my father."

Skypilot took note of the fact that she was referring to her baby in the present tense. He'd heard other people do that during the early days of grief. He had no idea if having Ayasha here to play with and help care for would help lessen her grief or add to it.

"This baby is light-colored for an Indian," Isabella commented.

"His father was white. Moon Song was married to a French-Canadian trapper."

"Oh. That would explain it."

With the moss evenly distributed around the fire, Moon Song got up to leave the shelter.

"Where are you going?" he asked.

"To find bowl."

"A bowl? Where do you think you're going to find a bowl?"

"You like tea?"

He threw another branch on the fire. "Of course, I like tea, but there are no bowls here."

She smiled knowingly. "You see."

What she came back with was nothing more than a rectangular piece of birch bark.

"That's your bowl?"

"You see soon," Moon Song said.

He didn't say anything. Instead, he simply kept watch, even though what she was doing made no sense to him.

She warmed a corner of the bark, which seemed to soften it, and then she creased and folded it along all the corners. With a small, sharp twig, she punched holes in each of the corners and used tiny young grapevine stems to tie the holes together — creating a sort of rectangular bowl. The only thing he could see that the bowl would be good for was perhaps picking berries, had there been any berries this time of year.

As something to make tea in, it was useless. If it had been anyone else he knew, he would have made a joke, but with Moon Song, he decided it would be best to keep his mouth shut. Who knew what she might have up her sleeve?

She then took the container down to the lake and came back with about a quart of water in it. It surprised him that it did not appear to be leaking. She raked the main flames of the fire over a few inches, creating a small bed of coals covered with ash, and then she did something he would never have believed had he not seen it with his own eyes — she set the birch bark bowl flat upon the ash-covered coals.

"Won't it catch fire?" he asked.

"Wait," she said. "Watch."

And so he watched. The side of the bowl closest to the body of the fire got darker from the heat but did not catch fire. Within about ten minutes, curls of steam rose from it. Within twenty minutes, steam was rising in earnest. At that point, Moon Song took a handful of something from her pocket, chopped it up, and then sprinkled it over the hot water.

"And what is that?"

"We call it 'little sturgeon-fish plant.' White people call it 'mountain mint.' "

"Is it some sort of healing plant?"

"No." She glanced at him, concerned. "You sick?"

"Not yet."

She shrugged. "Taste good."

While the herbs steeped in the steaming

159

liquid, Moon Song's hands were not still. She worked with three other pieces of birch bark, which she cut, warmed, and shaped into small cups.

He could soon smell a minty aroma arising from the thin wooden basket.

She took one of the smaller birch cups then dipped it into the steaming water. She handed it to Skypilot, who cradled it in his palm. This time he did not say "ladies first," but he did wait politely to drink. Isabella took the woodland cup and examined it carefully. "This is beautiful, Moon Song, and I've always been partial to mint tea."

Moon Song smiled and held up an invisible pretend container. "Sugar?"

Isabella played along. "Well, I don't mind if I do. Three lumps, please. I've always preferred my tea extremely sweet."

Moon Song, like a small child at a doll's tea party, pretended to drop three lumps of sugar into the cup of tea. Then she looked at him questioningly.

"Two lumps, please." He held out his cup for his imaginary lumps of sugar.

Moon Song giggled as she pretended to drop them into the water. To amuse her, he made exaggerated splashing sounds.

He was finding himself absolutely entranced with this daughter of the lake

160

country with her combination of competency, courage, and innocence. No doubt Katie had served Moon Song tea in a real china cup with sugar and . . .

"Cream?" Moon Song tipped her head to one side and held up an imaginary pitcher.

"I would love some!" Isabella said, enjoying the game.

"Me too," Skypilot agreed.

After pouring the imaginary cream, Moon Song, smiling, took Ayasha onto her lap, cuddling him as she sipped the minty hot water.

He was astonished at how heartening the civilized action of drinking hot tea could be, even if the sugar and cream were imaginary. With a fire, dry clothes, cooked fish in his stomach, and now a hot liquid to sip, life seemed manageable, even if they were far from civilization and rescue.

The two rabbit snares she'd set early that morning had taken much skill and time to perfect, but the time spent had been worth it. They would be having two juicy rabbits for supper tonight. She gave thanks for the blessing these little rabbits would be for them. She was also grateful that her grandmother taught her how to make an effective trap that did not rely on string or wire. She made them out of small, threadlike roots she knew how to find.

The braves of her tribe were experts in bringing down deer, bear, and moose. After a productive hunt, the men spent time sitting around, reliving the kill while the women butchered the animal and carried the meat into camp.

The women of the tribe were the experts in snaring small game, something with which the men seldom bothered. The squirrels and rabbits her grandmother had caught had filled in around the edges of their hunger between her grandfather's bigger kills. The rabbit skins had many uses as well.

Unfortunately, many of their people had come to rely on white man's string and wire and his metal cooking pots and guns for such a long time that the old ways of survival were being forgotten. Not every Chippewa woman had these skills anymore. Many no longer wanted them.

Instead, they waited for the yearly annuities that the government had promised them for their land. And they waited, and they waited. Too often the payments were late. Too often the people spent their money on the cheap, brightly colored goods set up by hawkers outside the government offices. More often than not, an entire year's worth of annuity was wasted on the liquor that some of the more unscrupulous salespeople brought.

Her grandmother had quietly despised the whites for what they had done to her people, but she equally despised those of her own tribe who had allowed themselves to become more and more dependent on the government. It was not war that had wrested the land from the Menominee and Chippewa nations, but the desire for more European trade goods. Grandmother had taught her that too many animal skins had been traded for items their people thought they could not do without but had lived without since time began.

Fallen Arrow had fought back by keeping as much of their traditions and skills alive in her granddaughter as possible. Now those very skills were helping keep Moon Song's baby and two white people alive.

All this she pondered as evening fell and as she watched over her basket of rabbit stew steaming on the soft coals. It was a larger basket than the one in which she had made tea, and not something in which to cook quickly, but if one had the time, it was possible to create a wonderful stew.

She had fashioned a cover for it to make it come to a boil sooner. Once the rabbit cooked for a while, she began cutting chunks of something that looked like a parsnip on top.

"What is that?" Isabella asked.

"Burdock root. My people eat much."

She sprinkled on a chopped herb, and within the hour, the stew she had fashioned had begun to bubble and steam.

"That's smelling really good," Skypilot said.

"Where I see woods," Isabella said, "Moon Song sees a larder."

In the Chippewa culture, everything was sacred, and everything had a circle. Skypilot and the others had saved her and Ayasha's life. Now she saved his. The rabbit would nourish all of them as it was meant to do.

Eventually, she took the makeshift lid off the birch bark pot and stirred the stew with a stick. The meat fell off the bones, and she knew it was done. She dragged the basket off the fire and was gratified to see there was still some gravy juice from the rabbit in it.

"It is ready," she said after it had cooled enough to eat.

They ate from the same container, dredging up the meat and burdock with their fingers and drinking the liquid. When it was gone, they gnawed at the soft ends of the bones and sucked out the marrow.

With the good shelter, a clear view of the lake in case a ship might pass, and plenty of fish to catch and eat, they continued to allow their bodies to recover from their ordeal. They rested and took turns looking out over the lake, ready to start yelling and waving Isabella's voluminous white petticoat if any sort of boat was sighted.

In the distance, they heard the howl of wolves.

"What is that!" Isabella asked.

"Don't worry," Skypilot said. "There were always wolves howling around the lumber camps, but none of us were afraid of them."

"Of course not," Isabella said. "With sturdy log cabins to sleep in at night and axes ready at hand during the day, I'm certain you felt very safe."

"You have a good point, but I don't think they'll bother us. They sound very far away, and we have a good fire."

As she sipped more tea, Moon Song gazed out at the moon shining off the lake as she listened to the music of the wolves.

"What are you thinking about?" he asked.

"Thinking we walk tomorrow." She pointed west, along the lakeshore. "We walk close to lake. If ship come, we see. If not, we walk and walk."

"Can I be part of this conversation?" Isabella asked.

"Of course," Skypilot said.

"It seems to me that we should stay here until we're rescued. We have fish. We have water. We have fire and shelter. It feels foolhardy to do anything else."

"You like mosquitoes?" Moon Song asked.

"No. Why?"

"You like blackflies?"

Isabella shuddered. "Of course not."

"Weather get warm. Much bite."

"Oh." Isabella absorbed this thought. "Then I guess we'll start walking tomorrow."

"We might be closer than we realize." He handed Isabella her newly heelless shoes.

Isabella put the shoes on, stood up, and rocked back and forth on them. "Not bad. Not wonderful, but not bad. And just in time. I need to . . . go."

Neither he nor Moon Song paid much attention to Isabella's absence until several minutes later when they heard a shriek and Isabella ran into their rock shelter.

"Eyes!" She was panting. "So many eyes!"

She grasped one of the logs he'd brought inside before it got dark and dragged it onto the fire. "Make the fire bigger. Hurry!"

12

Moon Song, who seldom showed fear over anything, sprang up, whipped her knife out of her boot, grabbed Ayasha against her, and shoved her back against the back of the rock shelter, holding her baby with her left hand, her knife in her right.

He had no idea what was going on. "What's wrong?"

"You hear?" Moon Song's eyes were wide with fear.

"Hear what?" he said. "It's quiet out. The wolves finally stopped that incessant howling. There's nothing to hear now except the lake."

Then he felt the hair on the back of his neck prickle, and even without turning around, he knew that something was standing directly behind him.

As Moon Song said, the wolves had quit howling.

This would not have meant a thing to him

except for the fact that two women were cowering against the back of the shelter and something deadly was staring a hole through his back. He could almost feel the thing slavering as it anticipated the snap of its jaws around his neck. He'd heard many stories about wolves in the bunkhouses of lumber camps late at night and had discounted most of them. The veteran shanty boys enjoyed making up bloodcurdling tales to frighten greenhorns.

When he first came into the northwoods, he had made it his business to find out from a couple trappers he trusted just how dangerous these wolves were. He was told that they were relatively shy, incredibly intelligent animals and under normal circumstances did not attack humans.

Unless they were hungry . . . like right after they had gotten through a long winter.

Or unless the prey was a woman.

Or a small child.

The only weapon he had was fire. Slowly, he reached for one of the larger tree limbs they'd stuck into the fire earlier. With no axe to cut wood into smaller sections, they had been feeding the larger tree limbs into the fire a little at a time. Now he slowly grasped it in both hands and lifted it, dripping a trail of sparks and embers behind it while turning to face the thing standing behind him.

The wolf was gray, and up close, it looked like a rangy dog, except this animal was bigger than any dog he had ever laid eyes on. He had never seen a wolf close-up before, not close enough to measure against himself. The top of this wolf's head came nearly to the middle of his chest, and when he looked into those yellow eyes, it was as though he were looking into an intelligent, malevolent force.

There was going to be a battle tonight, and it was a battle he wasn't sure he could win. Except he had no choice. He had to win it. There were three lives behind him that he had to protect. His only weapons were this half-burned tree limb, the muscle and sinew in his arms, and his bare hands.

The large wolf was standing stiff-legged now, its ears forward, its hackles raised, and yet it did not attack. Instead, it looked almost as though it were smiling.

Then he heard a scream.

He glanced over his shoulder and saw that it was not Isabella screaming this time. It was Moon Song, backed up against the rock wall, as far away as she could get from the outer perimeter of the shelter, and he saw why — several gray shadows were skulking toward her as she held Ayasha in her arms.

The large, leader wolf had chosen him as the biggest threat and was deliberately keeping him distracted while his wolf minions stalked the two women and the baby. These wolves were not shy, and they were not afraid of humans. They wanted food and saw an easy supply.

Her grandmother had worked hard to teach her to be courageous. Fallen Arrow said that women needed twice the courage of men. Unfortunately, she had one fear that she could not rid herself of — her terror of wolves. Where that fear had come from, she did not know, but it was very real, and right now, it was serious.

Her knees felt weak as she backed away from the silently moving shapes skulking about. They wanted her and they wanted her baby, and the more fearful and cringing she appeared, the more a target she became in their eyes.

She knew this — and yet she could not make the hand with which she held her knife stop shaking.

"Let me hold Ayasha," Isabella whispered hoarsely. "Then you will be free to fight if they come."

Moon Song gladly handed Ayasha over to

170

Isabella. As young as he was, he seemed to sense the terror in the air, but instead of crying like many babies would, he kept silent and watched all that was going on with eyes too wise for his age. A faint part of Moon Song's brain saw that even at eight months, her son had more courage than most. He would make a great brave some-day. Perhaps he would even lead their people. Her life at that moment became unimportant compared to protecting his.

Watching those animals milling about, stalking her, staring at her with the light of the campfire reflected in their yellow eyes, brought a great terror. Her heart pounded so furiously she wondered if it might ex-plode, but it was no longer fear for herself. Her life had ceased to matter to her. The terror was for her son. The wild protective-ness that came with loving a child gave her the strength to face the wolves with steadi-ness and calm. She held her knife, ready to fight to the death.

Then she saw the leader wolf leap straight at Skypilot.

She had seen Skypilot swing an axe before. She'd admired the way he used those mas-sive arms and shoulders to fell trees that would have taken lesser men days to chew through even with the sharpest of axes.

171

There was power in those arms, and skill. There were those at camp who had boasted that Skypilot could split a toothpick with his axe.

She wished he had an axe now. The wolves would have stood no chance against Skypilot with an axe in his hands, but all he had was that tree limb. He swung just as the wolf leaped, and struck it square in the shoulder, making it spin out into the night.

The leader wolf was not used to being thwarted in its plans. With a vicious growl, it leaped again, as fast as lightning. Once again, Skypilot struck it a full blow.

The lesser wolves saw the attack and edged closer to Skypilot.

It was a scene she would remember for the rest of her life — the vision of that big man, his legs planted firmly in place, fighting off the wolves with nothing except a sturdy tree limb and his bare hands. He swung over and over. She saw wolves' bodies flying through the air, but there was always another to take their place.

Then tragedy struck. The limb broke in half, and the stub was not enough for him to use for protection. There was nothing left in the shelter that was an appropriate length, and they were hours away from daylight.

The leader wolf saw the situation and began to creep closer and closer. One of Skypilot's blows had made one leg go lame, and it limped as it went toward him while Skypilot looked around frantically for something to use as a weapon.

"Here!" She tossed him her knife. It left her defenseless, but all she could think about was getting a weapon into Skypilot's hands. If he did not survive, there was no chance for the rest of them.

He caught the knife just as the wolf once again launched itself straight at him. Its great front paws hit his chest, knocking him over, and Skypilot was down.

Just as its great jaws were closing over Skypilot's throat, she found herself standing over it with a large rock in both of her hands, ready to bring it crashing down on the wolf's head.

Then she saw it fall over sideways, and Skypilot crawled out from under it.

"Thanks for the loan of the knife." He stood up. "Looks like the rest of the pack decided to reconsider."

Hardly able to believe her eyes, she glanced out at the darkness and saw no sign of wolves. As silently as they'd come, they'd melted back into the forest.

"Are you all right?" He tipped her chin

back and looked deep into her eyes.

"I think you die," she said. "I think we all die. I think we be food for wolves."

He chuckled. "I'd have given those wolves a really big bellyache if they'd tried."

No Chippewa or Menominee brave could have fought any harder. This big man had saved her and her baby's life. Her overwhelming gratitude, combined with an enormous feeling of relief, overcame her good sense. She practically flew at him, grabbing his head, bringing it down toward her for a kiss. He was surprised, but it took less than a second for him to respond. He dropped the knife, wrapped his arms around her and lifted her off her feet, deepening the kiss that she had initiated.

When they finally pulled apart, they gazed into one another's eyes with a mixture of awe, surprise, and wonder. He was the first to break the spell.

"Where did *that* come from?"

She had no words. She did not know. That was the last thing she had expected to happen. He set her down gently, and she backed away from him, almost like she had backed away earlier from the threat of the wolves.

No one said a thing, not even Isabella. Moon Song grabbed Ayasha out of her arms and laid down on the ground and curled herself around her child as the silence grew thick and heavy.

She was staggered by what had just happened. That kiss was not just about relief and gratitude. That was the kiss of a woman who was in love with a man, and her actions and fervor had stunned and shaken her even more than they had Skypilot. She had fought her attraction to him all winter in the lumber camp, and with good reason. This was *not* someone with whom she could allow herself to fall in love. They were too different, their lives had been too different. There was no way Skypilot could fit into her tribe, and she had already failed to fit into his.

Besides, to fall in love with a white man was to leave herself open to more heartbreak than she had the strength to endure.

French-Canadian men didn't count. Many — although not all of them — were a little more liable to treat their Indian woman as a true wife and lifetime companion. Most had no desire to live anywhere else except the North. Some of them were more Indian than white.

Even though her husband had had a weakness for alcohol, when he was sober they got along well enough. They had much in common and she had never been afraid that he would abandon her.

Yankees or English men? Without realizing it, she made the same grunt of disgust her grandmother always made when she talked of this. They had a reputation of building families with Indian women while they were in the North country, but the minute they could go back to their homeland, they abandoned them. Sometimes with hardly a backward glance. It was called a "country marriage," and since it had not been sanctioned by the church, the men figured there was no legal reason to worry about the wives and children they left behind.

Some of the men had a little more conscience than others. They would "trade off" their woman to another man, giving her and their children as a sort of gift to someone without a family. The woman, unless she was very strong willed or had a family that could take her in, had no recourse but to go with whomever her "husband" gave her to.

Moon Song finally fell asleep to the sound of the crackling fire, waking up from time to time to see Skypilot sitting vigil, keeping the fire alive. From what she could tell, he didn't close his eyes all night.

The carcass of the wolf did not look appetizing, but he figured meat was meat.

"Are we going to butcher this thing?" he asked when Moon Song awoke.

"To eat?" Her eyes did not meet his.

"Of course to eat. We could roast it over the coals like you did that rabbit yesterday."

"No." She wrinkled her nose at the thought. "Wolf meat taste like mouse nest smells."

Mouse nest? That was a puzzling thought. "Why?"

"Wolf lives on mouse in spring."

"How do you know it hasn't been living on other animals?"

Moon Song shook her head. "If he could find other animals, he not need to eat us."

As they packed up to leave, he stood over the giant wolf for a moment. He supposed some men would take a souvenir to remember the battle they'd fought, but he had no desire to do so. He would be happy if he never remembered those blazing yellow eyes ever again.

He would much prefer to remember that kiss from last night. He was as surprised by his own response as he was by the fact that Moon Song had flown at him like she did. That had never been part of their relationship, and yet when their lips had touched, he felt as though some floodgate within his heart had been opened, and he wasn't all that sure he could ever shut it again.

This journey, even apart from all the dangers, was turning out to be a lot more complicated than he had ever dreamed. He tried shoving away the feelings he'd had when he'd held Moon Song in his arms by trying to remember Penelope. Her lovely dresses. The smell of her expensive perfume. Her father's library.

It didn't help. No matter how hard he tried, he could not forget the way Moon Song had looked at him with such passion in her eyes. It made the few chaste kisses he'd shared with Penelope pale by comparison.

No, he would not be forgetting that kiss. Not soon. Not ever.

In some ways, it was hard to leave the rock ledge that had sheltered them and strike out for the unknown. He did not know where they would shelter come nightfall or what dangers they might be facing as they trekked north.

He felt a bit as he thought Moses and the Israelites might have felt as they faced the wilderness with no idea what challenges they would face.

"Lord, protect and keep us in the hollow of your hand," he said as they departed.

"Amen," Isabella responded.

Moon Song simply looked at him quizzically for a moment, then lifted Ayasha to her back and led them at a steady pace along the lakeshore.

Isabella tried hard, but she was not used to walking long distances. She didn't complain, though; he would give her that much. There were much worse companions with whom he and Moon Song could have been left.

No one talked much as they walked. Hour after hour they followed Moon Song through the woods, on the lip of a cliff, down on the shore. Always with the lake in view. He agreed with Moon Song that their best bet was to follow the lakeshore. It would be foolhardy to take off cross-country even if it would cut off some miles. He hoped they would find something or someone who could help them long before they actually made it to Marquette. He did not think Isabella or her shoes could hold out for long.

At one point, Isabella began to hum a little tune.

"That's nice," he said. "What is it?"

"Oh, it's just a little lullaby Archibald likes."

He noticed she still spoke of her baby in

179

the present tense.

They camped, if it could be called that, in a small glade around noon. Moon Song built a fire and fashioned a fishing spear again. A half hour later, she came to the fire empty-handed.

"Fish hide," she said. "Try again later."

Isabella didn't complain about hunger, or anything else. Except for that short exchange about the lullaby, she didn't talk or even seem to notice that she had companions.

They all kept an eye out for another place to camp that was as protected as the rock shelter they'd left, but nothing presented itself. By late afternoon, their hunger was so great that Moon Song halted their trek and went back out into the shallows of the lake again, standing in that cold water for over an hour. That hour produced only one fish, which she quickly cooked and divided into three pieces, all the time using her words sparingly, communicating only what was absolutely necessary. He would have talked with her about what had happened the night before, but the effect on him had been so profound, even he didn't know how to give words to what he felt.

Isabella ate her portion of fish quietly, also without initiating any conversation. The woman he had met on the boat seemed to be disappearing.

He wondered if the change in Isabella's behavior might be a delayed reaction to her grief.

The wisest choice for all of them as far as he could see was to keep putting one foot in front of the other until they got to a place where they could make sense of all that they had been through. Now was not the time for words. When it came to what had happened between him and Moon Song last night, he wasn't sure there were any words.

The emotional terrain through which he was traveling was not an easy one, but neither was the physical one. He guessed they would do well to cover ten miles a day. With Isabella limping along on her broken shoes, probably less. At that rate, according to his very rough calculations, it could take them more than a week to make it to Marquette, assuming he was even close to correct on how far it was.

He prayed that they could continue their journey with no more visits from the wolves. He intended to continue to stop early enough to gather plenty of wood each night to keep a fire blazing — just in case. He also intended to sleep in the late afternoons while Moon Song foraged and fished, so that he could keep watch all night over the baby and women.

Each day consisted of the same thing: walking until Isabella gave out. They were starting to camp wherever Isabella lay down on the ground and refused to move. This was hard for Moon Song to accept because everything within her wanted to keep going.

Still, it was strange how quiet Isabella had become. Now, she seemed barely to notice she had companions. Moon Song wondered if fatigue and hunger could completely change a white woman's personality. The one positive thing about the shortened days was Moon Song had more daylight every afternoon in which to fish.

Walking and fishing kept her from having to look at or talk to Skypilot. The easy camaraderie they had enjoyed for months had evaporated in that one moment. Unfortunately, she could still feel the kiss on her lips, could still feel the roughness of the short beard he had grown in the few days since he had appeared, clean-shaven, to keep her from killing old Stink Breath back in Bay City.

They camped early enough each afternoon to give her time to build a fire, fish, and forage for their dinner. They had fallen into the habit of Skypilot pulling out his water-stained, misshapen Bible, untying the leather string, and reading a story each night. This became a comforting routine. It felt familiar to her, hearing stories of great men and women. She had grown up hearing her own people's stories around the campfire every night.

Tonight, she cuddled a sleeping Ayasha and waited eagerly for the story Skypilot would choose as he riffled through the Bible pages, looking for something to read to them. She had known little about this book until she met him, except a vague knowledge that it was sacred to some of the white people she had met.

She used to think the book held a list of rules, or even incantations. It had never once occurred to her that it was mainly a book of stories. She had shared this discovery with Skypilot as they walked along the shoreline, and he had told her that at heart, the book was a love story bridging thousands of years — a love story about the Creator and his great love for mankind. Skypilot told her that the Bible taught that the Creator *was* love and that in putting the need to love and be loved in people's heart, he had shared a piece of himself.

This was something she pondered long

and hard. The idea of love was high on her list of things to think about as they plodded along. Her affection for Skypilot was growing in spite of her determination to ignore it. It was getting harder to shove it away, though.

Skypilot was the most patient man she had ever known. Her husband had been handsome and brave — good traits in a husband — but he had also often been dismissive, abrupt, and easily annoyed. There had been times when she tried to share her thoughts with him about things that troubled her, and he had grunted and walked away.

This big white man listened as though what she said held importance to him. Each time she came back to their camp from fishing or foraging, he was happy to see her and listened carefully to every word she told him about her small excursion. It was obvious that the big lumberman respected her, and that knowledge made her walk just a little taller.

"Ah. Here's a good one. I think you'll like it," he said. "Especially after what we've been through."

He began reading the story of a man named Noah, who built a great boat and saved his family from a great flood. The more she heard, the more excited she became.

"My people tell same story," she interrupted. "My people tell about a flood so big it cover the whole earth. Higher than mountains. Very, very long time ago."

"I had no idea your people believed that." Skypilot paused and stuck one finger in the Bible to hold his place. "Tell me more."

Moon Song felt proud to share her people's story with him. "A bad, evil snake cause a flood to fill world. A good man build big, big raft and put family and animals on it. Save lives. They on raft many days before floodwaters go away, but evil snake never come back. Great flood kill it and other evil things."

"That's really interesting," Skypilot said. "Do your people have any other stories?"

"Oh, so many!" Moon Song exclaimed.

"Like what?"

"Lots of stories about Gitche Manido and others."

Skypilot smiled at her enthusiasm. "And who is this Gitche Manido?"

"Gitche Manido is the Creator, or the Great Mystery," Moon Song explained. "First sound he make is thoughts. His thoughts make moon, sky, stars, earth. Then he make other sound. His heartbeat. Life.

185

Heartbeat put in every living thing. My people use drum to make heartbeat and honor Gitche Manido with ceremonies."

Skypilot looked at her for such a long time that she thought she had said something strange. Perhaps she had been wrong to share so much of her people's beliefs.

"I had no idea you believed in one Creator, Moon Song."

"Somebody make all this." She waved her hand around. "We call him Gitche Manido."

"Does Gitche Manido have a son?" Skypilot asked.

"You mean like the man you call Jesus you talk about when we at the lumber camp?"

"Yes. Like our Jesus."

"No, but we have Nanabozho." She grinned. "Nanabozho is great trickster. Sometime he turn into big rabbit. We tell children many stories of Nanabozho." She paused. "But I think he not real."

Skypilot chuckled. "Well, our Jesus was not a trickster, and he definitely did not turn into a giant rabbit, and I've pretty much based my life on believing that he is real."

"Could you two please stop talking now?" Isabella said. "I want to go to sleep." Those were the first words Isabella had spoken all day.

"Of course." Skypilot tied the string back around his Bible and put it in his pocket. "I apologize. We all need to get some rest."

They had found a place on the beach where they could sleep on sand with their backs against another rock cliff and the fire throwing heat and flickering shadows against the stone. The beach was a softer place to sleep than they'd had previously, and exhausted by the walk and feeling comforted by the security of having the cliff behind them, Moon Song fell sound asleep while Skypilot kept watch for wolves.

Moon Song slept so deeply, she did not awaken until after the sun had crept above the horizon and found Skypilot shaking her.

"Do you know where Isabella and Ayasha are? I dozed off for a few minutes around dawn, and when I woke up, they were gone."

Moon Song was instantly on her feet. She did not see Ayasha or Isabella. She searched in her mind for a good reason this should be, but there was nothing. Isabella had left their side only for the few minutes it took each day to relieve herself. Had she alone been missing, Moon Song would have assumed she was answering a call of nature, but there was no reason for her to take Ayasha with her.

The cradle board lay empty beside Moon

Song. Isabella had evidently taken him in her arms. As Moon Song looked around, a trail of footprints led off toward the west.

"Look!" She pointed.

"Let's go get them," Skypilot said grimly.

13

The tracks led at least a mile down the beach and then they stopped. For a moment, Skypilot was afraid Isabella had walked right into the lake with the baby in her arms. The mind could do strange things. Perhaps she'd thought that if she couldn't have her baby, Moon Song couldn't have hers either.

If anything happened to that child, he would never forgive himself for falling asleep.

Moon Song saw something and motioned for him to follow her up a rise. The woods were sparse here, growing on earth that was more sand than dirt.

They moved as quietly as possible. He thought there was a good chance they might find Isabella. A mile was a long way for her to walk carrying the baby.

And then they heard her singing the words to that lullaby they had heard her humming incessantly for the past two days. It was in French.

"Do you understand the words?" he whispered to Moon Song. He knew that French was a language over which she had some command.

"Hen lay egg in church." Moon Song listened closely. "Children eat egg." She looked at him. "Words not make sense."

"Maybe she just wanted a chance to hold the baby and sing the lullaby," he said softly. "Without us hearing her. Maybe it comforts her."

Moon Song shook her head. "This not right."

They watched quietly as Isabella talked to Ayasha. "They thought I couldn't tell the difference between you and that Indian woman's baby, Archibald." Isabella chuckled. "As though I wouldn't know my own child." She had wrapped Ayasha in the petticoat that she had used to try to signal a ship. She was sitting on a fallen tree, rocking back and forth, looking down into Ayasha's face. "They tried to convince me that you were dead." She kept rocking. "But I knew you were alive. I knew all along, and I was right. They had hidden you in that Indian baby's cradle board. It just took me a few days to recognize you. But Mama's here now, Archie, Mama's here and she'll never leave you alone again."

Moon Song looked at Skypilot with real fear in her eyes. "Not her baby, *my* baby."

"I know that, but evidently she doesn't right now. If you try to take Ayasha from her, she might hurt him. Let me handle this."

Isabella's expensive velvet dress was already tattered and soiled from sleeping on the ground. Her hair hung in straggles around her face. She had lost weight and her eyes looked sunken. He pitied her, but he had to get that baby away from her.

"Good morning, Isabella." Carefully, he sauntered into her line of vision with his hands in his pockets, as though he didn't have a care in the world and that it was normal for him to find her here.

She clutched the baby tightly to her chest, and her eyes darted back and forth as though deciding where to run. That was one thing he was trying to avoid, Isabella running. He didn't know what Moon Song might do to her if she had to chase her down.

To keep that from happening, he sat down on another fallen tree several feet away from her. He did not want her to feel threatened.

"Did you sleep well?" He yawned and

191

stretched his arms above his head. "That's the best night's sleep I've had since the explosion."

She watched him with wary eyes.

He searched for something to say that she would not perceive as a threat. "That's a pretty song you were singing. What's it about?"

"It's a children's song I learned in Paris. Archie likes it. He always has."

"What's it about?"

"A hen. An egg. A church. Children."

"I never heard that lullaby before," he said.

"You can't take my baby away from me again," she said. "That was mean, telling me he was gone when it was the Indian woman's baby who was dead. It was horribly mean to switch babies and trick me."

"You're right. If we had done that, it would have been a very mean trick, indeed, but we didn't. I'm sorry you are in so much pain, Isabella."

She held the baby's head against her neck and began to rock again, faster this time.

"You're lying," she said. "I saw you two kissing. I know you two plotted to steal my baby."

He picked up a twig and began to break it into pieces. "How are you going to feed him, Isabella?"

This seemed to puzzle her. Her forehead furrowed as she thought.

As though on cue, Ayasha began to whimper and root around on her chest.

"I think the baby's hungry now," he said.

She looked around, panicked.

"Moon Song?" he called. "Isabella needs for you to come nurse her baby."

It was a long shot, playing along with her illusion, pretending the baby was hers until Moon Song could get her hands on him. But it was the only way he could think of to pry the baby out of Isabella's arms without the possibility of endangering him.

Moon Song walked out from behind a tree. She'd figured out what he was trying to do. "You want me to feed the baby, Isabella?"

Isabella looked at Moon Song and then back at Skypilot.

"You two are trying to trick me!"

"No, Isabella," Skypilot said. "We're trying to help you."

Isabella stood up, wrapped the petticoat more snugly around the baby as though preparing to hand him to Moon Song, then gathered up her skirt with one hand and with Ayasha in the other took off like a shot.

Never would he have believed that Isabella could move that fast.

She was taller and her legs much longer than Moon Song's. The unnatural strength that sometimes comes with great fear or with insanity sent her practically leaping through the forest with as much agility as a deer. Moon Song was driven by the wild desire to protect her son, but she was smaller and it took everything she had to keep up with the larger woman.

As he took off running after them, he remembered how last night Isabella was so exhausted he was half afraid he was going to have to start carrying her if they were ever going to get to Marquette.

Her spurt of energy propelled her up the hill and over onto the beach. When he topped the hill, he saw Isabella standing hip deep in the water. Moon Song was wading out to her with her arms outstretched.

"Please," Moon Song kept saying, her heartbreak so audible in that one word. "Please!"

Isabella backed away farther into the lake. She was up to her waist, and a corner of the petticoat Ayasha was wrapped in was dragging in the water. She lifted the baby onto her shoulder. "Stay away. You can't have him. He's mine!"

Skypilot was in the water now, standing beside Moon Song.

"Please don't go out any farther," he pleaded. "We're not going to take the baby away from you, not until you give us permission to hold him."

Her eyes were slits of suspicion. "You keep trying to trick me."

Moon Song was creeping closer. Isabella noticed and took another step backward.

"Stop it, Moon Song!" he said. "She'll go out too far if you don't."

His warning came too late. A wave came in, larger than the others, enough to cause Isabella to lose her footing. She thrashed around, trying to keep her balance and save herself, and in so doing, she dropped Ayasha into the water.

In a flash, Moon Song dove headfirst into the lake and started swimming under the water to where Isabella had dropped the baby. Skypilot waded farther in, following Moon Song. Isabella came up, spluttering and gasping.

"Help me!" She grabbed hold of him.

"Stand up!" He shook her off. "It's not even over your head."

He was no swimmer, but he held his breath and ducked beneath the crystal-clear water with his eyes open, trying to find the baby.

All he saw was Moon Song.

The same wave that had knocked Isabella over had evidently sucked Ayasha back out into the lake before Moon Song could get to him.

Again Isabella grabbed at him. Again he shoved her away. He might not be an expert swimmer, but he would help Moon Song find that baby or he would die trying.

He went under the water over and over, holding his breath as long as he could, casting about wildly, trying to get a glimpse of the child. Ayasha had been wrapped in that white petticoat, but that had drifted off and now floated by him with no infant in sight.

"I find him!"

He rose up and saw Moon Song trying to swim while holding on to her baby's limp body. He was a full foot taller than Moon Song, and his feet were planted firmly when she got to him. He grabbed the baby from her and, using his greater strength, plowed through the waves, holding the child by the feet, head down. The minute he was out of the water enough to do so, he turned the child upside down over his knee and squeezed his belly, expelling the water from his lungs. Then he tilted the baby's head back, covered the baby's mouth and nose with his own mouth, and began to puff air into the infant's lungs just like he'd been taught by those wonderful volunteers so long ago.

Moon Song had dredged herself out of the water and was pulling on his arm. "What you do? What you do?"

"Stop it!" Skypilot shook her off and continued puffing air into the child's mouth and nose.

Moon Song backed away but kept circling him, wringing her hands and reaching for her child, which Skypilot refused to give up.

And then came the moment that he had been praying for desperately. He felt Ayasha stir. He took his mouth away and watched as the child took his first breath and began to wail.

Moon Song put the child up over her shoulder and bounced and patted him, her face a study in relief. "How you know how to do this?" she asked.

"I saw a demonstration when I was in college." He sat down in the sand, completely wrung out.

Moon Song stood over him. "Where is that white woman?"

He glanced around and saw Isabella wandering down the beach. The waist of her red dress had torn, and now the hem of it dragged in the sand. The elaborate up-swept hairstyle she had worn on the boat had long ago turned into a ragged mass. It streamed down her back, wet, tangled, and matted. She walked with a limp.

"Please hold Ayasha?" Moon Song's voice was low and deadly. "I go teach lesson to that baby-stealer. Big lesson!"

"No, Moon Song. Don't hurt her. She isn't right in the head. She didn't know what she was doing."

"She steal Ayasha again."

"We won't let that happen," he said wearily.

"How we keep it from happen?"

"Neither of us will sleep at the same time or leave him alone with her for an instant. She was a nice person until she snapped. You don't know how you would react if you were in the same situation, Moon Song."

Moon Song stared at the apparition limping down the beach and gave his words consideration.

"Keep white woman away from me."

They spent the rest of the day with the three of them spread out in a thin and ragged line. Isabella limping along in front of them. Skypilot in the middle. Moon Song bringing up the rear. He strode ahead once, to try to talk to Isabella and see if she was snapping out of it. She wasn't. She stared at the ground and did not acknowledge his presence or his questions. She did not speed up or slow down, she simply kept putting one foot in front of the other as her limp grew worse and worse. By midafternoon, Isabella's walk had slowed until their journey became little more than a crawl.

"I go ahead," Moon Song said. "Find food."

"That sounds fine," he said. "I'll stay behind and keep an eye on her. I don't want her to wander away."

Moon Song took off at a mile-eating trot with Ayasha bouncing along on her back. Skypilot hoped that if he ever had a baby, it would be as good as Moon Song's son. That little boy had been through so much and yet rarely whimpered unless he was hungry or cold. It was as though those black button eyes were too busy absorbing everything he saw to complain or cry.

Moon Song soon disappeared around a curve in the lakeshore, and he didn't see her again until they came upon her as she bent over what looked to be a steaming hole in the ground.

"Mussels," she explained. "Found wild onion too."

When he got there, he was amazed at what she had been able to accomplish. She had dug a hole, built a fire, and dredged mussels from the sand and water. When she saw them coming, she scraped away the hot rocks and, using pieces of driftwood as utensils, offered the half-opened steamed mussels to him and Isabella.

"Very good," she said, cracking the shell all the way open and scooping a tender morsel into her own mouth to show how it was done.

"Look, Isabella." He put his hand on Isabella's arm to stop her plodding, onward progress. "Moon Song has made a meal. You can stop and rest awhile and eat."

"Here." Moon Song tried to put a cooked mussel into Isabella's hand. "Give you strength."

Isabella allowed the mussel to drop from her limp hand and kept walking.

"You need to eat something," Skypilot said. "This will help you stay alive."

Isabella wouldn't stop. She just kept plodding on. Annoyed and hungry, he grabbed her arm and forced her to stop. It was only then that she seemed to notice him. She looked straight at him, and her eyes were as wild as the wind. Then, with no warning, she opened her mouth and began to scream.

He'd heard Isabella scream the night of the steamship explosion, but this was different. There was no emotion in this scream. It was as though she had become a sort of force of nature.

He dropped her arm and took several steps back as she continued to scream and scream. It was the single most hair-raising thing he'd ever experienced, and that included the years he had spent trying to help slaves escape.

What was this . . . this *thing* Isabella had turned into? Nothing in his experience, from his Bible college training, to his time in the ministry, to working in the lumber camps, had prepared him for this.

Finally, when he'd gotten far enough away from her, she stopped abruptly, like a teakettle that had been taken off the fire, and once more began to walk west along the shore.

He walked back to the fire where Moon Song was consuming aromatic mussel meat, and then he turned back around and watched Isabella walk away.

"Huh," Moon Song said. "Look like she not hungry."

It was such an understatement in the face of such bizarre behavior that he glanced at her to see if she was joking. A look of dry humor flickered behind her eyes.

"I have no idea what just happened," he

said. "But I certainly won't try *that* again!"

Moon Song simply shrugged and kept eating as she squatted beside the small cooking pit. Without another word, he joined her in breaking open the mussels and throwing the shells over his shoulder. After they finished, refreshed and reinvigorated by the food, it was no problem to catch up with Isabella, who had slowed even more. It touched him that Moon Song folded some cooked mussels into a scrap of the sheet fabric she'd saved.

"For Isabella," she said. "If she change mind."

There came a time in the middle of the afternoon when Isabella stopped and simply sat down.

"Do you want to rest, or are you ready to camp?" Skypilot asked her.

Isabella did not reply.

"You hungry?" Moon Song offered her the little bag of mussels she'd been carrying, but Isabella did not acknowledge them.

Moon Song gave up. "I go find firewood."

Skypilot sat down beside Isabella, but she did not acknowledge his presence. She just kept on with that empty stare. He glanced down at her feet and saw that her shoes were coming apart. No surprise there. They had never been made for walking long distances. Then he saw blood seeping out of a busted seam.

"You're bleeding!"

She didn't appear to hear him. Carefully, and making no sudden moves, he got on his knees and began unlacing her high-topped shoe. She didn't seem to notice. It was as though she had gone far away in her mind and had forgotten that she even owned a body, let alone realized that it was hurting. What he saw after he unlaced her shoe sickened him.

One side of her right foot was so blistered and raw it looked like someone had poured boiling water over it.

"Moon Song," he called. "You'd better come see this."

In spite of her anger with Isabella, even Moon Song was appalled.

"She no walk anymore, feet like that."

When he took off her other boot, he found it was not quite as bad, but it had been rubbed raw in several places too.

"We won't be going any farther today," he said.

Moon Song did not have her grandmother's expertise, but she knew a few plants that could heal a wound and immediately went in search of a sage plant she had seen awhile back. While gathering the sage, she also saw a newly fallen birch tree, from which she cut two large rectangles of bark.

When she got back to the camp, she shaped the first rectangle of bark into another cooking pot, just like the one she'd had before, dipped water into it, then tore the sage leaves into shreds and allowed the mixture to simmer. When that was finished, she set it off to one side to cool. She picked up the second sheet of bark, but Isabella, who had been practically comatose since nearly drowning in the lake, snatched it away.

"No," Moon Song chided, holding her hand out for it. "This is for tea water."

Isabella ignored her and smoothed the bark out on her lap.

"What is she doing?" Moon Song said.

Skypilot had managed to spear a large fish and was roasting it over the fire just as he'd seen Moon Song do. He turned the fish over and continued to roast it. "I have no idea why Isabella is doing anything she's doing."

A piece of half-charred wood that had fallen away from the fire caught Isabella's eye. She snatched it up, even though a tiny curl of smoke still rose from it. She flattened the birch bark on her knees and began to make quick, slashing marks with the blackened stick upon the smooth, white inner surface of the bark.

Moon Song looked over her shoulder and watched.

Using birch bark as drawing paper, or to record rituals or maps, was not new to Moon Song. Her people had been doing that for centuries. They had many birch bark scrolls they treated as sacred.

Still, she had never seen anyone making such fast and furious marks before. It was as though Isabella was possessed. She frowned as she drew, and spittle flew from her open mouth.

Moon Song continued to peer over Isabella's shoulder, astonished. Chippewa women loved to make intricate decorations upon their clothing. Some made intricate designs on birch bark by folding it and leaving bite marks that when unfolded blossomed into lovely patterns, but she had never seen any of her people do anything remotely like this.

With quick, sure strokes, Isabella had drawn a picture of a man's face. To be exact, it was Colonel James Hatchette's face, and it was so lifelike that it seemed almost like magic. Moon Song could not imagine how anyone could make a face appear with a burnt stick and some birch bark.

Isabella finished the drawing, stared at it, added a couple more strokes to perfect it, and then tossed it onto the fire.

It was such a miraculous piece of work in Moon Song's eyes, she almost snatched it out of the fire to save it, but Skypilot grabbed her hand. "That's her picture and she should be allowed to do with it as she wishes."

Isabella closed her eyes and relaxed against the boulder behind her. A big sigh escaped her.

Moon Song's head was still reeling from what she had seen. How could anyone make a man's head just appear like that?

"Is that stew you were making ready?" Skypilot asked. "It's certainly smelling good."

"Stew?" At first, Moon Song had no idea what he was talking about, then she understood. "Oh, that is medicine for Isabella's feet."

She had gotten so caught up in watching Isabella draw that she'd forgotten the poultice. It had cooled to the point that she could put it on the bad places of Isabella's feet without hurting her.

"Pity." Skypilot smiled. "For a moment, I thought you were whipping us up a Thanksgiving dinner."

"You joke?" She wasn't sure.

"Yes, Moon Song. That was a joke. Sage is one of the spices my mother used when she was cooking turkey."

"This medicine help maybe." Moon Song knelt before Isabella. "I try help?"

Isabella didn't protest. She merely watched with mild curiosity as Moon Song smoothed the healing poultice on the blisters and sores and raw skin and bound them up with strips of cloth.

"No walk. No move," Moon Song instructed. "Let medicine work."

Isabella merely closed her eyes and leaned back against the boulder again.

"Is she going to be all right?"

Moon Song shrugged. She had bigger worries than Isabella's feet. She was starting to get the feeling that wolves were following them again. The smell of blood from Isabella's foot would most definitely interest them, and who knew how long that trail would linger. She could imagine a wolf pack sniffing along the trail they'd taken. They were on flat ground. No cliffs for shelter. Her great fear was that they might be regrouping, getting ready to attack again once night fell.

"This not good place," she said. "Not tonight."

"Tonight? Are you picking up on something?"

"Maybe. Maybe not. Just feeling."

"Then we can't stay here, and I can't carry her far. I doubt she can take more than a step or two on those chewed-up feet."

"You stay here. I will try find better place before it get dark."

"Don't go far," he said.

"Why?" she teased. "You scared stay here by self?"

"No," he said. "But I am afraid of losing you."

The tenderness in his voice when he said that made her heart feel funny, and she did not want her heart feeling funny around this man. She was still trying to forget that unfortunate kiss. She left to do her explorations without another word.

She discovered that they were on a small peninsula. It didn't go very far out into the lake but far enough that the trees were stunted and scraggly from being exposed to the cold wind coming off Lake Superior's winter water. At first she was disappointed. She had come nearly a mile, and there was no sign of a cliff or even any large rocks that they could use to fortress themselves in for the night.

There was no reason to continue farther.

This was as far as they could bring Isabella. Then she saw something that made her heart leap up, and she started crashing through the underbrush, shoving limbs away from Ayasha's face, hoping she was seeing what she thought she was seeing.

What a discovery! The scraggly trees sheltered a Chippewa longhouse. This was one of the more permanent structures that her grandmother's people constructed. They built them to house several families when the smaller family groups met together to work at a specific task. Just like the longhouse her grandmother's people had in the stand of sugar maple they tapped and boiled down into sugar and syrup. Or the longhouses they built in favorite fishing spots to catch their winter supply. Or near the wild rice fields when that harvest was imminent. Her people were not nomads, but they did move around through the various seasons to be closer to whatever natural supplies they needed to cache a larger variety of food.

The camp was cold and abandoned but looked as though it had been used as recently as last summer. She entered the longhouse through a piece of leather hung over the doorway. It had been well built and was still sturdy. It even had sleeping benches built into the walls, which would be a great improvement over sleeping on the bare ground.

She investigated every inch, evaluating the possibilities.

There was an old bearskin that had been left behind. Far beneath one of the sleeping benches, she found a small iron cooking pot. It was quite a prize. Her guess was that the woman who left this behind had missed it when she got home. A pocketknife with one blade broken but one working blade left was wedged in the crack between another sleeping bench and the wall. Although she scavenged around the longhouse one more time, nothing else came to light. Still, those two items were quite a find. She walked back outside and stopped in her tracks, wondering if her eyes were playing tricks on her. There, leaning against a tree, was what looked like a perfectly sound birch bark canoe.

She ran to it, overjoyed. Wouldn't Skypilot be thrilled with her discovery! Her joy turned to disappointment when she saw that it had a great hole in one side of it. That was the reason, no doubt, that it had been abandoned.

Still . . . a sturdy shelter, another knife blade, a ratty bearskin, a small cooking pot, and a useless canoe were a whole lot more than they had an hour ago. If they had to camp for a few days, she was grateful that Isabella had chosen to collapse near this place, otherwise they might have passed by without ever seeing it.

She wondered if Skypilot would consider this an answer to the prayers she'd heard him whispering throughout the night last night as he sat vigil over all of them. If so, she was going to enjoy telling him of her discovery.

"You were gone for a long time," he said when she got back. "Were you foraging?"

"No. I find good thing."

He listened intently as she described the Chippewa camp she'd found. "How far did you say it is?"

"Mile maybe."

"It would give us some decent shelter while we wait for Isabella's sore feet to heal up?"

"Oh yes." Then she looked up at the sky and sniffed the air. "Better start. It rain soon."

He glanced up into the sky.

"Isabella?" He bent over the sleeping woman. "It's time to wake up. We need to see if you can walk."

He helped her stand while Moon Song kicked the fire apart so it would burn out and then picked up her flint and the bundle of dwindling moss.

As happy as she was about finding the longhouse, it was the damaged canoe that was making her heart sing. Much of the building of canoes was considered women's work among the Chippewa. Therefore, she knew exactly how to repair it. It took a long time to make a good, waterproof craft, but once built, a birch bark canoe was buoyant and sturdy and would be the very best way to get them out of here.

It would be a relief to hand Isabella over to her own people. Moon Song could hardly wait.

14

Skypilot had never had the chance to examine an Indian dwelling up close before. He was intrigued by the workmanship and the intelligence that had gone into making this one. There was a fire pit in the center, just like the woodstove in the middle of the logging camp bunkhouse, with an opening at the top — again, just like the bunkhouse.

He had anticipated that the log structure he and the other shanty boys normally lived in would be the better shelter, but now he wasn't sure. That shanty at Foster's camp was better than most, but the walls still leaked moisture. The smell of dozens of dirty bodies and unwashed feet never went away. He wondered if the cattail mats he saw layered upon the outside of this longhouse might not be better insulation in the long run than the green logs that grew frosted in the winter with condensation from the men's breath. He and his lumber

213

camp buddies knew the value of wearing layers of clothing, trapping the air between each layer for maximum warmth. It stood to reason that layering cattail mats over a longhouse would have the same effect.

He sat Isabella down on a sleeping bench.

"Stay here," he instructed.

Then he took the cast-off bearskin outside and shook it out. The thing was filthy — but at least it would provide a bit of cushion.

The minute he and Isabella entered the longhouse, Moon Song disappeared to look more closely at that canoe she was so excited about. He was excited too, except that he had never been in a canoe and wasn't looking forward to getting into this one.

"Is it usable?" he called out of the longhouse opening.

"I can fix."

"You know how to repair a birch bark canoe?"

"No."

"Then how in the world do you think you can . . ."

"I help Grandmother *build* one." Her hands explored the ragged edges of the hole. "I think I know how to repair."

Moon Song peeled and split the shallow

black spruce tree roots that she ripped up out of the ground. Then she drilled holes through the canoe with the tip of her knife as well as through the new birch bark patch she had cut off of a tree. She threaded the root strips in and out, so close together that they almost overlapped.

"Is there anything I can do to help?" Sky-pilot asked.

"Get sap from spruce tree."

"How much?"

She nodded at the iron kettle beside her. "Fill it up."

An hour later, they had a fire built, the patch had been stitched onto the canoe, the sap had melted, and Moon Song had feath ered the end of a small branch and used it as a brush with which she'd redaubed not only the patch but every seam in the canoe.

He inspected the lightweight bark boat. How could it possibly withstand the punish-ment Lake Superior could give it? "Will it hold all of us?"

"Yes."

"Won't the lake tear it apart?"

"No. We fine." She laid down the brush. "Canoe dry while we sleep."

There was still supper to accomplish — more fish. Afterward, she cleaned out the small iron pot, then put all the fish bones, skin, and heads into it, along with anything else she deemed edible, including the left-over mussels that Isabella had ignored, covered it all with water and set it to simmering on the coals. It was a noxious-looking liquid.

"What's that for?" he asked.

"Fish broth. Drink in morning. Very good." Then she left him to go hunt some more moss for the baby.

Moon Song was grateful for the sleeping benches. This made it possible for her to put the baby in between her and the wall of the longhouse, with her back to Isabella, her knife at the ready in case the woman tried anything else. She felt sorry for Isabella, but Ayasha came first.

She could tell that Skypilot didn't know what to do about Isabella. Finally, he tied her to the bench, for fear she'd awaken and try to do some damage to one of them. That cloth rope was not going to hurt her. In fact, she doubted that it would do a thing to hold her back if she wanted to escape.

Moon Song slept little during the night. The wolves kept howling. Her instincts had been correct. The wolves had regrouped after the loss of their leader, they were near, and they were hungry. The shelter they were in wouldn't keep out a determined animal, but it had afforded enough protection to make them think twice.

She also slept little because she was planning what had to happen tomorrow.

The canoe would be fine. It was a well-built craft to begin with, and she had repaired it well. She knew Lake Superior's moods and knew she could make many miles safely in that canoe if the weather held. Her greatest concern was Isabella. It was a risk to take that crazy lady with them. It took skill not to accidentally tip a canoe over. If Isabella suddenly decided to jump out, and who knew *what* she might get in her head to do, she could capsize all of them.

Toward morning, she decided that if they were going to get safely to Marquette, they would have to leave Isabella behind. Her fear was that Skypilot would not allow it. If so, she would be forced to leave without him, even though she desperately needed his strength for the long canoe voyage.

The next morning, she and Skypilot carried the canoe to the water, slid it in, and tethered it. The fishing was good, and they caught several large trout, enough to feed them and leave some behind for Isabella. As they ate, she kept an eye on the white woman to see if there was any spark of sanity coming back into her eyes. There wasn't. It was as though her body was alive but the rest of her was dead. Isabella did at least feed herself, but the whole time she did, she sat there staring into space.

"She stay here." Moon Song nodded toward Isabella. "We go on alone."

Skypilot's head jerked up. "You can't be serious."

"You want to drown?"

"Of course not."

"She stay here. We will have others come get later. One, two days maybe."

"We can't leave her here by herself for two days," he said. "There's no telling what she'll do."

"In canoe she is a danger."

His jaw set stubbornly. "I won't abandon an innocent woman. We have to take her with us."

"You ever paddle a canoe?"

"No. I've paddled small rowboats, but I've never even been in a canoe."

"Canoe tricky."

"I'll stay here with her, then."

She frowned. "You think the townspeople listen to this Chippewa woman? You think they send help because Moon Song say so?"

He hesitated. "I don't know."

"You are strong. We get to town faster."

He looked relieved. "If it's only muscle you need and someone the people from town will listen to, I'll go and you stay."

The man had never handled a canoe in his life. He had no idea what he was talking about. They could stand here and argue, or he could find out for himself that there was more to this than he realized.

"You do that." She stood up and crossed her arms. She could hardly wait to watch him try.

"You mean now?"

"Here." She picked up one of the paddles she'd found beside the canoe.

He took it and looked at it doubtfully. "You do mean now."

He finished the last piece of fish and then followed her down to the lake.

It took exactly six seconds for him to turn the canoe over and get dunked. He came up out of the water, spluttering, and then righted the canoe. She could tell he was angry, and couldn't help rubbing it in a little.

"You want help?" She smiled. "I hold it steady for you."

"You will *not*!" His face was grim. "I'll get the hang of this if it kills me."

She stood back and watched as he tried

several more times and overturned it each time. His bulk, lack of experience, and the buoyancy of the craft made it a difficult task. She kept quiet as Skypilot learned a lesson, and it was an important lesson to learn. It hurt her to see this good man struggle, but a canoe could save a life or take it. One clumsy move could capsize everyone.

Finally, he was in the canoe, but barely. He sat like a child, with legs outstretched before him, grasping the sides of the canoe, trying to balance himself. So far so good, but he had managed to get himself into a difficult position from which to paddle.

"Here." She handed him the paddle. "Try Indian way of sitting on knees."

She held the canoe steady while he repositioned himself, then she gave it a gentle shove out into the water.

It was hard not to feel sorry for him. He knelt in the middle, trying to paddle while the canoe acted as though it had a mind of its own. It didn't take long before he was going in circles. When he floundered close enough to shore, she waded in and caught the nose of the canoe.

A lesser man would have been cursing by now, but instead, Skypilot simply admitted defeat.

"You were right," he said. "This is much harder than I imagined. You pretty much grew up in one of these, didn't you?"

"Yes."

"Do you really think we can leave Isabella alone here?"

"Only choice."

"I'll try to talk to her."

She waited while he had his little talk with the crazy lady. She could hear him reassuring her that they would send someone soon to come back and get her.

Moon Song wasn't convinced that Isabella cared whether they came back or not. From what she could tell, the woman would lie on that sleeping bench until she starved to death unless someone made her get up and move.

"I think she understands what we're planning to do," Skypilot said. "At least she nodded that she did. I removed a couple of the sleeping benches and braced them against the door when I left. If she'll leave them there, I think they'll be sturdy enough to keep the wolves out if they come sniffing around later on."

"We hurry." Moon Song tied a long piece of white cloth to a branch that hung out over the water. "There," she said. "Make easy to find longhouse."

Once again, she held the canoe while he climbed in.

"You sit in front," she instructed.

"In front? I figured you would want to be in front since you'd be steering."

"The person in back steer." She leaped in, positioned herself in the back, pulled the paddle from the bottom of the canoe, and began to paddle. She saw Skypilot reach for his.

"No," she said. "Wait. Get feel for canoe. Then you help."

Skillfully, she set the canoe's nose out into the lake. The water was calm. If the big timberman in front of her could keep from capsizing when he started to help, they would make good time.

"You think you can paddle now?" she asked. "Without falling out of boat?"

"I hope so."

"Try."

He dipped the paddle in and gave a mighty shove, making the canoe tip to one side. She sighed. She was afraid of that.

"Not so hard. Long way to go. Make muscle last."

It took a few more instructions, but eventually they worked out a rhythm, and soon the canoe was skimming across the water.

"You do realize there are things that I'm good at, don't you, Moon Song?" His voice, usually so filled with confidence, was subdued. "I'm not a complete dunce about everything."

"Oh yes!" she said brightly, as though praising a small child. "You read marks on paper very, very good."

He laughed out loud. "That doesn't amount to much in a situation like this, does it, Moon Song?"

"You fight wolves good too." Her voice grew husky at the memory. "You save our lives."

"You've also fed us and saved our lives," he said. "I am sorry if I've ever treated you like you were ignorant."

She didn't say anything.

"I have treated you like you were ignorant in the past," he said. "Haven't I?"

She thought back. Had he? He had been kind, but he had frequently treated her like she was one of the children he had taught at the lumber camp during his convalescence.

"Moon Song not a child."

"No, ma'am." He glanced back at her, and that glance made her feel warm inside. "You are most definitely not a child."

■ ■ ■ ■

Hour after hour, they paddled, fueled only by that morning's fish broth and desperation. By early afternoon, he was hungrier than he had ever been in his life. Moon Song, however, never complained. Even the baby did not cry. Finally, they stopped at a small spit where there was some sand upon which they could pull the canoe.

That was when he discovered he could not get out of the canoe. Usually, the only time he ever knelt was in prayer. Spending so much time kneeling in the canoe had left his legs numb. Moon Song was already out of the boat, of course.

It was a little hard not to resent that fact. Everything she did seemed to be so effortless, even carrying the child with her everywhere.

"Get out," she said.

"I'm not sure I can. I've tried. My legs have gone to sleep. I can't get them to move. The only way I'm going to get out of this canoe is if I fall overboard."

She gave the canoe a yank to one side, and he did exactly that, fell out into the water. It was sudden, and the water was shocking, but he decided it really was the

224

only way. It would take a much bigger man than himself to lift him out of the position he was in.

Now he wasn't just hungry, he was hungry and wet. It seemed like he'd been hungry and wet forever.

He hoped Moon Song had planned for them to eat, but the only thing she seemed to have on her mind was nursing and changing the baby. He waited, hopeful. She'd made things to eat practically materialize out of thin air before.

"Aren't you hungry?" he prompted.

"Yes."

"Do you have any ideas?"

"No time to hunt or fish. You walk around. Drink water. We leave soon."

He did exactly as she instructed. He walked and got plenty of blood back into his legs. He drank water, and he ignored his hunger, or tried to. It was hard. He had seldom been truly hungry in his life unless he was waiting on a meal that was late. But there was no meal coming. No time in the future that he could depend on that there even would be food. Hunger would simply have to be ignored, indefinitely, while they paddled to Marquette.

By the grace of God, there were no storms, heavy winds, or catastrophes. Just mile after mile after mile of blue sky, blue lake, and eventually, groaning muscles. After discovering that his legs had become paralyzed from kneeling for so long, they stopped approximately every hour so that he could stretch for a few minutes. Moon Song took the opportunity to feed Ayasha and allow him to toddle about and get a bit of exercise.

The sun sparkled off the water like diamonds, shining in his eyes, nearly blinding him. He coped by perpetually squinting, watching through his eyelashes, trying to save his eyes from the constant onslaught of sun.

During one of their stops, Moon Song dug around in the bank of a little rivulet that emptied into the lake, and there she found some sticky mud, which she smeared all over his face and neck.

"There. That better?"

The coolness of the mud upon his already burning face felt wonderful — until it began to dry. Then it just itched. Moon Song ignored her own skin but shielded the baby by rigging a small canopy of balsam boughs.

He was sick of seeing nothing but trees and lakeshore. Years ago, in Richmond, he'd sometimes longed to be someplace where all he had was God's beautiful handiwork all around him. Sometimes he had even fantasized about living at the edge of a lake in someplace wild, just him, the Lord, and nature.

This fantasy had been fueled partially by Henry Wadsworth Longfellow's poem "Hiawatha," which had become immensely popular ten years earlier. Longfellow had touted the beauty of the Michigan North country and wrote a poem about a lovely Indian maiden, and primeval forests, and sparkling big seawater.

He was in the heart of what Longfellow had called Gitche Gumee, and he had his very own Indian princess paddling along behind him. All right, so she wasn't exactly a princess, but she was Chippewa and she was beautiful.

Unfortunately, his particular Indian "princess" had spent the biggest part of the past few days telling him what to do in order to survive.

He scratched his sunburned nose. It wasn't quite the idyll that Longfellow had described.

Longfellow hadn't mentioned mosquitoes or no-see-ums. He didn't talk about what hunger felt like when the lining of your stomach rubbed together. Living in the lumber camp looked like the lap of luxury in comparison to what he was presently going through.

He had thought he was roughing it when he went north and got a job as a lumberman. He had thought sleeping in a sawdust-filled bunk was rough. He'd even felt a little sorry for himself when the axe had blistered his hands and he had to buy itchy, leather-lined wool gloves until his hands got calluses. What he wouldn't give for a pair of those gloves now!

His hands had grown tender during the weeks of relative inactivity. Now, he had to paddle, no matter what. He pulled his shirtsleeves down far enough to cushion the paddle and endured.

The first sign of civilization came around nightfall. At first there were a couple of unoccupied fishing shacks, obviously built by white men. Then there was a pier and many houses way out in front of them.

After being a castaway for so many days and under such trying circumstances, he had almost begun to doubt the fact that such a thing as a town existed. Marquette, with its stores, houses, and churches, seemed unreal, like a mirage when it began to appear.

He glanced back to see if Moon Song was as excited and relieved as he was at this oasis of civilization ahead of them.

All he saw was a stalwart woman, rowing in an unbroken rhythm. No person he had ever known, male or female, had one-tenth of Moon Song's grit. She'd done everything he'd done, and she'd done it while carrying a baby on her back.

He remembered Penelope swooning over things great and small, which had become the fashion among well-to-do ladies of the South for a while. A doctor friend mentioned once that he attributed such behavior to corsets that were so tight they brought on a lack of oxygen, but Skypilot thought it probably had more to do with the fact that Penelope's friends swooned, and so she swooned.

It was supposed to make a man feel big and strong, and it worked. He'd caught Penelope in his arms more than once when a comment or scene overcame her.

He could just imagine the look of contempt in Moon Song's dark eyes if she ever witnessed such behavior.

The town didn't come a minute too soon. Moon Song felt as though she would drop. In fact, her fatigue had grown so great she had begun to despair of having the strength to continue one more hour. The lack of food and the constant labor had left her feeling weak and disoriented. When they nosed up to the pier, Skypilot was able to crawl up and out of the canoe, but she sat stationary, hardly able to move.

Her legs hurt. Her arms hurt. Her back hurt from carrying the baby continually on the cradle board. Had an experienced rowing partner been in the canoe, she would have felt more comfortable taking the cradle board off and leaning it up against the side of the boat. But with Skypilot and his great bulk and inexperience? Never. She had to be ready to be thrown into the water and swim at all times.

"What's wrong?" he asked.

"Now it is me who cannot move."

Skypilot helped her out of the canoe, and both sat on the pier getting their bearings and absorbing the fact that they were here. Wondering what came next.

What came next was a middle-aged man in a black robe who walked over and stood staring down at them. She'd had some contact with the Black Robes in the past and respected them. The Jesuits did what they could for her people, even though what they could do was seldom enough.

"My name is Father William Slovic," the Black Robe said to Skypilot. "It looks like you two have had a long and arduous journey."

"We have."

"My housekeeper can provide you with food and shelter."

Food and shelter sounded mighty good to Moon Song, but she had no energy left for talking. All she wanted was a place to lie down and rest her raw hands. She knew how to endure, and she would never speak of her pain, but her hands hurt terribly.

"We would appreciate anything you could do for us." Skypilot dragged himself to his feet. "My name is Isaac Ross. My friends call me Skypilot. This is Moon Song and her son, Ayasha."

"When you are rested enough to follow me, I'll take you and your wife to my home."

It was an understandable assumption, but Skypilot did not feel like he could ignore it.

"She's not my wife."

"Well, we can fix that." The priest rubbed his hands together.

"You don't understand," Skypilot said. "We were in a shipwreck east of here a few days ago."

"The *Belle Fortune*?"

"Yes."

"We were anticipating the arrival of that ship, but when it didn't come, we hoped that it was merely delayed."

"It was most definitely delayed," Skypilot said. "Permanently."

Moon Song was surprised at the bitterness she heard in his voice. He was always so strong of heart. The fatigue must be getting to him too.

"There were many souls lost?"

"At least forty."

"Did anyone besides you survive?"

"One woman. Isabella. She was the wife of Colonel Hatchette, who was to take over command of Fort Wilkins. We had to leave her behind."

"How far behind?"

"A day's journey by canoe. Isabella has not been right in the head since losing her husband and child. We were afraid to bring her with us for fear she would capsize the canoe."

"Can you draw us a map of how to find her?"

"Yes, plus we tied some white cloth to a tree limb that you can see easily if you go by boat."

"We'll get a group of men together immediately to go get her."

"Tell them to pack some food," Skypilot said. "They'll need it. And so will she."

"I will take care of it," the priest said.

"How do you happen to possess a canoe?"

"Moon Song found it, repaired it, and trained me how to use it. Both Isabella and I would be dead by now if it wasn't for this amazing woman."

"Ah. I see." The priest looked back and forth between the two of them. "Well, now. Please come with me. While my housekeeper tends to your needs, I'll get some men together to rescue this Isabella."

Moon Song had never been so grateful to see another woman in her life as she was the priest's housekeeper. Mrs. Veachy was middle-aged and portly, and told Moon Song that she had been providing hospitality to stray people the priest brought home to her for the past three years.

Moon Song was almost beyond caring what happened. Her arms and back ached. Her baby needed to be fed. Her stomach was beginning to growl yet again.

"You're safe now, dear," Mrs. Veachy said. "As soon as we get some food down you, you can have a nice bath and then get some sleep. I'll be happy to take care of this little pumpkin for you a few hours."

Moon Song was grateful for Mrs. Veachy's ministrations. The first thing the housekeeper did was ladle up two large bowls of thick, nourishing beef soup with plenty of fresh bread and butter. Moon Song had to caution Skypilot not to gorge — she had known true hunger, but she suspected that he had not. She did not want him losing his supper from eating too much. As soon as she'd finished her food, Mrs. Veachy saw to it that she had a good bath, and soon she was tucked away beneath clean-smelling blankets on a bed filled with fresh straw that felt like heaven. She had no doubt that Ayasha would be well taken care of by that bustling, kind woman. She gave herself permission to sink into blessed and complete oblivion.

It was after noon when Skypilot awoke to voices. He threw on his clothes and went outside to the kitchen.

Father Slovic was standing in the middle of the room, still in his black frock coat. The tail end of it was wet and his black boots were mud splattered. Three other men were with him, along with a bedraggled Isabella, who was sitting at the kitchen table, eating what appeared to be a bowl of bread and milk.

Mrs. Veachy was seated in a rocking chair, holding Ayasha, who was sound asleep.

"Did you have any trouble finding her?" Skypilot asked.

The three other men waited respectfully for Slovic to speak.

"No trouble finding her, although we were a little surprised to find her pointing a rifle at us."

"A rifle?" He was dumbfounded. "Was anyone hurt?"

"No," Father Slovic said. "It was broken."

"But where would Isabella find a rifle?"

Isabella sat eating, as though unaware that they were talking about her.

"She hasn't spoken a word yet, but I'm guessing she found it lying around the camp. Part of the annuities the Indians got this year from the federal government in return for the lands they ceded is food, clothing, and a rifle," Father Slovic said. "Each brave was given a gun and a pouch of shot to help him hunt and feed his family during the winter. The rifles were so cheaply made that many blew up in their hands. More than one warrior has been maimed by them this year. That's why the Chippewa abandoned that fishing village so fast and ended up leaving behind a damaged canoe. I recognized it when you came in. The owner had a son who was blinded by that rifle. They brought him here to see our doctor."

Skypilot was concerned. "Did the doctor help?"

"He tried, but the young brave will never see again. Others will try to keep his family from starving." The Jesuit's jaw clenched. "I've sent letters of disapproval to government officials, but I doubt it will do any good."

"I'm so sorry." Skypilot felt sick over such greed and injustice.

Moon Song entered the room. "I take baby now."

She had been transformed. She was wearing a long, ruffled gown. Her hair had been washed and brushed. He did not know what had happened to the clothes that Delia had purchased for her, but without them, she looked like a different person from the one with whom he'd escaped from the steamship.

The three men who had gone with Father Slovic eyed her hungrily. Whether they were good men or bad, he did not know, nor did he intend to leave her alone with them long enough to find out. He was grateful she had not been there earlier. Hopefully, she had not heard about the defective guns her people had been given.

"Ayasha good baby?" Moon Song asked Mrs. Veachy.

Mrs. Veachy handed him to her. "He's been an angel."

Skypilot noticed that Ayasha was dressed in diapers and a long blue dress, the kind most white baby boys wore until they were old enough to wear britches.

"Father Slovic says that woman there has no man." One of the men pointed at Isabella. "Is that true?"

"Her husband and baby were killed a few days ago," Skypilot said.

"I don't care if she's only been a widow a couple of minutes," the man said. "I'm laying my claim on that woman."

"Leave her alone," Slovic said. "She's not right in the head yet."

"Don't matter none to me," the larger one said. "She's kind of draggy-looking right now, but I bet she'll clean up good."

"It's time for *you* to go home," Slovic said. "I apologize. My friends here mean no insult, but there are a lot more men than white women in the Upper Peninsula. When one shows up, sometimes there are brawls."

Isabella gave no indication that she had heard a word. Instead, she merely shoved her empty bowl away from her.

"Would you like some more, dear?" Mrs. Veachy said.

Isabella reached for a lead pencil lying on

a side table near a large Bible, and began to draw on the priest's snowy white tablecloth.

"Isabella!" Skypilot scolded. "Don't draw on the priest's good tablecloth."

She ignored him while her pencil flew.

"Leave the poor child alone," the Jesuit said. "If drawing gives her a sense of relief, then that tablecloth is a sacrifice I'm willing to make."

Skypilot noticed that Mrs. Veachy didn't look quite as willing to make that sacrifice, but she held back her words. Soon, even she did not seem to care about the sacrifice of a tablecloth for the awe she felt as she saw it transformed.

This was no child's drawing. It was a professional sketch, and it was fascinating to watch it come to life before their eyes. This reminded him of the picture she'd drawn of her husband on birch bark, only much, much better.

Mrs. Veachy was an impressive housekeeper, and the tablecloth had been starched and ironed to within an inch of its life. On the hardwood table, it made an almost perfect drawing surface.

With a few deft strokes, Isabella was turning the tablecloth into a priceless canvas. All stood there, amazed, as a baby's face emerged, laughing, happy. Skypilot could almost hear him giggling.

In one corner, she drew the same baby's face asleep, his eyes closed on rounded cheeks, innocent, mouth poked out as though in deep thought while he slept, a tiny hand curled under his cheek.

While they marveled at that picture, another emerged from the other corner, the same baby looking all dewy-eyed as though he had just awakened from a nap.

Isabella drew feverishly as she immortalized image after image of her child on the makeshift canvas of the linen tablecloth. From time to time she would stop, grab a paring knife off the sink, and sharpen the end of the pencil. Then she would start in again, shading, forming, creating a masterpiece of a mother's love . . . and grief.

"We will have to purchase another tablecloth after today, Mrs. Veachy," Slovic said. "Or do without. We shall never wash this one. It has become a holy thing."

"I agree, Father," the housekeeper said.

Isabella didn't stop until every square inch of the kitchen table was filled with images of her child, studies of his hands, his tiny feet, a dimpled knee, a perfect, shell-like ear. It was as though she was driven to immortalize every feature, every wisp of hair. It was almost magical watching her create those images, and Skypilot was unable to turn away, as was the priest and Mrs. Veachy. By the time she finished, the pencil was nothing but a nub.

She rose from the chair and stood looking at the entire space of the four-by-four-foot square. It was as though she were trying to memorize every detail. She gave one last flick of her wrist, perfecting an eyelash. Then she crumpled to the floor.

Moon Song had hung back, clutching Ayasha to her heart as the rest in the room gathered around Isabella while she drew.

Now, as the Black Coat and Skypilot carried Isabella into a room off the kitchen where Mrs. Veachy said she usually slept, Moon Song went over to see what it was that Isabella had done.

What she saw broke her heart.

The poor woman had captured every nuance of her baby's face and expression. She wondered if this is what Isabella had been brooding about all this time. Had she been trying to remember? Trying not to forget what her child looked like?

There were no similarities between her baby and Ayasha at all except their ages. Isabella's baby had light-colored hair and light-colored eyes. Ayasha had dark hair and dark eyes.

She had hated Isabella for the terror she'd felt when Ayasha was missing. But would she have been any saner than Isabella had she lost little Ayasha? She didn't think so. If anything, she might have been worse. In her heart, she forgave Isabella. It was something that the Jesus in Skypilot's book had said a person should do. Forgive. She understood the wisdom in forgiveness. Especially when a person, like Isabella, couldn't help what she had become.

15

"Another ship is due in soon." Father Slovic rose, black robes rustling, and paced the floor.

The Jesuit was a tall man and wore his wavy dark hair parted in the middle. He was slender to the point of emaciation and had a craggy face that seemed to be permanently windburned. There was an air of restlessness around him, as though he were aware of having too much to do in too little time. Skypilot guessed his age at anywhere from forty to sixty. His face was not young, and his eyes had the look about them of someone who had seen too much, but his movements were that of a younger man.

"I hope it makes it here safely."

"I'm sure the steamboat captain will take you north to Copper Harbor, or on his return visit take you back down to Bay City, whichever you prefer."

"I'll have to go on to Copper Harbor," he

said. "I promised my boss that I would see Moon Song safely with her people before coming back."

"Do you know which tribe she is part of?"

"She says she's Chippewa."

"What do you know about her?"

Skypilot told Slovic the story of her coming to the lumber camp and their journey together. He left out the part about the stiletto as well as the kiss they had shared.

"Thank God you and your friends were there for her. Did they treat her well?"

Skypilot was not Catholic, but he definitely had respect for the dedication he saw in this Jesuit priest.

"I have thanked God many times that she was able to find her way to us, and yes, she was treated very well."

"Good." Slovic nodded his head thoughtfully. "Good."

"How long have you been here in the North country?" Skypilot asked.

"I have been here most of my adult life, although I was born and raised in Slovenia."

"So far away," Skypilot said. "It cannot have been an easy ministry for you."

"I did not become a Jesuit because I wanted 'easy.' I prayed to God for a people to serve who needed me, and the Lord saw fit to give me the native tribes of this area."

The priest fingered the large cross he wore around his neck.

"Mrs. Veachy tells me that the people around here call you 'the Snowshoe Priest' because of the hundreds of miles you travel every winter to check on the various tribes. She also says you've learned the languages of several Indian tribes and even written a book on those languages."

"I have been blessed with a strong body and a mind that picks up the tongues easier than most," Slovic said. "I believe the Lord deliberately gave me the gifts and strength I needed to minister to these particular people."

Skypilot thought back to his own aborted ministry, and how easily he had been rejected by those he had once hoped to serve. How unwilling he felt to go back to such a life. How had this man done it? How had he stayed the course all these years? Especially here where things were so primitive?

"But what about the blackflies and mosquitoes? What about the blizzards? The wolves? The snakes? The loneliness? The resistance to your message?"

He was truly hoping for an answer. Something profound. Something to make sense out of his own reluctance to go back into the ministry.

"Why would any of that matter?" Slovic's voice sounded puzzled, as though he did not understand the question.

Skypilot started to clarify and then realized he had already been given his answer.

What would any of that matter, indeed?

What did danger, discomfort, and discouragement matter when one felt called to carry the message of Christ?

He felt infinitely inferior to this man who had devoted his life to the unforgiving North country. Slovic had a steely quality in his eyes that spoke of the endurance it took to walk long distances to far-flung villages in spite of much danger and hardship. Compared to Father Slovic's, his own ministry in Richmond looked like child's play. Bible study and books and social events. None of these particularly strained a man's emotional, spiritual, or physical resources. Everyone spoke English. It wasn't until he preached an unpopular sermon that things got difficult.

"I used to be a minister," he confessed.

The priest stopped and stared at him. "*Used* to be?"

"I'm just a timber cutter now."

"Oh?" Slovic said. "Tell me about this journey you have had from minister to timber cutter."

This was not a casual question, and Sky-pilot knew that the priest would not accept a casual answer.

"I was in Virginia, back before the war." Skypilot closed his eyes, remembering. "I was foolish enough to preach against slavery to a people who had spent their lives defending it. I was young and at that time was still arrogant enough to think that I could make a difference with my words."

Slovic threw his head back and laughed. "The arrogance of our youth. I remember it well. What happened after this brave sermon?"

Skypilot smiled. "Oh, the usual thing when a young preacher thinks he knows more than the older leaders of a church. Within three days I lost my job, my home, my reputation, most of my friends, and my fiancée."

"Ah." Father Slovic sat down in the chair beside him, crossed his hands over his stomach, and gazed at him with calm, wise eyes. "But did you lose Christ?"

Skypilot thought it over. "No," he answered truthfully. "My faith in people was damaged, my faith in myself was destroyed, but my faith in the Lord was unshaken."

Father Slovic smiled. "Then you really lost nothing of importance, did you?"

The fire crackling in the grate was the only sound in the room.

"No." The truth of this dawned so bright it lit up his soul. "I lost nothing at all of importance."

Slovic leaned forward. "A true minister of the gospel does not have to possess a pulpit or be an eloquent speaker. He does not have to have the Holy Scriptures memorized or be able to dissect various doctrines. There is a simple powerful holiness in giving a cup of water to someone who is thirsty. Or a bite of food to someone who is hungry. My guess is that you have done much of this."

During his lifetime, especially during the months he helped escaping slaves, Skypilot remembered giving many cups of water, many bites of food.

"I have."

"Then you never left the ministry at all, did you?" Slovic said. "You simply carried it with you."

In spite of having no church. No pulpit. No congregation. In spite of having no "reverend" or "pastor" to hang in front of his name, he was still . . . a minister?

"Living a life of service to others," the weathered-looking priest said, "is the most powerful sermon of all, don't you think? My 'church' encompasses thousands of acres and includes hundreds of souls — many of whom are not Catholic or even religious in any way."

The priest's words struck a chord in his heart. Suddenly, Skypilot felt the need to move, to do something with his hands. He got up and put another log on the small fire in the kitchen grate. "I thought this trip was going to be a simple, up-and-back journey. I planned to take Moon Song to her people and then get back to my life."

"And instead?"

"It's turned out to be more complicated than I ever dreamed. As I've been walking those many miles to get here, I've discovered that I'm not sure what kind of life I want to go back to. Bay City is not my home, but it's easy to find work there. I could drift along, working in the woods until a tree took me down, but I know that a man's years on this earth should have more impact than simply making a living, eating, and sleeping." He moved the log a bit with the poker, and flames licked over it. "The problem is, although I have the skills and the knowledge, I have no desire to be a minister again — at least not the kind of minister I was before. I lost the desire to preach a long time ago."

"Then don't. Instead, simply find a way

to serve the people the Lord puts in your path," Slovic said. "For instance, this Moon Song woman. Is she a Christian?"

"No."

"Have you taught her about Christ?"

Skypilot thought back. Had he?

"I've read several biblical stories to her — some of which were about Jesus."

Slovic nodded approvingly. "Have you treated her well?"

"I think so. I've certainly tried to."

"Not every white person who professes Christianity has treated the Indian well." Slovic steepled his hands and gazed at Skypilot, his brow creased in thought. "It has made my job very difficult."

They spent another night with the priest and Mrs. Veachy, waiting for the expected steamboat to arrive. When Moon Song awoke the second morning, she felt like her old self again. Two good nights' sleep had given her all her strength back. Her spirits were high with anticipation of the last leg of the trip, which would take her back to her people. As she entered the kitchen, she saw the Black Coat and Skypilot in the process of tacking the tablecloth Isabella had drawn on to the kitchen wall.

"Good morning," Slovic said. "Are you

feeling better?"

"Yes."

"Ah. That is wonderful." He put a couple more tacks in. "I'm putting this up where your friend can see it whenever she wants. It appears to give her comfort."

"Isabella like that."

"Mrs. Veachy went to some neighbors to purchase eggs. She'll be back soon to fix breakfast."

The door opened, and Moon Song expected to see Mrs. Veachy walk through the door with an apron full of eggs. Instead, an elderly Chippewa man came in. He was not of her tribe and she did not know him.

She expected the priest to exclaim at the sudden appearance, but Slovic merely nodded toward a cabinet against the wall. "It's in there."

She had not yet braided her hair this morning and was wearing white woman's clothing, so the old man did not greet her. He seemed too intent on his mission to look to the right or left.

He opened the cabinet door as though used to rummaging inside the priest's furniture, and brought out eight loaves of bread, which he put into a large sack he'd brought with him. Then he nodded his thanks and disappeared.

"That's the man who owns the canoe that brought you here," Slovic said. "Since it had served its purpose, I gave it back to him. He was grateful for the repairs."

"Thank you."

Mrs. Veachy came through the door with a basket of eggs in her hands. "Did Crooked Foot get his food?"

"He did."

"Oh good. His wife has been so ill, and she loves my bread. Perhaps it will help."

"I'm sure his son will be grateful for it too."

"Do many Chippewa live near here?" Sky-pilot asked.

"There's a settlement nearby," Father Slovic said. "The government is insisting that they learn how to be farmers. Last year's potato crop did fairly well. It helped get them through the winter."

It made Moon Song's heart ache to think of those fine braves who had once roamed this land being forced to turn themselves into dirt farmers in order to live. They were growing potatoes now? In a brave's mind, that would be women and children's work. No wonder her people drank!

When Isabella entered the room, she looked as rational as she had been the first time Moon Song had seen her. Her hair was brushed and her face washed. Mrs. Veachy had evidently loaned her a dress too. It was not fancy, but it was a vast improvement on the stained red dress she had been living in.

However, the most arresting thing about Isabella was the fact that there was a person behind her eyes again. She took one long, lingering look at Ayasha and then her eyes sought Moon Song's.

"I remember what I did now," she said. "And I apologize."

Then she went over to the tablecloth that the priest had tacked to the wall and traced the largest picture of her child with one finger. "Good morning, little one. Mother will never forget you."

16

The soldiers at Fort Wilkins were fascinated by the fact that a white woman was stepping off the ship. Moon Song was of some interest to them, but they gazed at Isabella as though she were a mirage.

It had, Skypilot assumed, been a long, long winter.

There were two other women in the garrison. The doctor's wife had accompanied her husband here, as had the wife of one of the other officers. As the commanding officer's wife, even though her husband was deceased, Isabella outranked the other two women socially, at least for now. A new commanding officer would be found eventually.

The two women gathered solicitously around Isabella and ushered her into one of the buildings, completely ignoring Moon Song.

Somehow word had gotten back to Detroit

about the loss of the *Belle Fortune,* and provisions had been hastily gathered and sent by the U.S. government. Barrels of everything from salt pork, to salted herring, to salted soda crackers were taken off the boat and carried into the fort.

As Skypilot looked around the fort, he decided that if there was a more beautiful spot on earth, he had not seen it. The neat, whitewashed buildings formed a *U* around a parade ground, and all faced Lake Superior. The buildings and parade ground were protected and surrounded by upended logs, sharpened into points, and dug well into the ground, creating a wall behind which, presumably, the fort could be protected.

The soldiers did not seem to be in any imminent danger of being attacked on this bright spring day, though. The gates were thrown wide open and appeared as though they had not been closed for a long time. There was an easy flow of foot traffic as Indians and soldiers mixed freely. Everyone watched the fascinating unloading of the steamship that had brought provisions.

"Are any of these your people?" he asked Moon Song.

"They are not of my tribe," she answered.

"What are they doing here? They're not soldiers."

"They're here for handouts," an officer standing nearby responded. "That's always why they're here. Hungry beggars, every last one of them."

Skypilot felt embarrassed for Moon Song, who stood close enough to hear what the officer had just said. Her face was impassive.

The officer seemed to be unaware of her presence even though she had cleaned her doeskin outfit and was wearing it again.

"The squaws are the worst," the officer said. "They'll offer themselves to you for nothing more than a loaf of bread. These people have no sense of morality whatsoever."

Skypilot saw Moon Song's eyes narrow, but she kept her impassive expression. He wondered what she had endured through the years in the way of rude and unthinking comments.

"My friend and I will need a place to stay until tomorrow," Skypilot said. "I would appreciate the use of a couple horses until I can get her to her tribe."

The soldier spit a used-up wad of tobacco on the ground. "Why do you think you have to take her there?"

"Because she is a special friend of my employer's wife, and I promised to see her

255

safely home."

"She don't know how to ride," the soldier said.

"What do you mean?"

"Chippewa don't have horses. Never have. Let her loose outside the gate and she'll find her way home, just like a lost dog." The soldier laughed at his own joke and walked away.

The soldier never knew how close he had come to being felled by Skypilot's fist.

"I'm sorry for that, Moon Song," Skypilot apologized.

"What he say is true." Moon Song shrugged. "Some of my people *will* sell themselves for a loaf of bread. We do not own or ride horses. And if you let me loose outside this gate, I *will* find my way home, just like a smart dog. You go back to Bay City now. You have been a good friend, but it is time to say good-bye. I not stay here."

Then, without another word, she began to stride toward the gate.

She was leaving without him? Just like that? After all they'd been through together? He could not allow that to happen.

"Wait!" he called. "Don't go!"

She did not turn around.

"Moon Song!"

She did not slow down. If anything, she

walked a little faster toward the gates.

"Please!"

He saw her stop, but it took her a few beats to turn around. She didn't turn until he got to her, and when she did, he saw that she had been crying.

"Moon Song," he said in a softer voice. Despite everything they had been through, he had never seen her cry. Most white women he had known cried easily. He thought perhaps it was part of the Indian way to not cry. Now, he saw that there were tears streaming down her cheeks. What was going on inside of this woman? He could not guess. He had never been able to guess.

This was not the place to show any sort of affection for her — he knew it would be misconstrued by everyone around who saw them — but he could not help putting one hand on her shoulder and looking into her eyes.

"What's wrong? Why are you leaving like this so quickly?"

"You good friend to me," she said. "But I go now."

"Let me go with you."

"You have life in Bay City."

"I really don't, Moon Song," he said. "I don't have to be anywhere except back at Robert's lumber camp this October, and then only if I want to be. There will be men lined up for my job, and you know it."

"You have woman in Virginia. Woman who writes on pretty paper."

He was stunned. "How do you know that?"

"I see you sneak looks at letter on boat. You smell like woman's perfume after."

"Penelope and I were in love once, but no more. I'm not going back to her."

"You abandon your woman?" Moon Song turned away from him with disgust. "That just like a white man!"

"Where did you get that idea? She broke it off with me a long time ago. Told me to leave."

"Oh." She absorbed that information and then shook her head. "No matter. You not follow where I go."

"Why? I want to see you and Ayasha back to your people. I have to tell Robert that you're safe or he'll never forgive me. Not to mention Delia and Katie. I can't possibly face those two women if I can't tell them for certain that you are all right. I know I'm not able to make food appear out of thin air like you can, but once I get some provisions from the fort, I'll be fine. A gun, an extra knife, and some hard tack and jerky and I'll be in great shape."

"No. I go rest of way alone. You my good, good friend, but I must go rest of way alone."

He was perplexed. It was obvious from her tears that her heart was breaking over their departure from one another, but she wouldn't budge on the idea of her going on to her people without him.

He took her hand, clasped it to his cheek, and kept it there covered with his own. "Will I ever see you again?"

"I must see to my grandmother. I worry she did not get through winter well."

She had not answered his question.

"Where does she live?"

He saw her hesitate. She was debating her answer. Debating whether or not to even tell him.

"She lives on a reservation." Her eyes shifted away from him. "The people are very poor."

It was then that it hit him. She was ashamed. His precious, valiant Moon Song was ashamed of how her people lived. It broke his heart. This was one woman who should never have to be ashamed.

Well, at least this was one thing he could fix. He could buy some food and gifts for Moon Song to take with her to her grandmother. He wasn't sure what he could get from the fort, but he was going to try.

"Stay here, Moon Song," he said. "I'll be back soon with whatever I can find for you to take to your grandmother."

"I have Ayasha." She looked alarmed. "Cannot carry big load."

"Maybe you won't have to. In fact, instead of staying here, come with me."

Skypilot had seemed so forlorn about not coming the rest of the way with her that Moon Song figured the least she could do was grant his request to wait a short while longer before leaving. She obediently followed behind as Skypilot went about his business.

She had no intention of changing her mind. It was easier for them to part now. She loved him, but there was no future for them together. She could not allow there to be a future for them. If there was one thing she knew to be true, it was that white men who married Indian women eventually left them.

She and Skypilot would have to say goodbye sometime — and now would be less complicated than allowing him to follow her to her home and being put into the position of having to answer all the questions Grandmother and the rest of the tribe would ask if she showed up accompanied by this big white man.

The problem was — Grandmother wouldn't just question, she would be furious, and a furious Fallen Arrow was not something she wanted Skypilot to experience. Skypilot had no idea how big a favor she was doing for him by not allowing him to follow her.

Besides that, Copper Harbor was at the tip end of the Keweenaw Peninsula, where there was nearly always a wind. Between Fort Wilkins and the reservation where her grandmother's people lived, there were miles of trails, swamps, wildlife, mosquitoes, and blackflies.

Skypilot had only a little experience with the pests of the Upper Peninsula. Staying along the coastline where there was much wind swept some of the little biting population away, but in the middle of the Keweenaw, where she intended to travel, he would find out what living in northern Michigan really meant.

It was kind of him to purchase supplies for her to take home to Grandmother. She stood quietly in the background while he struck a bargain with the sutler. He seemed especially delighted with an overpriced pack mule he purchased. He packed the mule's saddlebags with everything from hardtack to canned peaches, coffee, and evaporated milk. He also got some blankets and a tarp. An Indian family could have made it through a winter on what he purchased.

"I think this is about all the animal can carry. Do you want to say good-bye to Isabella before you go?" The sun had fallen low in the sky. Moon Song wished to get away from the fort and the eyes of the men as quickly as possible. In her opinion, she had already stayed too long.

"I say good-bye plenty," she said. "Isabella with white women now."

"I suppose you're right." Skypilot looked miserable standing there with his pack mule. "Give this to your grandmother with my thanks. Tell her that her granddaughter saved my life."

Moon Song smiled. "Oh, Fallen Arrow like squirrel with nut, digging meat out until nothing left. Grandmother not stop until she know everything."

"Everything?" His eyes searched her face.

"Maybe not." Moon Song smiled. "I not tell her I kiss you on night of the wolves."

It was the first time she'd acknowledged that the kiss had ever occurred. "Moon Song . . . let me come with you."

"No!"

■ ■ ■ ■

No? The woman was so adamant, she nearly hurt his feelings. In fact, it would have hurt his feelings if her eyes had not told him how hard this was for her. Did she love him too? He thought she might.

Her voice softened. "Indian woman always think white man not leave."

"What are you talking about?"

"You love Moon Song now?" She cocked her head to one side. "Think maybe marry?"

"I'll admit that the thought's crossed my mind."

"No."

"I didn't propose to you."

"Good."

"All I did was offer to walk you home."

"White man. Indian woman." She shook her head sadly. "Not good. White man leave some day. Always."

"Your husband was half white and you married him." Skypilot was immediately on the defensive, but he also couldn't believe they were having this argument. He had not said a word about marriage to her and hadn't planned to. At least not yet.

"Husband also half Menomenee. French-Canadian father leave him and mother.

Make him a very sad little boy." She turned to leave. "Go home. Go home."

Saying good-bye to Moon Song was the hardest thing he had ever had to do. The injuries he'd sustained the winter before when the falling tree hit him were insignificant compared to the pain he felt in his heart as she prepared to leave him.

As he watched her walk away, memories of their recent time together flooded his mind. He had never known any woman who could be so many different people wrapped up in one lovely package. He remembered the Moon Song who was the half-wild Indian woman he'd kept from killing the man she called Stink Breath. Then his mind flew to the half-frozen girl who had curled up in his arms after she'd swum the frigid waters of Lake Superior to save them. The tender mother caring for her child so faithfully. The wood sprite he'd admired, standing like a crane poised to spear a fish. The childlike woman who had created a tea party by pretending to put sugar and cream into their birch bark cups of tea. And most of all, the woman who had kissed him so passionately the night he had saved her from the wolves, and then pretended even more passionately that it had never happened.

All he knew was that whoever she was —

he loved her. He would always love her.

"You're wrong," he shouted. He could not let her disappear without saying it. "If we were married, Moon Song, I would never leave. Ever."

In reply, she simply waved a hand above her head without turning around, as though dismissing him.

Blast the woman! She had guessed correctly. He was in love with her. He did want to marry her and live with her forever . . . except for one very big thing that had been troubling him from the day he first realized he was starting to think about her as more than a little sister to be protected. It was the one thing that kept him from rushing after her and proposing right then and there.

Whose God would they found their life together on? He would not ever abandon his, and he wasn't sure she would ever abandon the religion she had been taught.

He'd tried to gently teach her about Christ, but he'd been too careful. All he'd really done — coward that he was — was read her Bible stories, hoping the power of the Word itself would help her believe. He did not want to coerce her into believing something simply in order to make him happy. If they were ever to be together, he wanted it to be real to her.

The problem was, he had never needed to convince someone who had absolutely no concept of Jesus that he was the Son of God. He didn't know how to do this. He'd spent his entire life with people who had at least a basic understanding of the Bible, even if they chose to live their lives apart from it.

The Chippewa did not live in a spiritual vacuum. He knew that fact from a conversation he'd had with Father Slovic. The priest had said that they followed a very ancient and intricate woodland religion. Even more worrisome, Slovic had found that sometimes they lived their lives with more integrity than many of the whites who had infiltrated their country. This made Slovic's job infinitely more difficult.

Skypilot had been trying to figure out how to approach the subject with her for months, and now he had run out of time. All he had managed to do was teach her some Bible stories. He had no idea if the two of them would ever believe the same, but if they actually ever married and had children, he did not want them to be raised by a mother who thought Jesus was nothing more than a character in a storybook.

Slovic had seen that he cared for her, and had privately asked him three questions. Was he willing to live with an Indian woman as his wife for the rest of his life? Absolutely. Was he willing to live in a wigwam for the rest of his life in order to be with her? If he was with Moon Song, of course . . . although he was confident he could build a decent cabin for them. Was he willing to marry someone who did not share his belief in a risen Christ and salvation?

No, and there was no guarantee she ever would. He couldn't chance it. Not yet. But if only she would let him travel the rest of the way with her, maybe he would find a way to talk with her in such a way that she would understand the miracle that had happened on the cross. Maybe God would give him the words.

He desperately needed the extra time that accompanying her to her people would give him, and so he caught up with her.

"Moon Song!" He grasped her arm. "Stop! Please let me go with you. Just to make sure you're safe. That's all. Then I'll leave."

She stopped but did not look at him. Instead, she stroked the mule's nose.

"Thank you for this gift," she said. "It will make Grandmother very happy. Perhaps I will teach him how to plow the ground. It seems that the white government wants

Chippewas to become farmers now."

He remembered the Chippewa braves Slovic had told them about who had been forced to become potato farmers. He had seen a cloud cross her face when she heard that and he'd wondered what she was thinking. Now he knew. From the tone of her voice, she was not happy.

"I'm sorry, Moon Song."

"Not your fault. I go to my people now." She looked up at him, and her eyes were pleading. "Go home. I cannot bear much more and still so many miles to walk."

He finally saw what he was doing to her and gave up. He would not allow his own selfish need to be with her to cause her any more pain.

"What will you do when you get back to the reservation?"

"I will miss you, Skypilot." Her eyes grew soft as she gazed up at him. "We have made many good memories together."

"I can hardly bear the thought of never . . ."

And then she astonished him once again by standing on tiptoe and giving him a quick, fleeting kiss on the lips. "You are a man who prays much."

"Yes, I am."

"Then pray for me, my friend," she said.

"Because I do not think my life will be easy."

"I will never stop praying for you."

She nodded in acceptance of this, tugged on the mule's harness, and turned away.

Watching that slim body walk away from him was wrenching, and yet he watched until he could no longer see the eyes of that sweet baby to whom he had grown so attached. He watched until he heard the sound of the steamship whistle blowing a warning blast, and he knew he would have to get on that boat or lose his mind and run after this woman who had asked him not to follow her.

He watched until her figure disappeared altogether, and then his heart quietly fell into a thousand pieces.

"This would have been an interesting place to live," Isabella said as the ship pulled away from Copper Harbor. "I would have enjoyed getting to know the other women of the fort better. They were so kind to me the short time we were here."

"Did you have any trouble getting the trunks you had sent ahead deposited on the ship?" He was trying to make conversation, but it was difficult. His mind was on Moon Song. His mind would probably always be on Moon Song. It felt so strange to be separate from her.

Isabella smiled. "It is not difficult for a widowed colonel's wife to get soldiers to carry things for her. The trunks are all safe and sound, although I have no idea what I'll do with them."

"How are you feeling?"

"Are you asking if I'm going to lose my mind again and steal someone's baby?"

Her comment made him uncomfortable, but he answered it truthfully. "Yes, I guess that's what I'm asking."

"I don't think so." Isabella looked at the fort as it receded into the distance. "But I honestly don't know what I might do. I never doubted my sanity before, but that episode has shaken me. I suppose any of us might lose our minds under the right circumstances."

"I suppose. For instance, right now I'm seriously considering jumping over this railing, swimming back to land, and going after Moon Song. That's pretty crazy. Right?"

"Completely insane." Isabella leaned against the railing. "She was magnificent though, wasn't she? I'll never forget her as long as I live. We both owe her our lives."

The lump in his throat felt like it might choke him. He gulped it down and went to find his cabin. He couldn't bear to talk about her anymore. Not even with Isabella.

In a few hours, the steamship stopped in Marquette, and Skypilot and Isabella once again accepted a few hours of the priest's hospitality.

While Mrs. Veachy prepared food and visited with Isabella, Father Slovic invited Skypilot to a small shed behind his house where he had a pair of snowshoes in need of repair. Skypilot had noticed the man seldom sat still. Even when he was talking or listening, he was usually moving.

"If I were a Chippewa brave," Slovic said after they'd gotten seated and he'd begun the repairs, "I would have a squaw who would expect to string my snowshoes for me. This is considered women's work among the Chippewas."

"I'm sure there are many Chippewa women you could hire to do so."

"Yes, but then what would I do when I'm traveling alone through these woods if these break? I have found it best to master many skills that were not taught in seminary."

"True." Skypilot's thoughts turned to Moon Song. If she didn't know how to make a pair of snowshoes, he'd eat his hat.

The priest glanced up at him. "A marriage with that girl would not work, you know."

Skypilot sighed. "My head knows you're right," he said. "But my heart doesn't seem to want to agree with you."

"The northwoods is such a harsh place. The insects alone are enough to drive a man mad during some seasons. There are animals that have never seen a human and have no fear of them. There is the snow, so many months of snow. You have not seen snow and cold until you have lived a winter in the Upper Peninsula. Then there is Lake Superior. So beautiful and yet so deadly."

Skypilot listened respectfully. Slovic was trying to tell him something important, but it was hard to give it much weight when all he could think about was the beautiful Chippewa girl he so desperately missed.

"The problem is, Father, I love her."

"No doubt." The priest's hands were surprisingly dexterous as he wove the sinew back and forth in the snowshoes. "I have watched many well-intentioned white men marry Indian women and start families, only to abandon them later. There has been enormous tragedy because of this. It may be easy for some men to leave a native wife after they have grown tired of her, but it has not always been so easy to walk away from one's children with her. Many mixed-blood children have been taken from their mothers by white fathers who believed it to be their right to do so."

"I would never do something like that."

"Of course you wouldn't. You are a reasonable and kind man. You would never put her at that kind of risk. Not all men are like you."

He heard a hesitation in the priest's voice, as though he were considering whether or not to say what was on his mind.

"Please, whatever it is — I'd like to know," Skypilot said.

"Did you know that Moon Song's father was white?"

Skypilot's jaw dropped. "No."

"I was talking about her the other day to another Chippewa who knows her family. They said that Moon Song's father was the youngest son of a wealthy man from Boston. He came out here to check into the possibility of buying some copper mining property for his father. He stayed four years, and when he left, he took his daughter, Moon Song, away from her mother and went back to Boston. The mother apparently killed herself from grief. The father brought Moon Song back at some point, dropped her off on her grandparents, and disappeared from her life."

"I can't believe it."

Slovic shrugged. "It's not the first time something like that has happened up here, and it probably won't be the last."

Skypilot was staggered. Of all the things Slovic could have told him, this was one thing he would never have guessed. No wonder she was so adamant about never marrying a white man. Both her and her deceased husband had been abandoned as children by their white fathers. Why had she never said anything?

He stood looking out at the lake, rethinking everything he'd known about Moon Song. How little he had understood. No wonder she clung to her child with such passion — she who had been wrested away from her mother.

So many pieces began to fall into place. No wonder she had picked up English so quickly. It had, no doubt, been at least part of her childhood.

He also understood why she had rejected him before he could convince himself to propose to her. It wasn't just her husband's father, it was her own.

"I can hardly bear to think of never hearing from her again. I wish there was some way I could know that she's all right."

"When she was here earlier, she mentioned that some of her extended family live

274

on the L'Anse Indian reservation, which is near here. I go there from time to time. Leave me an address, and if I hear something, I'll send you word."

"Thank you, Father." He watched the priest's hands work for a while longer. "Would you mind explaining something to me? Something I've wondered about but didn't know who to ask."

"I'll try."

"Why did the Chippewa and Menominee and the others sign the treaties that gave away their land? How could they have sold this beautiful country away for a few trinkets?"

"It isn't quite as simple as that," Slovic said calmly. "The northern woodland tribes did not trade land for beads and trinkets. They traded for survival."

"Because the white man had killed off all the game?"

"It was not just white men who killed off game. The Indians did much of that as well, and in the beginning, it wasn't necessarily for survival."

"Again — I don't understand."

"When traders first came, they brought good things with them: iron pots, steel knives, steel traps. All it took was a few beaver pelts to purchase them, and everyone was happy. Then the traders brought in glass beads and steel needles, so much finer and stronger than the bones they had used in the past, and fine-colored silk thread with which to do fine embroidery. All of it affordable — only one or two beaver skins. Then some traders enticed braves to go into debt to them. They would outfit a brave with traps and supplies. Some Indians worked all winter and still did not have enough to cover their debt."

Although Slovic's voice remained even, Skypilot saw that his hands were jerking the sinew he was weaving with more force than necessary.

"As the fur became less plentiful, the braves had to find some other way to provide for their families. The government was happy to buy their land on what some would consider the payment plan. A certain amount each year for many years, enough with which to support their families. The Indians signed hundreds of thousands of acres away for pennies per acre, thinking it would give them financial security. Instead, what they received, for the most part, was shoddy goods — like those exploding rifles — and reservations upon which they were expected to live."

The priest finished the repair, tied it off,

and cut the sinew.

"You're angry," Skypilot said.

"I live angry because of what I've seen," the Jesuit said. "Righteous anger is a powerful force. That is what gives me the strength to keep going."

The steamboat whistle blew, and they both looked toward the source.

"It is time for you to depart, my friend." Slovic clasped his hand.

He was surprised a few moments later when Isabella informed him that she was not getting on the ship with him.

"Why?" he asked. "I thought you had family you planned to visit for a while until you decided what to do."

"That can wait," Isabella said. "I have some . . . other things to do first. I'll be fine."

"Other things?"

"I'll be fine," Isabella repeated. "Don't worry about me, Skypilot. You have done enough."

17

Moon Song was not easily frightened, but for several miles she had felt that someone was following her. Friend or foe, she knew not. To be on the side of caution, she fastened Ayasha's cradle board to the side of the mule, freeing her hands in case she had to fight.

It would have been nice to have the big lumberman beside her. He might not know how to fashion a snare for a rabbit, but he would be deadly with his fists. Her decision to send him away had been more of a struggle than she could ever allow him to see. He had no idea how badly she wanted him to come with her and to love her, but that was the problem. How long would he stay? How long before he tired of her? How long before he would want to return to his old life, the one he'd had before she'd ever met him?

And yet, alone in these woods, and espe-

278

cially with a baby to protect, it would have been a welcome thing to have him beside her.

She heard a twig snap. And then another. That told her nothing of value. It could mean that she was being followed by a white man too clumsy to cover the sound of his own footsteps. It could mean that it was an Indian who was being polite and allowing her to hear them approach. Or it could be a four-legged predator. Her horror of wolves was always near the surface.

She eased the knife out of her boot and held it tightly in her right hand as she led the mule with the other. She did not look back over her shoulder. Surprising her opponent by not giving away the fact that she knew he was there would give her an advantage.

"Wife of my brother," a voice said.

"Rising Star!" She whirled around. "Oh, it is good that it is you."

The feeling of relief was great. This was a man she had always liked and trusted.

"My brother is not with you."

This was one of the things she had dreaded about coming back: telling her husband's family that he was gone.

"He sleeps with your ancestors."

There was no change in the expression on

the face whose features were an echo of her husband's. She noticed that the lines in his face had grown deeper since the last time she had seen him, and there was more gray in his hair.

"How did he fall?"

"He went to set traps and never returned. A white man who looks for trees for lumber camps later found him caught in a beaver trap. Drowned."

One eyebrow went up. "My young brother was more skilled than that. He would never have allowed himself to get caught in a trap."

"He left our camp with a full bottle of whiskey in his pack. He thought I did not see him put it there, but I did."

"Oh." Rising Star's face fell. "He loved the white man's liquor too much."

"In the end, he loved it more than me. I gave birth alone, with no food. I waited but he never came back."

"This man who found him?"

"He buried my husband's body and brought his knife to the lumber camp where I worked."

"Is it the one you hold in your hand?"

She handed it to him. "It is."

Rising Star handled the knife with as much reverence as if it had been a lock of hair from his younger brother's head.

"I gave this to him," he said. "He was twelve."

"I know. He often mentioned that. I now keep it with me always. Last week it cut the throat of a wolf that would have eaten Ayasha."

"I am grateful that my brother's son will be raised by such a courageous mother."

Those kind words from a man she had always liked and trusted was her undoing. The months since she had walked out of the woods with her starving baby had been difficult — but she had underestimated how much of a toll they had taken. She had worked so hard for so long . . . just to survive and keep Ayasha alive. Now, here with her husband's brother — their voices and faces so alike — the memories she had kept at bay came flooding back. Not the bad days after the drinking had begun, but the good days together when she had loved him, and when he had loved her and only her.

She turned her face away from him. "I must go."

Quickly, she left him with the mule and Ayasha and ran into the woods. Instead of relieving herself, as she wanted him to think, she found a huge oak tree, deep in the forest, sank down behind it on a cushion of old leaves, and began to sob. She'd been trying to hold back the tears all day — and with the exception of a few that had leaked out against her will, she had succeeded. Now, she could hold them back no longer. With Rising Star safely guarding Ayasha, she cried her heart out in the greatest flood of grief she had ever felt.

She grieved her love for her young husband, and the white man's whiskey that had taken him from her. She grieved the fact that he would never know their young son, or teach him to hunt and to become a man. She grieved over the way she had been treated in Bay City by Stink Breath — how he and his son had acted like she was a thing instead of a person. She grieved the fact that she would never see Katie or Delia or Robert and Katie's children whom she had grown to love. She grieved the life she saw stretching out before her as her people's way of life grew more and more difficult. She grieved the fact that her son would grow up in a world so strange and different from that of her and her grandparents. And then a fresh wave of sobs wracked her body as thoughts of Skypilot washed over her. He was the finest and truest man she had ever known — and she would never see him again.

When she emerged again from the forest,

Rising Star kindly made no mention of her appearance, even though she knew he could tell from her swollen eyes what she had been doing.

Rising Star was not a young man. He was a much older brother of her husband and full Menominee. He had not been happy that his little brother had been fathered by a white trapper but he had loved him.

Now, he looked at her with sad eyes. "It would be best if in the future you did not marry a man who loves whiskey as much as my brother."

Her thoughts ran immediately to Skypilot, whom she had never seen take one drink.

"I agree."

"You are going to your grandmother?" Rising Star asked by way of speaking of happier things. Neither of them acknowledged the amount of time that had elapsed while she cried her eyes out.

"Yes. I hope to find that she survived the winter."

"I have heard that it was a hard one for her, but she improves now that spring is here. Seeing you again will be good medicine for her."

"As she has always been for me. I will stay and care for her."

"She is worthy of your care. Our people

could learn much from her instead of relying so heavily upon the government's annuities."

Moon Song nodded. "Those are true words."

"May I continue to walk with you?"

"I would very much like the company, Rising Star."

He looked at Ayasha. "Your son is a fine child. He reminds me much of my little brother at that age."

It brightened Moon Song's heart to hear Ayasha praised. "He is very strong and bright. Like his father."

"I saw you saying good-bye to a white man back at the fort," Rising Star said. "May I ask who he is to you?"

She answered honestly. "He is my friend."

"A very good friend, I think." Rising Star's voice was mild, but she heard the underlying tension.

"We will not see him again," Moon Song assured him.

"That is good," Rising Star said. "That is best."

Having Rising Star find her had been a good thing. Not only was he good company, he also had a valuable rifle that he had paid money for, not one of the government-issued guns. With it, he shot enough small game to make it possible for them to eat well without waiting to set snares or dipping into the provisions Skypilot had given her. She looked forward to surprising her grandmother with such a bounty of gifts, not to mention the unexpected possession of a good mule.

After several days' travel, during which they carefully avoided the copper mining towns that dotted the Keweenaw, they drew close to her grandmother's village. There, Rising Star left her.

"I must see to my own family now," he said. "They will be much saddened to hear of my brother's passing. Now that I have found you and know what happened, I can stop searching. But we will meet again." Then he melted into the shadows of the trees and was gone.

Much had changed since she had seen her grandmother. They would have so many things to talk of. Finally there would be someone to whom she could pour out her heart.

Living in a one-room log cabin had been one of the many changes the whites had brought about now that most of the Chippewa had moved to the reservation. Instead of moving from place to place with the seasons — to the rice fields when they were ready to harvest, to the sugar bush when the sap flowed in the maple trees, to the lake when it was time to catch and smoke a winter's supply of fish — they lived in one place.

Instead of the efficient and relatively mobile wigwams that could be taken up and put together in less than a day, they were expected to stay in one place and live their lives from these dank structures.

Tuberculosis was rampant among her people. She did not know if the change in their living situation had caused the disease, or if it was caused by being in too much proximity to the whites, but it was a scourge of her people. Venereal disease had taken a terrible toll, especially to the children born of diseased parents. Even measles was life threatening when one's body had few defenses against it, especially if that body was already weakened by hunger.

Her grandmother, wiser than most when it came to medicinal plants, tried to help as much as she could, but these were diseases for which she could do little.

Worst of all, in Moon Song's opinion, was the hopelessness she saw in her people's eyes. Too many had given up. They were so tied to the land that when it was no longer theirs to roam at will, it was as though they no longer knew who they were. And so a people who believed in visions sought those visions in the bottom of a whiskey bottle.

Hollow-eyed children peeked out at her from some of the gaping, dark doorways as she passed. Young men, who years ago would be out hunting for game, lounged in the yards. She avoided engaging in conversation with any of them. That would come later but not now. First she must see her grandmother.

She was surprised to see two of the tribal women sitting outside her grandmother's one-room cabin, busying themselves around Fallen Arrow's outdoor campfire.

"Where is Fallen Arrow?" Moon Song asked in Chippewa.

"Is it you, Moon Song?" The younger woman blocked the sun from her eyes with one hand. "Your grandmother has been waiting for you. One who had seen you at the fort came to tell her. She's inside."

Moon Song found it strange that her grandmother had not come out to greet her. The sound of her voice alone should have brought Fallen Arrow to her side after so many months apart.

"Is something wrong with her?" Moon Song asked.

The older woman, a relative known as Fighting Sparrow who was preparing a small meal over Grandmother's campfire, glanced up but did not answer the question directly. "It is good that you have come."

What exactly did that mean? A feeling of dread entered Moon Song's stomach. The fact that the two women watched her so closely instead of immediately exclaiming over Ayasha struck her as odd.

She ducked into the low doorway of her grandmother's cabin. Fallen Arrow had always been the strongest person Moon Song had ever known, and had once been the wife of the great chief Standing Bear.

Now she found her grandmother lying upon a thick bear rug placed upon a sleeping bench. This was not normal behavior for her grandmother to lie down in the middle of the day unless she was extremely ill. Moon Song's worries that Fallen Arrow would have difficulty getting through the harsh winter had been justified.

"I brought someone to see you, Grandmother," Moon Song said.

Her grandmother reached out a trembling hand and placed it on Moon Song's sleeve. "You're home."

"I am home and I have brought my boy child to you. You must get stronger so that you can teach him as you taught me."

She slipped off Ayasha's cradle board and positioned it so that her grandmother could see him. Fallen Arrow smiled and touched his face and hair.

"What a fine young brave you have brought into my cabin," Fallen Arrow said. "He looks like his father."

"His father no longer walks among us."

Her grandmother's eyes widened at this news. She struggled to sit up, and as soon as she did, she started coughing. The cough was deep and racking, and it frightened Moon Song.

The younger woman, Snowbird, who had been outside, came in and knelt down beside Fallen Arrow with a wooden bowl of broth in her hand.

"How long has she been like this?" Moon Song asked.

"She has been ill ever since the Sap Running in the Trees Moon," she said. "She was not able to make our annual trip to the sugar bush, and you know how much she always loved being part of sugaring."

"I have cones for you," Fallen Arrow said. That small speech seemed to exhaust her.

"She asked those of us who went sugaring to bring some back for her to save for you," Snowbird said. "She told us that you had loved those as a child, and that if you came back, she wanted to have some for you."

If Moon Song had thought that finding Fallen Arrow so weak and ill was heartbreaking, it was nothing compared to discovering that her grandmother in her illness had still been thinking of her. Moon Song could not allow her to escape from this earth — not yet. She was the only person left who loved her that much.

"My grandmother was strong and healthy when I left last summer. Did she have sufficient food to eat over the winter?"

"None of us did." Snowbird looked at the ground as though afraid to meet Moon Song's eyes. "The government payment for our land did not arrive on time. Our braves were without ammunition. Our chief gathered all the food together and divided it up to get us through the winter. Your grandmother made the same choice that many of our old ones have made in the past. She gave up her own food so that the children could survive. It weakened her body. She has not been able to get rid of her cough, no matter how carefully we prepare the herbs we gather."

"Thank you for taking care of her," Moon Song said. "I will take over her care now."

"You are back to stay?"

"I am back to stay."

Snowbird gave a small sigh of relief, set the bowl down, and left. Moon Song looked around her grandmother's cabin. She was grateful that she had not allowed Skypilot to accompany her here. This was not his world. These were not his people. He would not understand an old woman who had starved herself so that food could be put into the mouth of a child. And yet that had been her way and her ancestors' way forever. The survival of the tribe was always more important than the life of the individual.

She knew that Fallen Arrow had not sat idly by, though. Her grandmother would have set out snares and dug roots until there was no more small game to capture and the snow was too deep. If she knew her grandmother, even if the old woman had been able to capture enough rabbits to fill her own belly, she would have taken only a few bites to remain strong enough to continue to hunt for food until she knew for certain that it was futile.

Oh how grateful she was to Skypilot for the wealth of food he had sent with her. She found herself almost wishing that the big timberman was beside her now just for the sheer strength of his great heart to encourage her. The responsibility for her grandmother as well as for her child was now on her shoulders. This was not a good time to be an elderly Chippewa, nor was it a good time to be a little Chippewa brave.

She knelt beside Fallen Arrow with the wooden bowl in her hand. "You must sit up and drink this broth that Snowbird made," she said in Chippewa. "You must get stronger."

Her grandmother turned her head and answered in their precious native tongue. "Have you and the child eaten? Have all the children of the village eaten?"

"Yes, Grandmother." Tears stung her eyes. "Everybody's bellies are full except your own. It is your turn now. You must regain your strength."

"I am no longer hungry," Fallen Arrow said.

"You must eat anyway." She smoothed back her grandmother's gray hair. "You must regain your strength so that you can teach my son the way of the old fathers. I need you here to teach him how to be strong and brave and proud of his people."

"He will be a leader of our people."

"What do you mean, Grandmother?" Moon Song asked. "Have you seen a vision?"

"A vision is not needed." Fallen Arrow

roused herself and grasped her arm. "Fight for your son. When I am no longer with you, fight for him. Do not let him become one of the young men who give up their manhood for empty promises from the government."

"I won't, Grandmother. But Ayasha is still very small, and right now I'm more concerned about getting you to eat something. Please take a sip of this good broth that Fighting Sparrow and Snowbird made."

Her grandmother did as she asked, taking a small sip, then she laid back down. "His name will no longer be Ayasha — Little One. He must be called Standing Bear."

Moon Song gasped. Fallen Arrow was bestowing the name of Ayasha's great-grandfather upon him. This was an enormous and rare honor. She had known of it happening only once before, many years ago, when a chief had proudly given his own name to his son after a great feat of courage had been executed by the young man.

She wasn't entirely sure her grandmother had the right to do this thing.

"Are not the elders supposed to choose his name?" Moon Song asked.

"Too many have died this winter. I am now the oldest of my people. Your little son needs a strong name. Standing Bear was a strong man. In the days ahead, our people will need for your son to be as strong."

Moon Song did not like all this talk of her baby son fighting. She wanted to be able to enjoy his laughter and chubby cheeks and sweet smiles. "If my son fights, I will stand beside him."

"Oh, Granddaughter." Fallen Arrow turned sad eyes upon her. "Don't you realize? You will have to fight long before little Standing Bear eats his first mouthful of solid food."

18

Bay City held no attraction to him anymore, but he didn't know where else to go. His heart was walking around someplace on the Keweenaw Peninsula while he was stuck here, at loose ends until the lumber camp started back up in October.

The only bright spot in his life was Robert and Katie's happiness. Sarah and her husband had found their own little place nearby, and Katie was busy keeping track of the three children. From what he could see, it wasn't easy, given all the freedom the children had enjoyed at the lumber camp. Robert's son and daughter and Katie's little brother were like wild Indians after spending the winter among the roughshod shanty boys.

He stopped himself. Wild Indians? What a foolish thought when thrown up against the reality of Moon Song and her concerns about her people's very survival!

Strange how once you loved someone, you began to perceive the world through their senses. The native men and women he saw living at the edges of Bay City now took on a whole new significance in his eyes. The lives of the women, especially. He saw Moon Song in each one. Less than a month earlier, he would have barely noticed them.

He couldn't stop wondering how she was doing. If she had enough to eat. If she was warm. If she was safe. If Ayasha had cut those teeth yet, or if he was still gumming that little fist. He found himself noticing every baby he saw who was close to his age, and each time he felt as though someone had wrenched his family away from him.

What did you do when you loved someone and couldn't be with them? Shouldn't be with them.

He missed her so badly, if he thought there was half a chance Moon Song would take him, he would go to the reservation and begin combing the woods for her, but would she accept him if he came back? He didn't think so. He had given her a choice, and she had made it.

October couldn't come soon enough. He needed something to throw his weight into that would make him tired enough to fall into bed every night and lose consciousness.

He needed something that would take the memory of watching her walk away from him out of his mind.

"Another letter came for you today," the boardinghouse mistress, Mrs. Wilcox, said. "It's the same curlicued handwriting from Virginia you got before. Frankly, if I were a man, I wouldn't trust a grown woman who has the time on her hands to fool around with all that fancy nonsense. I got too much work to do to mess with something like that. Just write it out plain is what I say."

"It would be considered odd to most of her friends if she didn't write with that sort of penmanship."

"Humph." Mrs. Wilcox washed her hands, dried them on her apron, and set to work punching some bread dough down. "If you have a mind to get tangled up with some-one, I have a perfectly good granddaughter of marrying age who can't write fancy, but she'd make a good wife."

Skypilot had met the boardinghouse mis-tress's granddaughter, and she was lovely. The girl was also every bit as opinionated and forceful as her grandmother. A man who had someone like her in his life would lose all control of it.

"She's a lovely girl, but I'm not looking

for a wife right now."

"You ever gonna preach again?" the mistress asked.

The question took him by surprise. "Why?"

"I heard the Methodist church is looking for a preacher." She stopped her kneading and looked him over head to toe. "You'd probably clean up good enough to get the job, and my granddaughter would make a real good preacher's wife. That girl is like me," she said proudly. "She could run the church for you and all you'd have to do is stand up in the pulpit once a week and spout off a few big-sounding words and bury or marry someone every now and then. It'd be a nice soft job. You wouldn't have to get your hands dirty again."

He put his hands in his pockets, leaned back against the dry sink, and stared at the woman's back while she continued kneading.

Stand up in the pulpit. Spout off a few big words. Show up and marry or bury someone every now and then.

He supposed some ministers could get by with living like that, but he could not. He had found that feeling a responsibility for people's souls, minds, marriages, broken hopes, guilt, and doubts was much harder than the clean, sweeping feel of swinging an axe into a pine tree.

The pressure of being a woodsman wasn't even a close second to being a preacher. Soft job, indeed!

"No thanks," he said. "I think I'll just head back into the woods when summer ends."

"I could put in a good word for you with the hiring committee."

"The problem is, Mrs. Wilcox, I was never all that good at spouting big words." He pushed away from the sink and headed up the stairs to his room. "I'll leave that to someone else."

She had a good heart and meant no disrespect, but his mind flew to Father Slovic and his snowshoes and his mastery of Indian dialects and his seven-hundred-mile treks through the northwoods every year. Not exactly a soft job.

He wondered if the Jesuit had heard any news about Moon Song. He wished it was a letter from Slovic he had received instead of one from Penelope.

He went upstairs to his room, laid down on his bed, and read Penelope's letter. It was basically a repeat of what she had already written. She said she was sending it because she feared that he had not received her earlier one. The woman must indeed be desperate.

He ran a hand back through his hair so roughly that he nearly yanked some strands out. The slight twinge of pain felt good. It helped mitigate the pain he was feeling inside.

He missed Moon Song! How was he going to live without her? He was so tired. He was tired of trying to do the right thing. He was tired of praying. He was tired of reading his Bible. He was tired of worrying about other people.

For the first time in a long time, he felt the need to go out and get roaring drunk, and there wasn't a reason in the world for him not to do so. He was no one's preacher anymore. He was just another shanty boy. He could get drunk if he wanted to, and so help him, he was going to!

The sound of piano music spilled out onto the infamous section of Water Street that the lumbermen referred to as "Hell's Half Mile." On the main floor of the three-story Catacombs, where nearly every vice known to man was rumored to exist, inside the Steamboat Saloon there was raucous laughter.

The female laughter was brassy and contrived. The male laughter was coarse and drunken, but at least inside that establishment there was the illusion of enjoyment. One thing for certain, there would be enough liquid refreshment to help a man forget his loneliness and confusion.

Or maybe he should go back to Virginia after all. Just give up and go the direction that would seem the most . . . normal? Would it be that hard to accept the carefully couched offer he'd been handed by a beautiful woman? Penelope was exquisite in a drawing room or dance. She could converse with anyone without saying anything that mattered. She, who was always aware of how she looked, and dressed, and appeared to others, was a master at flirting and making a man feel like a man. She and he would, as someone had once remarked, make very pretty children.

Even though they would be impoverished, compared to sleeping in a lice-infested bunkhouse, it would be a relatively comfortable life. He couldn't be a shanty boy forever. There would come a time when he could no longer swing an axe. More than one old shanty boy had lived out his days in total poverty, sweeping out saloons for a pittance and a drink. Compared to the specter of that sort of end to one's life, the alternative of going back to Virginia didn't seem so bad.

Going home to Penelope and letting bygones be bygones would make sense in so many ways.

A smart man would go back. A beautiful, willing, contrite woman. A graceful, comfortable home. A few loyal servants who had nowhere else to go to help keep it that way. The lovely, lush countryside. Ragged now, perhaps, but beautiful in his mind. It had been a sort of paradise to him when he'd moved there with dreams of having his first church. With dreams of making a difference.

His head and common sense told him to follow that second letter back to where it originated and make a life for himself.

His heart said otherwise.

His heart longed for the sweep and majesty of *Kitchigami,* that brooding lake that had nearly swallowed him whole. He longed for the wild, whistling, mourning sound of loons at dawn. He longed for a campfire made from sparks knocked off a flint in the hands of a serious young woman so intent upon her work that she was not even aware that his admiring gaze was trained upon her. He would never forget the look of joy he'd seen on her face when that first flame had caught and leaped into life, nor her look of triumph when she smiled at him over her accomplishment.

Longing for her made no sense at all. The whole time they had traveled together, she had bested him over and over in everything they needed to do to survive, and she had done so with no apology or attempt to cover up her cleverness. He smiled and shook his head at the memory of her allowing him to show his ignorance of handling a canoe before she calmly got in and showed him how well a canoe could slice through the water when an expert was wielding the paddle.

Moon Song's hair had never known the touch of a curling iron. Her skin was not the peaches and cream that Penelope had always kept in perfect whiteness with various lotions and potions and parasols. Moon Song did not shy away from the sun or apparently give it much thought.

Penelope was completely feminine in the way she walked. It was something carefully studied and practiced. Tiny, elegant shoes peeking out from beneath layers of fabric and petticoats.

Moon Song walked with toes deliberately turned slightly in, wearing worn moccasins, head down, always scanning the forest floor or lakeshore for food or signs of small game.

Penelope smelled of lilac and smelling salts.

Moon Song smelled of campfire smoke and fish and sometimes of a soiled baby.

Penelope had worn watered silk.

Moon Song wore stained doeskin and probably had no idea what watered silk was.

Penelope's eyelashes fluttered demurely when she talked to him.

Moon Song looked him square in the face, openly, as though she were taking his measure the entire time.

Marrying Penelope would open up polite society to him. A society that he might not always agree with but that he at least understood.

Marrying Moon Song would plunge him into a world that he did not understand and probably never would. Marrying her could quite possibly mean becoming a castaway from his own people for life.

Going back to Penelope would be familiar.

Going back to Moon Song would be like deliberately stepping off a cliff into the dark thin air.

Being with Penelope would mean sharing a hymnal at church and Sunday dinner with friends.

Being with Moon Song would eventually mean discussions where his religious beliefs would be called into question and so would her own.

Penelope wanted him.

Moon Song did not. She had made it clear that she did not want him to follow her.

A sound of broken glass, a shout, and then tinkling laughter bled out onto the street. He had not been an angel in his younger years. Everything within him wanted to go in. He knew the illusion of comfort that he could find inside that saloon. It would be so easy to bury himself there tonight.

"You ain't trying to make up your mind whether or not to go in there, are you?" Delia strolled up and gazed into the dimly lit saloon window beside him.

"You shouldn't be out walking around here at night, Delia," he said. "These sidewalks aren't safe for a woman alone."

Delia looked up at him in surprise and then spluttered with laughter. "Honey, you are just too good to be true. You act like a gentleman even to someone like me. You realize I've spent the bigger part of my life working around these Catacombs. Don't you think I know how to take care of myself?"

He gave her his full attention. "I think if you knew how to take care of yourself, you wouldn't have had to spend all those years

305

working on Water Street."

Delia was reputed to be in her midfifties, but devoid of makeup and finery, she looked much older. The woman had "hard life" written all over her, including the scowl she gave him now.

"That's easy for you to say," she said. "Men have choices. Most women don't. In case you ain't looked recently, there's not a whole lot of help-wanted ads for women in the *Bay City Journal.*"

"At least you have a different life now."

"I do, don't I?" she said brightly. "Thanks to your employer. Robert Foster is one of four truly good men I've ever known."

"Who are the others?"

"Two are men you never heard of, but they gave me hope that mankind wasn't quite as bad as I had grown to think. The fourth is you, Skypilot. That's why I'm here."

"Me? Good?" He was startled. "Far from it."

"Are you feeling bad about yourself because you're standing here wanting to go in and having trouble keeping yourself from it?"

"There are better ways to spend my time."

"Most men wouldn't think twice, you know that, don't you? Instead, here you are, listening to all that laughter, hearing the clink of glasses and the happy sound of the music, and probably knowing exactly how smooth the whiskey would go down — and yet I've been standing there in the shadows, watching your face, seeing you struggle these past fifteen minutes. Most men would be into their second bottle by now. And I got a feeling the battle you're fighting ain't all about whether or not to go inside. What's wrong? You look like you got a war going on inside of you, and I'm itching to find out what it is."

"Sorry, but you wouldn't understand, and it's my concern, not yours."

"Oh, I beg to differ with you on that," Delia said. "You're one of Robert's best axe men. That is very much my concern. I need to know if you're going to be able to work this fall or if I need to find someone to replace you when the lumber camp starts up again."

"I can still swing an axe. Don't worry about that."

Delia took a stance in front of him and looked him full in the face as though trying to read it.

"You just got back a few weeks ago from taking Moon Song and Ayasha back to the Keweenaw, didn't you?"

"Yes."

"I hear the two of you got stranded for a while along with another passenger of that poor ship *Belle Fortune.*"

"We did." He really didn't want to be having this conversation with her. It was his own private misery, fighting to forget about his love for Moon Song, wondering what he was going to do with the rest of his life . . . without her.

"Robert told me Moon Song saved your life."

"She did."

"Along with that artist woman who lost her mind and tried to steal Moon Song's baby?"

"Is there anything you don't know about, Delia?"

"Not much. That's my job." Again that close, appraising look. "You miss her bad, don't you?"

"Who?" He glanced away.

"The beautiful Indian girl who hovered over you half the winter taking care of you after the accident."

"We became good friends," he said defensively. "Of course I miss her."

"Then you're a fool if you don't go up there and find her again. She is a prize and so is Ayasha. That little boy is going to make some man a fine son with Moon Song as a mother."

"She told me not to follow her. What if she doesn't want me, and what would I do for work? They aren't timbering all that much up there yet. Not like around here."

"Do you remember how our Katie got here?" Delia asked.

"She rode the train as far as it would go, praying for a job all the way."

"And the Lord opened the door for the exact job she needed."

"True."

"I've heard you're a praying man, Sky-pilot," she said. "Is that true?"

"It is." It embarrassed him that she asked this question when he was standing outside the saloon wrestling with whether or not to go in. "Most of the time."

"Then for heaven's sake, hop on the next boat north and start praying."

"I can't. I'm telling you, she does not want me to come find her."

"You must be as stupid as you look, son," she huffed. "You need to trust me on this. I've spent time with that girl. I know her. I've known a lot of women, and if you have any sense at all, you'll go after her. Marry her!"

Delia's voice usually had a light, mocking

edge to it, even if she was talking about the weather, but now her voice tightened down into such intensity she was nearly shaking from the emotion of it.

"You can learn to fish or weave baskets or whatever it is you have to do to make a living up there."

"I'm telling you, she won't have me."

"And why not?"

"Because she believes that I'll eventually abandon her when I get tired of living there, like her father abandoned her mother and other white men have abandoned their Indian wives. She seems to think we're all alike."

"Her father was white?"

"Yes. Some rich man from Boston. Dumped her on her grandmother, from what I can tell, after her mother died, and he never came back. A lot of people up there think white men won't stick it out. I even had a Jesuit priest telling me to leave her alone so I wouldn't break her heart."

"A priest was giving you advice on marriage?"

"Yes."

"And you listened to him?"

"He's lived there a long time and he knows a lot about Moon Song and her people."

310

"All right. So here's the big question. Do you love her?"

"More than life."

He wasn't sure but he thought he heard Delia sigh a little when he said that. Could the old woman possibly have a romantic streak after all she'd been through?

"Then the answer," Delia said, "is as simple as the nose on your face."

"What is it?"

Delia hesitated. "You'll think I'm a meddling old woman."

"Go ahead and meddle."

"Don't leave her." She snapped her fingers. "Ever. It's that simple."

"I can promise her a thousand times that I'll do that, but she won't believe me."

"Of course she will. Go up there. Find work. Tell her you love her. And . . . just stay. Prove that you will never leave, that you'll never give up. Women love stuff like that."

"You think she'll have me?"

"No. Not right away. But if you prove that you can live on the Keweenaw without going stir-crazy or heading back south, I think you got a good shot. I probably shouldn't tell you this, but you need to know that every time your name came up in conversation, her face would light up. She cares

311

about you."

He couldn't help the sloppy grin he got on his face. He was starting to feel some hope, and see a future. Except for one thing.

"We come from two very different religions, Delia," he said. "It's a worry to me."

"Oh honey." Delia sighed. "Just go love the girl and continue to be the good man you already are. Let God take care of the rest." She gave him a little shove. "Now go and forget about this place. Nothing here to come back to anyway. Show the girl you ain't never gonna forsake her or desert that sweet baby."

He grabbed Delia by both arms and planted a kiss on top of her head.

"What was that for?" She stood in the middle of the street with her hand on top of her head where he'd kissed her.

"For being a meddling old woman!" Sky-pilot shouted as he ran down the street. "And thanks!"

"First time that ever happened!" he heard Delia mutter right before he turned the corner.

The thought of getting drunk was now the furthest thing from his mind. He needed to go back to his boardinghouse, find some writing materials, and scratch out a polite but firm reply to Penelope. The woman needed to know that he was not coming back so she could get on with her life.

Tomorrow he would make his good-byes to Robert, Katie, and the children. He would use his dwindling funds to purchase another ticket on a steamboat going north. Hopefully, it would not blow up and he would find his way back to Moon Song. She might reject him. She might accept him. He had no idea, but he was going to try.

19

He had written many letters in his mind to Penelope in the past few years. Long letters that would have filled pages and pages with hurt, and anger, and in some cases, longing. The one he now wrote bore no relationship to any of those imaginary letters.

Bay City, Michigan

Dear Penelope,
  I am honored by your kind invitation, and I regret to hear about the state into which your father's plantation has fallen. However, you need to know that the man you say you once loved no longer exists.

He stared at the paper for a few moments, debating whether or not to include the next sentence that his mind had begun to compose. Finally he put pen to paper and finished the letter.

I have fallen in love with this North country of Michigan as well as its inhabitants. I doubt that I shall ever have an occasion to visit Richmond again.

Kind regards,

Isaac Ross

He knew she would consider the abruptness of the letter to be rude, but he simply did not know what else to say. Twenty minutes later, he was on his way back from the post office, feeling nothing but relief. The way he figured it, if Penelope had truly loved him, she would not have waited so many years to tell him so.

Whether it was the occasional swallow of broth she had managed to get down Fallen Arrow or her and little Standing Bear's presence, her grandmother seemed to have gained a small amount of strength since they'd been living with her.

Fort Wilkins had not carried many delicacies, but it had carried some. Those it had carried, Skypilot had purchased in abundance.

One of the things he had packed was a small jar of orange marmalade. This would be a new adventure for her grandmother. Moon Song had never tasted marmalade until she had eaten in Katie's kitchen at the lumber camp. She well remembered late one night after finishing cleaning up a large supper, she and Katie had sat down and eaten a piece of Katie's good bread with a smear of marmalade and a cup of tea. It had been cozy and intimate and one of her fondest memories of her months in the lumber camp.

"I think you will like it, Grandmother," Moon Song said as she gave her a taste of it.

Fallen Arrow had always possessed a great sweet tooth, as did the entire tribe. These were not a people who used salt or any other condiment. Their main flavoring, whether it was on meat, rice, or cornmeal, was always the maple syrup and maple sugar they loved so much.

Grandmother's eyes opened wide. "What is that strange flavor?"

"It is from a yellow fruit that comes from far away. The white people call it an orange."

Fallen Arrow poked a finger in the jar and licked it off. "It has a strong flavor," she said. "But it is very good."

"Yes, Grandmother," Moon Song said. "It has strong flavor and it will help make you strong too."

She felt her eyes fill up with tears, and it surprised her because she had not cried since she'd come home. She must be more tired than she realized. Quickly, she dashed the tears away before her grandmother saw them.

Fallen Arrow sat up for the first time that night after eating the entire jar of marmalade, started asking questions, and listened with her full attention about Moon Song's time in lower Michigan.

Late that night, as Grandmother slept, and as she lay beside the newly named little Standing Bear, Moon Song felt such gratitude in her heart for having two of the people she most cared for in the world beside her.

She wished Skypilot was near so that she could tell him about her grandmother's improvement since she'd arrived and Ayasha's new, strong name. She tried hard to convince herself that her world was complete without the big timberman.

Perhaps, if she were lucky, in time his image would fade.

Skypilot passed the painted rocks in daylight as he went north along the shore in the *Temperance,* a brand-new steamship. With astonishing ease, they steamed right past the agonizing trail that he and Moon Song and Isabella had trudged.

The town of Marquette came up on the left, and the *Temperance* stopped for two hours to drop off supplies and to take on passengers. It had been several weeks since he'd seen Father Slovic, and he wanted to stop and see if there was any word on how Isabella was faring. With any luck, the priest might also have word of Moon Song.

He wasn't sure that Father Slovic would be there, but when he arrived, he was greeted with great joy by Mrs. Veachy, who said that Father Slovic had been desirous of seeing him again. He was home and did indeed have news for Skypilot.

She led him into the study, where Slovic was bent over several books open in front him. His quill was working furiously.

"Studying for Sunday's sermon?" Skypilot asked.

"Skypilot!" Father Slovic stood up from his chair and shook his hand. "I had hoped to see you again. You are an answer to my prayers."

"I'm glad to see you too, although I'm pretty certain I've seldom been the answer to anyone's prayers."

"As all good men of God should feel,"

Slovic said. "Those men who believe themselves to be God's gift to mankind are usually anything but. Please have a seat. I have word of Isabella that will interest you."

"How is she faring?"

"She told me that she was concerned the illness that overtook her during your journey might return. At my suggestion, she chose to spend some time with the Sisters of Charity in Detroit. They run an establishment there that cares for people who have various forms of . . . insanity, both mild and severe."

"Do you know if it is helping?"

"I know that they are taking good care of her. There is a new doctor there. His method with Isabella is basically to make certain she has drawing material and plenty of it. I stayed a few days on some church business, and when I went to check on her, her room was covered in the most extraordinary drawings. She seemed much calmer in spirit and says she believes she is making good progress."

Father Slovic walked over to a chest of drawers and pulled out a long tube wrapped in oilcloth. "I asked Isabella for this, and she was gracious enough to give it to me. I showed it to a friend of mine in Detroit while I was there who is an avid collector of art. He wanted to purchase it, but when I refused, he said that I should put it away carefully and keep it safe."

"What is it?"

Slovic unrolled the scroll of canvas on a table near a window. "Come look."

It was an oil painting done in sepia tones. It was of Moon Song bending gracefully over Skypilot, offering him a folded birch bark cup of tea. The expression of longing and love as he looked up at her, caught in the shadows of light from the campfire playing across his face, was staggering. Isabella had somehow captured exactly what had been in his heart at that moment.

If there had been any doubt left in his mind that he was head-over-heels in love with Moon Song — and there was none — that picture would have erased it.

"It's a perfect depiction of where we were, and yet it is done so simply."

"I know," Slovic said. "My friend confirmed my suspicions, which is that this woman is a rare talent."

"Will she ever be able to be sure of her sanity again?"

"I'm not entirely certain she was ever insane," Slovic said. "Sometimes I think that a true artist, the kind through whom our Lord allows his great creation to be interpreted, is not like the rest of us. We see only with our eyes and we experience life through somewhat duller senses. A true artist, one like Isabella, sees the world with an entirely different set of eyes, and it affects their heart and mind. I'm not sure but what there isn't always an element of madness in the greatest artists. Isabella did not have the ability to absorb the death of her husband and child and go on. Her mind retreated into that madness and she created an alternate world in which she could live, a world where Moon Song had stolen her baby and all she had to do was reach out and take him back."

"You mean she rewrote the script of her life? Like some theatrical play?"

"It's a theory the doctor and I discussed."

"Did she agree to that theory when you were there?" Skypilot asked.

"No," Slovic said. "I didn't even bring it up. I think simply keeping her in artist materials is the best course for now."

Slovic rolled up the oilcloth and carefully placed it in a drawer.

"My friend says that I should put this away and keep it for my old age. He says that there is a very good chance that Isabella's works will be worth quite a lot of money someday."

"Is that what you intend to do with it? Sell it?"

"Of course not." Slovic laughed. "I am a Jesuit, remember? The Lord will take care of my needs, which are small. This, I will use at the right time to help my parishioners."

As interesting as this conversation was, Skypilot had limited time, and there was something he wanted to know much more than anything else.

"Have you heard anything of Moon Song?"

"Yes."

Skypilot felt his pulse quicken. "Please tell me."

"Ah." Father Slovic lifted a finger into the air. "You have discovered that you cannot live without her. You must have her at all costs."

He had never heard Slovic sound sarcastic before, but the man was certainly skirting along the edge of it.

"Yes, actually, I have. I need to know if she and the baby are well. Did they make it to her grandmother's? Do you know where she is?"

"They are fine," Slovic said. "But before I tell you how to find her, please tell me — do you ever plan to preach again?"

"I have no ambition in that direction at the present." Skypilot was puzzled. "But what does that have to do with finding Moon Song?"

"It has a great deal to do with finding Moon Song. I have been working in this country for a long time and have grown weary of some of my own people's foolishness." Slovic gave a great sigh. "I like you, Skypilot, but I had great hopes that you would go away and stay away from my country."

"I have no idea what you're talking about. Why on earth would you say that?"

"Because I think you have no idea how much power you could have were you to start preaching again, and these native people are already plenty inundated and confused by our various forms of gospel."

"What do you mean?"

"In the last mining town I visited over on the Keweenaw, there was already a Methodist church, an Episcopalian church, and a Catholic church to minister to a very small town at war with itself."

"I don't understand."

"The Indians watch as Cornish men do battle with the Irish. They watch as the good churchgoing miners get roaring drunk every Friday and Saturday night. They watch as the same families go to their separate churches on Sunday and sing songs about Jesus.

"I show them my Bible, which I call sacred, and it is sacred. They then show me their writings that they preserve upon birch bark books that they also call sacred. I see their dances and songs of faith, and they hear us singing songs and lighting candles and sprinkling incense about, and they see no difference."

Skypilot glanced at his pocket watch. He had less than a half hour before he needed to be back on that ship, and yet Father Slovic showed no signs of slowing down.

"Do you realize that before the Europeans began to settle here, dishonesty was practically unknown among the Chippewa? So was selfishness. They greeted their visitors, gave them food and drink, and helped the first Europeans as they were used to doing for one another. I have to admit, I have not always felt justified in trying to teach these people the white man's religion. That's what they call it, you know, the white man's religion. As though Jesus himself was white."

"Father Slovic" — Skypilot glanced at his watch again — "I am grateful to you and for your hospitality, but exactly what are you trying to tell me?"

"That if you come into *my* country among *my* people teaching the gospel with words that you do *not* back up with godly actions . . ." Father Slovic's eyes blazed. "I will despise you, and so will Moon Song's people.

"Unless you know in your heart that you can live a life of dignity and honor here, unless you believe that you can pledge yourself to that girl for the rest of your life, then don't stay and add to the tears that have already been shed in this country. Don't be yet another man who comes here as a Christian only to dishonor the Lord's name."

Skypilot felt the heat and impact of Slovic's words and knew they came from harsh experience. One of his teachers in seminary had once said that the biggest stumbling block ever presented to people receiving the gospel was Christians acting badly.

"If she'll have me, I won't leave her. Ever. I will also try to live as close as humanly possible to the teachings of Jesus."

"Well, then." Slovic picked up a pen. "You have an education. Have you ever considered teaching school?"

"I did a little teaching this past winter when I was laid up at the lumber camp with an injury. There were three children in camp. Why?"

"Did you enjoy it?"

"A great deal."

"Then here is the name of an acquaintance of mine who is in charge of a school at the Minnesota Mine near Rockland, Michigan. It is at the base of the Keweenaw, near the center, so I'd suggest you find water transportation to Ontonagon. If you get off there, it will put you about twenty miles from Rockland instead of trying to walk in from Copper Harbor."

Father Slovic scribbled the name on a piece of paper. "They've been without a teacher for over two months. It is near the end of the school year, but you might be able to do some good in the next few weeks. The building they have is not much, and you'll have to share it with the Methodist church that meets there. Most of the parents I met are not particularly interested in their children's education. The children fight among themselves, Cornish against Irish, as do their parents. It does not pay a lot, but it does come with room and board and a chance to live close enough to see Moon Song from time to time. My advice is to spend the summer and winter there before you make a permanent decision. Make sure you have what it takes to stick it out before you do more damage to her than what has already been done. You need to, at the very least, experience snow like you have never experienced before in your life."

"I've cut timber in the Saginaw Valley. Trust me, I have experienced snow."

"You really have no idea what you are talking about, but you will. The Saginaw Valley is mild compared to the snow and cold we experience here. I've written a note on the bottom of this address recommending you."

The warning whistle of the steamboat blew. As Slovic was seeing him through the kitchen to the door, Mrs. Veachy triumphantly pulled a pan of small, crescent-shaped pies from the oven. "I hoped to have these finished for you in time."

"Ah," Slovic said. "Mrs. Veachy has made some pasties for your journey."

"Pasties?"

"The Cornish women make these every day for their mining husbands. They time it so that the pasties are coming hot out of the oven as their husbands go out the door. They put them inside of their coats to keep them warm as they walk to the mines."

"Thank you, ma'am." He tucked two of the savory-smelling, cloth-covered pasties in his pocket. "But are either of you going to tell me where Moon Song is?"

"No. I'll get word to her through some of

my Chippewa friends where you are," Father Slovic said. "If Moon Song wants to find you, she will. If she doesn't, you'll never see her."

The mining town of Rockland was little more than a few dozen log cabins huddled along the main trail, and the structures that supported the mine work along with one church/school, a general store, and a boardinghouse. Also, two larger frame homes with Gothic overtones rose apart from the rough log cabins. He assumed those were the homes of owners or overseers. Even around these loftier homes, the grounds were muddy, raw, and bare. Tree stumps were everywhere.

It was as though the earth did not exist to produce any living thing here but only to vomit up copper. The forests had been denuded all around. Smoke curled from a few chimneys where there must be cooking going on because it was far too warm to need a fire for warmth. These few acres compared to the sweeping grandeur of the lakeshore he had seen as he had sailed around the tip of the Keweenaw to Ontonagon was like comparing the pockmarked face of the moon he had glimpsed once through a friend's pair of strong field glasses to paradise.

Although he appreciated Father Slovic's note of introduction, he arrived at the Minnesota Mine footsore from walking, disoriented by how much his original plans had changed, and doubting in his heart whether the position was available. He also wondered if he would be up to the job. The teaching position here, at least the way Slovic had described it, didn't seem all that welcoming a proposition. Perhaps going into the copper mines would be preferable, although he knew nothing about mining, and the idea of going so far underground did not seem at all attractive.

Slovic's acquaintance, a Mr. Harvey Turney, turned out to be one of the foremen of the mining operation, and when Skypilot handed him Slovic's recommendation, he studied it, frowned at Skypilot, then studied it some more.

"You don't look like a teacher. You look more like a lumberjack."

"I've been both."

"And it says here that you go by the nickname of Skypilot?"

"That's what they called me in the lumber camps. It kind of stuck. My given name is Isaac Ross."

"I've heard that the shanty boys in lumber

camps call preachers Skypilots. Are you a preacher?"

"I used to be."

Mr. Turney spit a long stream of tobacco juice at a scroungy cat slinking by. Skypilot didn't know if that expressed the man's contempt for cats or for preachers. The cat stopped just long enough to hiss at Harvey Turney, so he chose to believe that this interchange involved a long-standing feud between the two.

"The former teacher here lasted three days."

Skypilot felt his stomach sink. "I'm sorry to hear that."

"Got the kids a two months' vacation, which is what they were aiming for. They'll be all cocked and primed for you."

He knew it was too much to hope for, but he had to ask. "Did the teacher leave any lesson plans behind?"

Turney switched the wad of chaw from one side of his cheek to another. "Don't know about that, but there's a pile of books still there unless them hooligans set fire to them."

Skypilot's stomach sank even further.

Turney handed the recommendation back to him. "Well, you got the job. If nothing else, you're big. That might scare them a little. Boardinghouse is over there. The pay is room and board and fifty cents a day if you teach. The pay is nothing if you don't show up."

That was less than half what he made in the lumber camps, and the way Turney spoke, it sounded nearly as dangerous. Slovic had said he should give it a year. He wished Moon Song knew what he was sacrificing for her.

He stopped himself. Sacrifice? He did not like the fact that that word had just cropped up. Tonight he would have to spend a good long time on his knees praying for forgiveness for seeing this opportunity that the Lord had handed him as a sacrifice.

"School would usually be closing in a couple weeks," Turney said. "But since it's already been closed all this time, let's plan on you keeping it open through the end of July. Teach the mean little beggers a lesson for running the teacher off. You can give 'em August off for summer vacation. Start back in September if you're still around."

"I appreciate the job," Skypilot said politely.

Turney gave a rough laugh. "You won't for long."

20

The bright eyes that surveyed him from behind the shared desks watched him studiously, but he got the distinct feeling that it had nothing to do with the subject he was trying to teach.

His neck hair stood up each time he turned his back on them, and there was a general feeling of uneasiness in the pit of his stomach.

So far the most he'd had to do was pull apart boys who were fighting. American-born kids against Cornish kids against Swedish kids, and all of them ganging up on the Irish kids, who were tough little nuts that could hold their own. Rocks were sometimes involved. Broken bones. Knocked-out teeth.

The last thing on any of these kids' minds was books and learning. With the exception of some of the sweeter, more serious girls, they were all too busy planning their next battle. At first he'd tried to integrate them within the classroom, a place where he thought democracy should hold sway, but that had turned into a disaster. Now the different factions each held to their own geographic location in the classroom, and the physical distance between those factions had become wider and wider as those on the outskirts imperceptibly scooted their chairs farther and farther away from those not of their own countrymen.

"The square root of —"

Something hit his neck. He smacked at it, and his hand came away with a spit wad. He whirled around to see who had thrown it.

Everyone feigned innocence, except two of the littlest girls who looked at him with sad eyes and three older girls who stared at the floor and blushed at the indignity he had just endured.

The hollowed-out tube that blew the spit wad at him was probably stuffed up someone's sleeve or pants leg right now. He'd have to inspect every last child to find out who the culprit was. How was one to teach under these circumstances?

Even though he was facing them, another spit wad hit him on the side of the face. Again, everyone on that side of the school feigned innocence, and the others snickered.

He'd thought it had been too quiet in the classroom but couldn't put his finger on what was bothering him. Evidently, he'd been sensing the fact that the children had called a temporary truce between themselves in order to get rid of the new teacher. They weren't happy about being kept in class during the month of July. Their truce gave them the energy to more fully concentrate on their objective.

He could have given any one of them a good shake or even a good smack. No one in this town would care one iota. Definitely not Mr. Turney. Such punishment was mild compared to what he saw some of the rougher parents doling out to their children on the street. But he had a feeling that if he did use his superior strength on them, things would only get worse. He would become the enemy indeed from that point, and the battle would be on.

On the other hand, he couldn't exactly call recess to get them out of his hair until he could reclaim his equilibrium. That would be rewarding bad behavior.

He glanced out the window, praying for inspiration, and saw something that gave him an idea.

"I believe we're all feeling a little restless

with summer here," he said. "Let's go for a walk."

"All of us?" the little girl on the front row said. She was still so small, her feet did not touch the ground when she sat on the school bench.

"All of us," he said. "I'm thinking about having a contest."

"What's the prize?" one of the bigger boys, an American-born boy named Rupert, asked.

Prize, indeed. He glanced around the schoolroom. Nothing much popped out at him. Then he remembered dinner last night.

"The woman who runs the boardinghouse where I live makes the best chocolate pies I've ever tasted. How about I buy a whole chocolate pie for whoever wins the contest."

There was a general affirmation at this. He had their attention. The spit wads, temporarily, ceased.

As they trooped out behind him, he hoped that he could keep this from turning into a free-for-all and prayed that he could finish out the day without anyone getting hurt — including himself.

The thing that had caught his eye outside was an enormous woodpile that needed to get chopped before next winter. Judging from the height of the pile, there was no end to the need for firewood here. He'd been whittling away at it himself at odd times, splitting the chunks of wood into smaller sections that would fit into the woodstove they kept at the back of the schoolroom/church building that the mining company had provided. There were two axes locked away in the storage shed. Both, thanks to his attention, were sharp as razors.

Most of the children, especially the boys, were used to being sent out to the woodpile to bring in kindling and firewood. They would know their way around an axe.

He divided the older boys and those girls who wanted to participate into two teams at random, after sitting the smaller children in a group off to one side far enough away to be safe once the chips started to fly.

There were complaints. He had anticipated there would be.

"I don't want to be on his team," one boy said, pointing to a redheaded Irish boy who immediately piled into him with his fists.

Skypilot pulled the two boys apart and held them by the scruff of their necks while they took ineffective swings at each other.

"Look at me. Does it look like I care if you want to be on the same team?" He gave them both a shake. "Does it?"

"No, sir," the older boy said. The Irish

boy simply put his hands in his pockets as his way of calling a truce. Skypilot let go of them.

"Whichever team wins today gets chocolate pie tomorrow!" he called out. Then he showed them what he wanted them to do.

During what was left of the school hour, the two teams tried to beat each other at who could split the biggest pile of wood. Skypilot used his watch and called "time" every five minutes, whereupon one would put down their axe, and another boy or girl would take their place. He kept the two teams far apart in case anyone's axe swing went wild.

From time to time, he would call out in a singsong voice, "Chocolate pie," and their efforts would be renewed. Some of the older children actually had some skill and did a respectable job. It pleased him when some of the children, getting into the spirit of the thing, called out encouragement to teammates even though they were from different backgrounds.

Finally he called it quits and measured the two woodpiles. The team that won happily congratulated themselves.

"I forgot to tell you." He rolled up his sleeves. "There's a third team. Those little ones over there. Since most of them can barely lift an axe, I'll be their team captain. If I win, the little kids' team wins the pie."

He handed his pocket watch to one of the smaller girls.

"Call out 'time' when fifteen minutes is up, Abbey. You" — he pointed to one of the older boys — "watch over her shoulder and make sure she gets it right."

Then he had all the children stand back. He spit on his hands and started splitting wood.

He had always had a special affinity for an axe. Like some men had a talent for playing the violin, he could practically make his axe sing as it sailed through that pile, splitting it into chunks of firewood perfectly sized for their school stove. When the little girl called out "time," his pile of wood was three times the size of either of the ones the children had cut.

"Guess my team gets the chocolate pie." He rested his axe over his shoulder. The smaller children started laughing, clapping, and hugging each other.

"That's not fair," one of the older boys said. "You're bigger and stronger than we are."

"Exactly," Skypilot said. "I'm bigger, I'm stronger, and I could break any one of you in half for the trick you pulled this morning. In fact" — he stood close to the boy and deliberately towered over him — "there's a big part of me that would love to do that. Fortunately for you, an even bigger part of me wants to march all of you in there right now and finish our arithmetic lesson for the day."

That was exactly what he did. Maybe it was the physical exertion that had calmed everyone down. Maybe it was the demonstration of his superior size and strength. Maybe it was simply the change in scenery for a few moments that helped the children concentrate. But they paid attention and did their work. He was surprised how proud he felt of this small accomplishment. Getting and keeping the attention of those ornery youngsters and beating them at their own game had given him a heady feeling that he seldom experienced. Teaching a room filled with wriggling children was one of the hardest things he had ever done, and strangely enough . . . the most satisfying.

He smiled thinking about the surprise he had planned for them tomorrow for their noon meal. It might cost him a week's wages, but he intended to have enough chocolate pie for everyone to get a nice, thick piece.

For once, they would all be on the same

team.

Fallen Arrow was still quite weak, but she was getting better. She could sit up for longer and longer periods of time. Her delight in little Standing Bear was limitless, and Moon Song felt great joy watching Grandmother play with him, as she went about organizing their small space by hanging supplies and clothing from the ceiling and walls where she could get to them quickly and not have to sort through the pile she'd brought with her.

She also religiously set and checked her snares each day, gathered the wild strawberries and anything else that was ripe and edible, and fished whenever possible. With the other women of her tribe, she had put in a large communal vegetable garden. Each woman knew that when the winter came, the strips of dried squash and the leathery beans and the dried corn and potatoes might be all that stood between them and hunger.

Moon Song had a bit of time now to do several housekeeping chores — gathering fresh rushes into mats to cover the floor, removing the old ones, sweeping out the dirt floor with a handful of twigs. She wanted to keep things fresh and clean for little Standing Bear, especially since he was toddling everywhere now and putting everything his hands could grab right into his mouth. She had to remove an earthworm only yesterday.

It was during her housekeeping, while Fallen Arrow was sitting outside in the sun keeping an eye on little Standing Bear, that she discovered a small cache buried in the ground beneath her grandmother's bed. Inside was a tin box she had never seen before among her grandmother's possessions. There were few secrets in Indian society, especially among close family members. She was surprised to discover this item. She drew it out, took it outside, and showed it to her grandmother.

"Where did this come from?" she asked.

Fallen Arrow looked embarrassed. "Oh, it is just something a white man brought."

"A white man gave you this? When?"

"One moon after you left."

"Why did you not tell me?"

"I was not sure what the box contained. There is much writing in there. I was afraid it held things we did not want to know."

"This white man, what did he look like?"

"I do not know," Fallen Arrow said. "I was checking snares, and Snowbird took it from him. She said only that he was a white man

341

and looked ill."

Moon Song fingered the box. In spite of being buried in the ground, it was still new enough to be shiny. "May I open it?"

Fallen Arrow looked frightened. "No good ever comes from white men's papers."

"What are you afraid of?" She could tell that Fallen Arrow was hiding something. "What are you not telling me?"

"Snowbird does not speak English well, but she says she thinks the man was sent by your father."

"My father?"

"If those papers are from your father, I'm afraid they will say something that will take you and Standing Bear away."

It broke Moon Song's heart to see the fear in her grandmother's eyes. Fallen Arrow had lost her daughter because of Moon Song's father, and now she was afraid even of a few papers he might have sent.

"There is nothing my father can do that will force me and my son to leave you." She laid a gentle hand upon her grandmother's arm. "Do you hear me?"

Fallen Arrow nodded, but Moon Song could tell that she was not convinced.

Most of Moon Song's cloudy memories of her father had been woven by Fallen Arrow after he brought her back following her mother's death. It was no secret to her or to the rest of the tribe that Fallen Arrow hated the man who had broken her daughter's heart. Because of that, Moon Song had no love for the man, either. The fact that he had sent papers here that had upset Fallen Arrow made Moon Song angry. He had been silent all these years, ignoring her existence. He should have continued to be silent!

"May I open it?"

Fallen Arrow took a deep breath. "Yes. Perhaps you can read it. I can make no sense of the marks."

Moon Song unloosed the latches on the shiny tin box and opened the lid. The item lying in the box appeared to be a large Bible. She sounded out the letters on the front of it. Sure enough. They said "Holy Bible."

Why in the world would her father be sending her a Bible after a silence of nearly sixteen years? And why should it give her such a stab of disappointment that this was all it was? A white man's Bible from a man who had abandoned her mother and then, upon her mother's death, had abandoned her. She shook her head and closed the box. White men could be such a mystery.

"There is something inside of that big

book," Fallen Arrow said.

"Oh?"

She opened the box and pulled the Bible out. Sure enough, there were two envelopes. She opened the larger one. It was very official looking and had handwriting that was extremely difficult to read and had a shiny seal upon it. The other one appeared to be some sort of a letter, but again, her ability to read was limited. With time she could sound out some printed letters, but it was impossible for her to read this fancy handwriting.

The envelopes and the writing looked important. She wished she had someone nearby who could read them, someone she trusted, but she didn't. Her tribesmen were even more limited in their ability to read English than she.

She wished Skypilot was here. He could read all these words, make sense of them, explain them to her, and would keep whatever was inside of them private if privacy was necessary. It was the gold seal that bothered her the most. She had a feeling those papers could be very important.

There were white men in town who could read this, of course, but she trusted none of them. Father Slovic could, but he was several days' journey away. She could not leave her grandmother alone for so long to walk so far.

"Can you tell what it is?" Fallen Arrow asked nervously.

"I think it is probably nothing," Moon Song said. "We won't worry about it for now."

She put the box back into her grandmother's hiding place and covered it with the mat. Her curiosity would have to wait until she could choose the right person to do the reading.

She did not know what she felt for the strange man who had fathered her and then walked away. She never had known what to feel or what to think about him. When she was little, she had sometimes pondered the fact that he had been so willing to leave her behind. She had wondered what was so wrong with her that he never cared enough to come back. As an adult, all she knew for sure about him was that regardless of her mixed blood, she was grateful that her heart was all Chippewa.

Skypilot was thankful when he made it to the end of July and closed the school down for a month. When he released the reluctant scholars to race into a late summer, they ran leaping out into the outdoors, practically drunk on freedom.

He didn't blame them. If he weren't the teacher, he would be leaping for joy right now himself.

Mainly, he was just grateful to have survived the past few weeks in the classroom. He would use the rest of August to prepare for the fall . . . and to find Moon Song.

Slovic said that he would send her word, and if she chose to come to him, she would. The problem was he had no way of knowing if Slovic's message had reached her or not. Right now he didn't even know if she was aware that he was back in her part of the country.

There was, however, a small tribe of Chippewa who lived not far outside of Rockland, and he intended to pay them a visit and see if he could find out anything. It might be like trying to find a needle in a haystack, but he needed to at least try to get word to her.

He felt awkward about walking into the Indian village, but he blundered in nonetheless. He did have the wisdom to carry with him a few items he thought the villagers might be interested in. A red blanket draped over his arm. A good pocketknife. A large cooking pot filled with several dozen sugar cookies he'd bought from the woman who kept his boardinghouse.

"You have whiskey?" one of the younger women asked hopefully when he walked into the middle of the small village of wigwams.

"No whiskey."

An older man, leather-faced and angry-looking, accosted him. "Why you here?"

Ah, this was more like it. A direct question. "I'm looking for information. There's a Chippewa girl and her grandmother I want to find."

"Why they hiding?"

"They're not hiding from me." At least he hoped not. "We're friends. It's just that I lost track of her. Her name is Moon Song. Her grandmother's name is Fallen Arrow. She has a small papoose she calls Ayasha."

The Indian walked away in apparent disgust. Skypilot wondered if whiskey would have sweetened his disposition.

An ancient-looking woman sidled up to him. "I know Fallen Arrow." She glanced at the pot filled with cookies. "Taste?"

He pulled one out and handed it to her, which she practically inhaled in spite of having no visible teeth. "Taste?" she asked again.

"Tell me about Fallen Arrow."

"Live near lake, that way." The old woman

347

pointed west. "On reservation."

He gave her another sugar cookie. "Can you take me to her?"

"Grandson, Little Gray Squirrel, take."

He glanced down; a small boy about ten had crept up beside his grandmother and was eyeing the pot of cookies.

"You know where Fallen Arrow and Moon Song live?" he asked.

The boy nodded eagerly, his eyes glued to the cookies.

"Will you take me there?"

The boy nodded again, holding out his hand.

"Me take pot," the grandmother said, grasping hold of the handle and the blanket, "and boy show you Fallen Arrow."

Skypilot had a strong suspicion he was being lied to, but he handed over the pot and strode off toward the west after the small boy, who appeared to know where he was going. His hope was that there would not be anyone waiting farther on to rob him or worse, but he had no other ideas about how to find Moon Song, besides going back to Marquette and wringing the information out of Slovic. He had a strong feeling that wouldn't work with the Jesuit.

To his surprise, several hours later, after following the child for many miles, he could hear the lake. They came upon a small village of cabins nestled into a grove of large hemlock trees. The boy, who had not said a word the whole time, led him straight to one cabin off to the side, and then stood back.

Skypilot stared nervously at the cabin. It was possible that Moon Song was behind that door. If she was, would she be happy to see him or angry? She had been so adamant that he not follow her here — and yet he had. He took a deep breath and knocked. "Moon Song?" Skypilot called. "Are you there?"

Moon Song was coming home with a fine brace of rabbits, the best she'd captured in a while. Even though the rabbits did not have the thickness of their winter coats yet, they would still make good eating, and she was already planning the fine small blanket she would make from the pelts. There were few things softer than a blanket made from rabbit fur, and her little son would enjoy such a blanket.

"Grandmother, I . . ." She walked into the open door to their cabin and nearly fell to her knees from surprise. There. Right there. In the middle of the cabin sat Skypilot, cross-legged on the floor with a little

Chippewa cousin who was chattering away, catching her grandmother up on all the family living over near the Minnesota Mine.

"Skypilot!" She dropped the rabbits inside the door. Her grandmother's eyes were watching her avidly and disapprovingly. "Where did you come from? I thought you were in Bay City or . . . or Virginia!"

He stood up, and he was so tall, his head was only a few inches from the low ceiling. In fact, his bulk felt like it filled up the whole cabin. But it wasn't just his physical size that filled the space — it was the enormous love for her that she saw in his face.

She had thought of him so often these past weeks and dreamed of him too. To actually have him here in front of her, the man she had never expected to see again, seemed so unreal. It was as though she was having a vision, but instead of melting away, he was there as solid and sturdy as she remembered. Everything within her wanted to fly to him, but she held her ground.

She needed to know exactly what this man wanted and why he was here.

21

The minute he saw her, he knew that no matter what Slovic might think, he had not made a mistake in coming. The priest was wise, but he could not read everything that was written within another man's heart. Or a woman's. He saw the way Moon Song's eyes lit up the moment she saw him. That told him everything he needed to know.

"How did you find me?" she asked.

"Good question." He smiled ruefully. "It wasn't easy."

He reached to touch her, but she gave a quick shake of her head, warning him that she was concerned about the fact that there were others around.

"Are you hungry?" she asked.

Now that he thought about it, he was. "Is there enough?"

"I have good hunting today. I think little cousin is hungry too, after long walk. I will get rabbit roasting and then we talk."

Little Gray Squirrel was most definitely hungry, and Moon Song quickly started a meal of the rabbits she'd just brought home, roasted over her grandmother's open fire pit.

Skypilot reacquainted himself with little Ayasha, whom Moon Song informed him was now to be referred to as Standing Bear, playing with the child by holding his hands and letting him walk toward him. Little Standing Bear chortled, delighted with all the attention. He wondered if the child's mind might hold some memories of their trek together, or even their winter together. He hoped so.

"I've been teaching school in Rockland," he told her as she worked over the food. "Father Slovic helped get me the position a couple months ago."

"You are in Rockland two moons?"

"You didn't know?"

"No."

"Slovic said he would send word."

She shook her head. "I hear nothing."

"I wonder what happened? Slovic isn't exactly a liar."

"Wait here." She disappeared into the cabin.

He heard her talking to her grandmother in a language he could not understand.

Then she returned, frowning.

"What was that all about?"

"Broken Crane tell Grandmother. Grandmother not tell me. On purpose."

"Ah. Grandmother is not happy about me being here."

Moon Song shrugged in reply.

"Slovic wasn't exactly happy about me coming back here either."

"I understand," she said. "But you are good teacher. Children are lucky you teach them."

He chuckled. "I don't know about that. But some of the children know a little more than when we started. School will start again in a month, and I plan to get better at it."

"You like to teach?"

"It is a challenge, but I like teaching. I'm making progress with the children. I plan to continue."

"You teach long time there?" Her hand was poised above the roasting rabbit, waiting for his answer. "In Rockland? You teach there forever?"

"No." Little Gray Squirrel broke into the conversation with English that Skypilot had not realized he possessed. No wonder she had warned him to be careful what he said. "The mine will close soon. There is less and

353

less copper. Many miners are moving away."

Moon Song did not seem to be surprised at Little Gray Squirrel's sudden mastery of English. "Is this true?" Actually, it was news to him. He had been so engrossed in keeping up with the lessons he had to prepare each night to stay afloat as a teacher, he'd had little time to talk with people about the mine. "If it closes, I suppose I could find another school somewhere."

The look she gave him was brimming with questions, but they were questions she obviously did not want him to answer in front of Fallen Arrow and the boy.

She knew that Fallen Arrow could not understand a word they said, but the old woman had grown morose and silent, and Moon Song knew why. She had lost her only daughter to a white man and she had no intention of losing her only granddaughter. Some Chippewa saw nothing wrong with intermarrying with whites and even encouraged it, but those Chippewa were not Fallen Arrow.

Fallen Arrow had been angry enough about Moon Song's marriage to her French-Canadian trapper husband, and he had been half Menominee. Skypilot? Grandmother was going to explode the minute he

354

left, if she even bothered to wait.

She didn't wait. "What is this big ox doing here?" Fallen Arrow asked in Chippewa.

"He's my friend, Grandmother."

"He is a white man!"

"It is his mule that brought all the good foods to you."

"Humph! White men like to give gifts . . . at first. Your father gave your mother many, many gifts in the beginning."

"I know, Grandmother. Skypilot isn't like my father. He is a good man."

Skypilot glanced up at the sound of his name. He knew they were talking about him. She would have to be careful and avoid the use of his name, even when she was speaking in Chippewa.

"All of them are like that."

"Not him, Grandmother."

"You already love him so much you would kill your own grandmother in order to have this love?"

"No one is killing anyone. I am merely roasting rabbit for a friend. You make a big story out of nothing."

"If you go with him and take Standing Bear, it will kill me."

"I will send him away with Little Gray Squirrel in the morning."

"And you will never see him again?"

"I cannot promise that."

"You will never see him again!" Grandmother pounded her frail fist against the outside of the cabin.

"I promise that I will never seek him out, but I cannot promise to run like a scared rabbit if he crosses my path."

That compromise seemed to mollify her grandmother for the time being, and the old lady accepted a crisp rabbit leg from her hand. She even smacked her lips appreciatively as she ate it, and then sucked the marrow from its fragile bones. Moon Song wished the good, fat rabbit would sweeten Fallen Arrow's attitude toward Skypilot, but she knew that was not going to happen. The wounds went too deep in the old woman.

As Moon Song looked at Fallen Arrow and then at Skypilot, she knew in her heart she would have to make a choice and that choice would have to be for the woman who had raised her and had taken care of her when no one else wanted her. Fallen Arrow had suffered too much. Moon Song would not add to her grandmother's sorrow.

Her grandmother napped often since her illness, and after the good meal, she wanted to be helped back into bed. Soon she was snoring. When Moon Song came back outside, she saw that Little Gray Squirrel had run off to play with the other children of the village. Little Standing Bear, tired out from all the attention and play, had already fallen asleep in Skypilot's arms.

It was still light outside. Light enough for Skypilot to be able to read. This was her chance, finally, to discover what her father had sent to her in the tin box. Best of all, she could find out without her grandmother's constant questions.

Quietly, she removed the tin from beneath her grandmother's sleeping bench and took it outside.

"I want you to do something for me," she said as she carried the tin outside.

"I would do anything for you." The tone of Skypilot's voice was so serious, it put a knot in her stomach. As did the image of him holding her little son so tenderly. She did not know if she would ever be able to untie that knot in her stomach. The man meant what he said. He always meant what he said. He would do anything for her, and she knew it.

She lifted Standing Bear from his arms as she handed him the tin.

"My father sent it to me. This box is here for me when I come. You read it to me, please?"

Skypilot opened the tin and pulled out the book inside.

"A Bible?" he asked. "Your father sent you a Bible? It might take me a few days to read it to you, but I'm willing."

"Two papers are inside," she said. "I cannot read the marks."

He pulled the first envelope out of the Bible and began to read.

Dear daughter,
If you are reading this, then it means that I have died and gone to my reward. What that reward might be is anyone's guess. I have not been a bad man, but I have been a weak man. I pray that my weakness did not destroy you like it did your mother.

"This says that your father is dead." Skypilot stopped and gave her a long look. "Are you all right?"

She wasn't sure. It felt strange discovering that her father was no longer on this earth, and yet it wasn't as though she had ever really known the man.

"Please read more."

Yes, I know about your mother. I have shed many bitter tears remembering my

358

love for her and how, in an ill-conceived attempt to make my own father happy, I tore you out of her arms.

I was twenty-four, the baby of my family, and a baby in more ways than I was a man, and I wanted so badly to please my father.

He had sent word that I was to bring you to him. He wanted to see his granddaughter, he said. He also sent instructions that I was to leave her mother behind.

I remember you playing with a small toy that day. It was the doll your mother had made to help keep you content on the journey. I remember holding your hand as we walked toward the ship on its way to the great city of Boston. You were such a good little girl. Your mother had spent weeks sewing beautiful little dresses for you that she thought would please my family. I remember how excited she was to get to meet my family. She had no idea that she would not be welcome.

She had no idea I had secretly made arrangements for her to be kept from following us onto the ship.

I should have turned back. When I saw the horrible grief on her face as the men

I had hired held her back from boarding the ship, I should have turned back. But I had promised my father that I would bring you, his only grandchild, to visit him — without your mother.

I had been too weak to tell her earlier, because I didn't want to deal with her hurt feelings, and because I was a coward.

She had even made a gift for my father. A beautiful beaded shirt. It took her weeks. He would not have touched it. He would have had a servant burn it had she ever gotten the chance to present it to him.

I did not realize at the time that the man was not fit to even look upon her face.

To my credit, at that very moment, as I saw her fighting to get to you, I regretted my decision and developed a plan. I would go home, confront my father, present you, in all your little girl finery, to him, and then go back to her, where I belonged.

I was proud of you. Never, ever doubt that I was proud of you. You were such a bright, happy, loving little girl. Smarter than a child your age should have been, and beautiful like your mother. You could already speak both Chippewa and English when we left for Boston.

Skypilot glanced up. "No wonder you picked up English so quickly last winter. You spoke it as a child!"

"I do not remember this." Her voice was strangled with tears. She was so grateful that her grandmother was asleep. "Please go on."

I had been sent to check on mineral deposits in the Keweenaw that my father and his business partners were interested in. I planned to give them a report, then take you and get on the next ship back to my wife and your mother. All this I was going to tell my father the minute he and I were alone.

It seemed so simple and so noble. A few days to sail to Boston, a couple days there explaining my intentions, a few days back. I envisioned apologizing to your mother, begging her forgiveness, and living happily ever after.

But I underestimated your mother's grief.

I also underestimated my father's deep understanding of my weakness.

Your grandfather was a brilliant man who made a fortune from his staggering ingenuity and his ability to read people. He listened to my pompous speech about going back to the woman I loved. He nodded and agreed and gave me no argument.

That was the most brilliant part of all — he gave me no resistance. I was ready for a fight, and when he gave me none, I did not see the danger.

Instead, he asked me to at least make a quick appearance at the parties he'd already scheduled to welcome me home. He gambled on the expectation that I would be hungry for the "civilization" I had left behind.

I enjoyed those parties and made quite a fool of myself all puffed up and telling my stories about the great frontier I had just left. Of course, this also drew many silly young females around me who made much of me. I fancied myself quite the brave fellow. You would have thought that I opened up the West single-handedly.

Also, my father was aware that one of my favorite activities had been attending theatres and plays. Those had also been arranged, along with the refreshments at various establishments afterward. Two days became a couple weeks, and I was the toast of the town with my grandiose stories and foolish posturing.

My father's parties and social engagements became like a spill of molasses in which a fly has become entrapped, struggling to lift itself from the sweetness until it no longer has the strength to try.

If I had been allowed free access to you during that time, perhaps your cries for your mother would have shaken me out of my own little self-centered world, but my father (and remember that he was the shrewd mastermind of a far-reaching financial empire) hired a virtual battalion of competent nursemaids who kept you nearly as entertained and occupied as myself. I convinced myself that you were having the time of your life and that you were too young to care about the short separation from your mother.

It was only later — much later — that one of the nursemaids confessed that they made certain to take you far away from my hearing so that I could not hear your cries each time you called for your mother.

One week passed, and then another. Nearly a month had gone by, and the parties and social engagements were finally beginning to pall. I grew tired of the conversations. I began to see myself as I truly was — a colossal bag of empty wind. I began to long for the clean winds of the North country, the rough-and-tumble inhabitants of the Lake Superior region, and most of all for your mother. I was packing to go back to her, and our tickets had already been purchased, when word of her death reached me.

It came through such convoluted channels that much of what had happened was garbled. My father broke the news to me. With such tenderness, he made it sound like it had been a tragic accident — the kind to be expected in such a primitive and dangerous place. I cried on his shoulder. He patted me on the back and soothed me, and I loved him for it.

I was so young. He was so shrewd. Neither I nor your mother were a match for him.

There was enough man in me that I did do one thing that he did not expect. I insisted on taking that trip back to Michigan. I wanted to see my wife's family. I wanted to apologize for that cruel trick I had played on her before we sailed away. I thought it would make me feel better.

I groan aloud at the thought now. I was still young enough to think that I could actually feel better.

What I discovered changed the direction of my life.

You have probably been told that your mother committed suicide because of her heartbreak over my abandonment. That is a lie. She was not that weak.

Your grandfather was an evil and selfish man. He had her murdered once he realized that I still intended to return to her. Your mother did not commit suicide. She was killed by a man my father hired. They poisoned her and made it look like it was at her own hand. My older brother told me in a moment of weakness. He had overheard a conversation between my father and the man he hired. My brother was too afraid of my father to stop it. By the time he told me, it was too late.

Neither my brother nor I said a word to my father about what we knew. My brother, because he was afraid. Me, because I wanted revenge.

If Skypilot could have absorbed the shock of those words into his own body and never let her know, he would have. As it was, he

365

had to sit and watch Moon Song stare into space. She sat on a log near the outdoor fire, her knees tucked up beneath her chin, rocking back and forth, back and forth.

"Moon Song," he said softly. "Are you all right?"

She gave a mirthless laugh, then held out her arm and pushed up the sleeve. "Why does color of my skin make me less than others?"

His heart broke for her. "Moon Song, my love, the color of your skin is perfect."

She ignored him. "My mother was not allowed in my father's home because she was Chippewa. She was murdered because she was Chippewa."

"I'm so sorry. You don't deserve such things to happen to you, Moon Song. None of your people do."

"Read."

"Moon Song, I —"

"No more talk." Her face was set and stony. "Read!"

My greatest concern became you. As small and innocent as you were, I knew that if my father perceived you as important enough to pull me back to my beloved Lake Superior region again, you would not be safe, either. I also knew, by then, that he hated you for no other reason than the fact that you were Chippewa. I did not want you to live in a home where you were barely tolerated.

I was terrified for you, because I now realized that I was no match for him. He was smarter and stronger and more ruthless than me. I could not fight him. There was only one nick in his armor that I could discover, and that was his own arrogance. He assumed that because he despised you, it would be easy for me to do so as well.

And so, as a shield to protect you, I feigned nonchalance toward your existence. I pretended that the only reason I went back was to leave you with your grandmother because I no longer wanted you.

Privately, I left you in the one place I knew you would be loved and cherished and taught the old ways. I never contacted you again because I knew my father had eyes and ears everywhere. My only contact with you these past sixteen years has been the daily prayers I send up for you. There has not been one day that I have not prayed for you.

It is because of you that I became my father's son. He chose not to pursue the copper mining he sent me to Michigan to be in charge of. I shrugged and said that we were well rid of that mosquito-infested wilderness. My two older brothers along with my father and I made mountains of money together, just as my father had always wished. I worked beside him every day, aware of what he had done to your mother, and I smiled every day because I knew a secret. My secret was that I was living my life for you.

The past sixteen years of my life since I left the land of your mother's ancestors have been a strange, emotionless dance that I have lived. Every morning I have put on a gray business suit, lived within the gray walls of my father's many lucrative businesses, and lived a gray life. I have not remarried because I could not see why I should have a life when your mother's had been extinguished because of mine.

One word sent to you or one word of news about you to me would have sent him sniffing after you. He would have found and devoured you had he any inkling I was trying to protect you by my apparent lack of interest. He had a vision of building an empire with his three sons, and he built it. He had no idea that the only color in my life was the vision of you living wild and free while I kept your grandfather satiated and at bay by my constant presence.

I waited a long time for his death. It came exactly one month ago. It was brought on by an overindulgence of all the good things that he loved to eat. He weighed so much at the time of his death that it took ten strong men to carry him to his final resting place, and even then, one staggered and nearly fell.

On the other hand, I deliberately ate sparingly. I had read the articles of Dr. Graham and about his institute. I lived on mixtures of whole grains, lemon water, fresh fruits and vegetables. I had one goal, to outlive my father and have the opportunity to safely see you again and tell you the truth.

There is irony in my attempt to stay healthy and well. I neglected one small thing. This week, my father got his own revenge. It appears that one cannot hate as intensely and as long as I have without one's body turning upon itself. The doctors say that I have a tumor growing and pressing upon my brain. They do not have the skill to operate. They say I have only a few days to live. Maybe weeks at most. I hate to tell them that my tumor bears my father's name. I am certain that my simmering hatred created it and put it there.

I had planned to come to you and see your face again now that the danger is over, but that will never be. I had long envisioned being present when you opened the gift I have spent sixteen years preparing for you. That won't happen, either. But the gift will remain. I hope it can remain for many generations.

I told you that I had lived a gray, nearly monastic existence. My brothers sometimes teased me about my less than lavish lifestyle. I, who could have afforded to live in a mansion, chose to live quite modestly.

My one luxury was putting every extra dime I could wrest from my father's business into purchasing as much as I possibly could of the most beautiful place on earth.

I am aware, however, of what has been happening on the Keewenaw. I know all about the mining that is going on there, not to mention the timber that is being removed for bracing up the mines.

Instead, there is a home waiting for

you in the Huron Mountains, my sweet girl, if you want it. The land is free and clear. The boundaries have been surveyed and well set. The timber is untouched.

I also made certain to purchase land that had no mineral value whatsoever, a tract of land that was far away from the ranges of iron and copper mines, so that you would never have to deal with the legalities of mineral rights or the problems that living next to the brawling mining towns can bring.

You will never have to live on a government-created Indian reservation. I have paid the taxes through your lifetime. You can live where you can breathe and where your children can run free. No one can ever take it away from you.

It seemed the least I could do.

Now, as I sit here dying, I keep remembering the call of loons at dawn on the lake, and I remember the smell of campfires, and the excited laughter and exaggerated boasting of your mother's people after a successful hunt. The happiest years of my life were spent with you and my beloved wife. As brief as they were.

These blessings I try to give to you

now, to enjoy forever, where no one can take them away.

Your loving father,
Benjamin Webster

22

How many acres had Webster been able to purchase for his daughter? A hundred? Several hundred? Maybe a large farm or tract of timber? Skypilot wondered if there was a house connected to it.

It would have been rude to pull the envelope with the deed out of the Bible without asking, but he had gotten so caught up in the story, he couldn't help but wonder.

He waited for Moon Song to absorb this earthshaking information and hoped that she could feel some gladness in her heart over a father who would sacrifice so much for her.

She was quiet, staring off into space, her hand automatically patting little Standing Bear's back.

Her father's Bible was old and well worn. He lifted the cover. Inside, on the flyleaf, the same hand that had penned a note, which he read aloud.

Dear Moon Song,

There are those among your mother's people who say that Christianity is a white man's religion. That is not true. Christ was not white. Jesus's skin would have been closer to the rich color of your mother's. Even though I am not of his race, I have drawn strength from his words. Perhaps someday you will find strength there too.

Your loving father,
Benjamin Webster

Skypilot decided he would have liked this man, and felt a sting of grief that he had never known him.

Moon Song reached out for her father's Bible, and he handed it to her. She hugged it to her heart for a long time, as though wishing she could somehow absorb her father's spirit. Finally, she stirred on her log as though coming out of a trance. "Read the other letter."

He fumbled the sheet out of the thick envelope he was holding, glanced at it, and then nearly dropped it.

"What does it say?"

"It is the deed."

"What does it say?"

He could hear the impatience in her voice,

but as he scanned the sheet of paper, he was suddenly having trouble getting his breath.

"It says that Victoria Moon Song Webster owns approximately sixteen thousand acres of land in the Huron Mountains."

She seemed unimpressed. "How much is that?"

He did some quick calculations in his head, grateful that his arithmetic knowledge had been well polished these past few months in the schoolroom.

"Twenty-five square miles."

"Oh."

Her tone of voice puzzled him. "You aren't impressed with that?"

"You do not understand. That is great wealth to a white man."

"Well, yes. It is."

"To Chippewa, it like saying that I own twenty-five square miles of the lake. I can fish in it. I can paddle in it. I can drink it and swim in it, but own it? How can one person 'own' sixteen thousand acres of land?"

"I don't know, Moon Song, but the reality is that your father took good care of you before he died."

"My father?" she said. "I do not know this father. He was not here when I fell from a tree or cried with a bellyache."

"No. He was trying to protect you from a vicious man the only way he knew how."

"I wish I could know that father whose voice you read." She gave a great sigh.

"Will you be going to see the land he bought you?"

"I must think what to do. Grandmother is still not strong, and it is a long walk to Huron Mountains for an old woman."

"You have the mule."

"I think Grandmother would not like to leave her people. It would be too lonely and dangerous to live there alone. I do not think the village would come with us."

At that moment, Grandmother called out for Moon Song. The old woman sounded irritated and querulous.

"Grandmother is not happy," Moon Song said. "She wants to know the meaning of our many words."

"Will you explain all this to her?"

"Yes. Someday soon. Not now."

For the life of him, he could not figure out why she seemed so emotionless and detached from that impassioned letter from her father. Most women would be sobbing by now, but Moon Song never seemed to react to anything the way he expected.

"What are you thinking, Moon Song?"

"There is only room for one thing in Moon Song's head right now," she said.

"What's that?"

"The name of the man who killed my mother."

Skypilot went to find Little Gray Squirrel while Moon Song tended to her grandmother and then fed Standing Bear, readying him for the night. Her child was able to eat wild rice porridge these days, which she seasoned with maple sugar. It kept his belly full longer than her milk alone had done, and he had begun sleeping through the night.

It was a warm night, which eased the awkwardness of what to do with Skypilot. There was no reason he could not sleep outside their cabin. She would gather balsam tips to make his sleep more comfortable. Little Gray Squirrel could stay inside with her and Grandmother. Fallen Arrow had once been a chief's wife, so she possessed several well-woven, good-quality Hudson Bay blankets that had been given to her husband in trade. These were highly prized items in her cabin. Skypilot would not grow cold.

Even though she knew Fallen Arrow was not happy with Skypilot being here, the

Chippewa were a hospitable people and her grandmother would not fuss at her if she took the time to make a comfortable bed for a guest. While the boy cousin once again played with little Standing Bear under the watchful eye of Fallen Arrow, Moon Song and Skypilot left to gather the balsam branches. Moon Song saw her grandmother look up and scowl as they walked away and knew that she would be soundly scolded when she returned.

She had things she needed to say to this man, and she did not want her grandmother listening. Fallen Arrow's knowledge of English was limited, but she knew enough to misconstrue the words she would hear.

It was one thing to sit at the campfire with her grandmother and cousin close enough to hear every word, and another to be completely alone with Skypilot. As they walked into the forest near twilight, neither of them seemed to know what to say. They, who had spent so many companionable hours together, were suddenly tongue-tied and awkward with one another.

It was foolish of her, and she knew it, but she did not stop walking until they had gone much deeper into the forest than necessary to simply gather a few balsam pine tips. Then she stopped and looked at this man who had haunted her dreams since they had parted at Fort Wilkins.

"The moon is so full," he said when she stopped. "It is a beautiful night."

"We have many names for the different moons."

"What is the name for this one?"

"Some call it Blackberry Moon," she said, "because it is the month when the blackberries grow ripe."

"That's a lovely name. What are some other names of your months?"

"There is Rice Moon when we gather wild rice for the winter. Falling Leaves Moon, when all the leaves fall to ground. Freezing Moon, when the snows come."

"That certainly makes more sense to me than the names of months we have," Skypilot said. "I'm glad I came to see you. I've missed you terribly."

"Why did you come here?" She held her breath, waiting. "I asked you not to."

His answer was as forthcoming and honest as any woman could want.

"Because I love you." His voice was matter-of-fact, as though he was saying that the lake was wet or pine boughs were green. He spoke as though she should already know this thing.

"You should go back to Bay City."

"I already did that. I was miserable. I couldn't stop thinking about you."

"You cannot stay here."

"Of course I can, and I'm going to. Maybe not here in this village right now, but close enough to see you."

"For how long?"

"Forever."

His answer took her breath away, but she couldn't trust it. Not even coming from Skypilot's truthful lips. He had not experienced what her people had. White people came to this land of *Kitchigami* to wrest minerals out of the soil, or to hunt for sport, or to cut down the timber, or to populate Fort Wilkins. Mining towns came and hundreds of people surrounded them. Then the copper gave out and the people left and the town died. No white person stayed forever in this demanding country except the Black Robes like Slovic, and even some of them left.

She turned away from him and began slicing balsam bough tips off the low-hanging branches.

He grabbed her shoulders and turned her around to face him.

"I mean it, Moon Song. I'm not leaving. I know we have a lot to overcome, but my hope is to someday be able to marry you and live with you, but even if you won't have me as a husband, I'm staying here anyway because this is where *you* are. I find it hard to breathe when I am away from you."

This was a hard speech to ignore. Then she remembered Fallen Arrow telling her that her father had said similar things to her mother before they married.

The vision of her mother trying to get on the ship and being held back by her father's men arose before her. What if Moon Song gave in? What if she married Skypilot and they had a child together? He would have the legal ability to take that child away from her forever if he so chose. She could not bear the thought of having to go through the nightmare her mother must have gone through after her father took her away.

"I'm not like your father, Moon Song," Skypilot said, as if reading her thoughts. "I am not a weak man. You know that. I'm not some young kid trying to please his rich father. I am my own man, and I make my own way. If you will have me, I will never desert you or forsake you. On this, I give you my most solemn promise."

Oh, this man had such good words. Her heart trusted him. She knew his goodness, his decency, his compassion, his loyalty, his courage. But her head kept telling her to be wise. To be cautious. To not trust.

Just like her grandmother had taught her over and over.

"No," she said.

"Do you love me?"

"Who could not love you?" She smiled sadly and shook her head. "You do not understand what you are saying. You do not understand how different our worlds are."

He glanced around and spied a long stick lying on the ground. He picked it up and drew a circle in the dirt as big around as the trunk of a large tree. "That is your world, Moon Song. Stand inside of it."

She wondered what he was doing, but she obeyed.

He drew another circle, this one intersecting with the first. "This is my world." He threw the stick away and then stepped into the space that had been made by intersecting the two circles and pulled her into it with him.

He grabbed her hands and held them to his chest. "Somehow, we will create our own world, here, together, where our worlds intersect. We will live in that world with little Standing Bear and Fallen Arrow growing stronger inside this circle with us. I will not leave you, Moon Song, ever."

"But all white men —"

"You have seen my Holy Scriptures, have you not?"

"Yes."

"The words in that book are sacred to me. When I say that I will never leave you nor forsake you, I'm not making up some white man's words that mean nothing, I am repeating sacred, holy words that are in that book. Those words have power. I want to teach you the power of those words. For me to ignore my Holy Scriptures and walk away from you, or to take a child from you as your father did your mother, would mean to me that I had lied to my God. I would accept death before I would leave you after making such a holy promise."

"But . . ."

With one strong arm, he drew her tight against him and stopped her protest with his lips. This was not their first kiss, but those two others were nothing compared to the passion that was within this. The man loved her. He had shown that love over and over. He had moved to this place and found work here even before he searched for her. He meant it when he said he was staying.

When they finally broke the kiss, she said, "The snow in winter is taller than four men standing on each other's shoulders."

"Then you'll have to make me snowshoes," he said, and kissed her again.

"Grandmother can be very demanding."

"Then we shall give her whatever she wants." He kissed her again. "She raised you. She deserves honor."

"You will be made fun of by some white people if you marry a Chippewa. They will call you insulting names."

"Names like what?" He laughed. "Names like 'squaw man'?" He took one step back. "Look at me. I can fell an ox with one fist. How many men do you really think are going to want to try and insult me?"

She knew that he did not realize what he had just said, but still, it cut her deeply. "You think being called a 'squaw man' is insult? Then maybe it is best not to marry a squaw." She put one hand on her chest. "I *am* a squaw! You *will* be squaw man."

"I didn't mean it like that, Moon Song." He was heartsick over the realization of how his words had sounded to her. Even to his own ears it sounded like he was ashamed of her. "You know I'm not . . . I would never . . . I was just saying . . ."

She stepped out of the circle and started picking up the boughs she had dropped on the ground. "Time to go back now. Grandmother will be worried."

■ ■ ■ ■

That night, she lay awake, her mind turning over this thought and that, like a child turning stones over, looking beneath, wondering which ones had worms beneath them or which ones might hide a small treasure.

Her father's letter had stirred up deeper emotions than she had allowed Skypilot to see. Her father was gone. Truly and irrevocably gone. She had always wondered if he might come back. As a little girl, she had longed for her loving father to come back. She had envisioned herself leaping into his arms and him telling her that trickster spirits had made him forget that he had a little girl, but that he had finally remembered and had come back for her, and that nothing would separate them now.

As she'd gotten older and more resentful of his long absence and silence, she envisioned a different scenario, one in which he came for her but she turned her back on him and refused to have anything to do with him, teaching him a lesson for having abandoned her for so long.

Neither scenario had come true. Instead, she was now left with a phantom father who had loved her desperately but whom she would not have the chance to love back. Time, illness, and an evil grandfather had taken that chance away.

It was strange how memories, long suppressed, came flooding back into her mind now as if they were breaking through a rotten dam.

Even though she had only been four years old when her father left her forever with Fallen Arrow, there were flashes of short, vivid memories. She remembered the nursery in the big house in Boston and how sometimes during the social whirl her grandfather had created, her father would remember that he had a little girl and would come to the nursery to visit with her. He would always have sweets with him. Sometimes he would sit on the floor and play with her. He would admire her dolls and her toys, and she remembered how they had played with teacups and pretend biscuits once.

He had been a handsome man, with kind eyes, and she felt safe whenever he was near her. It wasn't as though she felt unsafe with the nursemaids whom her grandfather provided, but she felt calm in his presence because she knew he loved her, and there was nothing better than to be held in his arms and to be told that she was precious to him.

Then he had taken her to Fallen Arrow and left her forever. When she finally realized he was never coming back, she had simply gone deeper and deeper into the culture that *had* accepted her until she had nearly forgotten who she was, even going so far as to suppress her little girl command of English. Her father's language was not something Fallen Arrow had encouraged or used.

A greater mastery of English surfaced naturally as the floodgates of her memory opened. She could hear now, with her child's memories and ears, the cadences and tenses of what had once been her native language, and she understood it all. Knowledge of her father's love for her had broken something loose inside of her, something that had been frozen in time for sixteen years.

A few memories now came, unbidden, to the surface of her mind. The feel of silk upon her skin. Velvet skirts brushing against her legs. Cool linen sheets and soft feather-tick mattresses. Thick damask tablecloths and heavy silverware and delicious foods that appeared magically out of nowhere. She remembered riding in a beautiful carriage with her father, her small gloved hand rest-ing in his as he pointed out the sights of Boston. Much of the time he smelled of cloves.

Now this father whose love had brought her into existence and whose weakness had destroyed her mother and nearly destroyed her, had given her this great gift. It felt very strange. Something that Skypilot said came back to her as she lay there, turning over the stones in her mind. He had said that she was now a very wealthy woman, and he was right. Sixteen thousand untouched acres was worth a terrible amount of money. More money than she could imagine. She had no idea what to do about it.

The ground was hard. He and Moon Song had brought just about enough boughs in from the forest to be annoying. His sleeping arrangements hadn't exactly been their focus. Not that he was going to be able to sleep anyway.

One slip of the tongue, and she had turned away from him.

Was this what being married to Moon Song would be like? Constantly being on his guard not to step his foot in something he did not see?

It felt as though he had been having a

lovely stroll down a shady path and accidentally stepped into a bear trap.

He had meant what he said. He was not going to leave. And he would never leave her if she would have him, but talk about getting the wind knocked out of your sails! Things had been going so well until that slip of the tongue.

A few minutes later, he saw her coming back outside. He was lying so close to the opening, she practically had to step over him. He felt immediate concern.

"Moon Song? Is everything all right?"

"I forgot to make water."

"Oh." He waited for her to come back from her little jaunt behind a tree on the outskirts of the village. When she came back, he was sitting up.

"Do you want me to leave in the morning?"

She didn't hesitate. "Yes."

"I don't understand what happened out there. I didn't mean anything by what I said."

She quietly thought this over. "You say you will not leave me. Did you mean that?"

"I don't say things I don't mean."

"Then you teach in that school awhile longer. See the big snow. If you are still in Rockland in spring? Then we talk."

"Can I come visit you?"

"If you are still here in the spring? You come visit."

"I'm staying at the boardinghouse. If you need me, you know where I am. I won't be leaving, Moon Song."

"Good." She patted his leg. "Maybe you will be smarter in spring."

23

Living in a fading mining town, knowing she was within a day's walk, was incredibly hard.

She had said for him to come see her in the spring, when she hoped he would be smarter. What had she meant by that? After a great deal of thought, he decided that he knew.

He had seen a beautiful, brilliant, compassionate, and competent woman and had fallen in love with her. It was as simple as that. The fact that she was Indian had little to do with his desire to spend the rest of his life with her.

However, in Moon Song's eyes, evidently being Chippewa defined her. He knew little about her people and he realized that unless he knew *and* loved the Chippewas, she would never trust his love for her.

He had hoped to convert her from whatever it was she believed in to Christianity —

without having any real idea about what those beliefs might be. He realized that until he learned more about her people's religion and beliefs, it would be unfair for him to expect her to show any interest in learning about his.

He prayed for guidance, and the answer he got was that if he intended to love Moon Song, he had to learn to love her people because, truth be told, he did not.

And so he decided that he would go to the small, depleted tribe of Chippewa who lived on the outskirts of the town, and out of love for Moon Song, humble himself and begin to learn from her people.

Moon Song had once again become part of a community of women who shared one thought and one purpose: surviving the winter with the tribe intact. Last winter had been a hard one. They had lost three of their elders and two new infants. The freezing moons were not a good time to give birth.

Fallen Arrow, however, had recouped her strength and was now, as one of the revered older women, busy teaching the younger ones in the proper ways of harvesting crops and preparing the gifts of their forest and waters as each food ripened.

Containers had to be created in order to

store food, and the best containers of all came from the bark of the birch, which kept food from spoiling for long periods of time.

"Waa!" Fallen Arrow pretended exaggerated upset with one of the younger girls who recently had her head in the clouds over a handsome brave. "Watch how you sew that food bag!"

Fallen Arrow jerked it out of the girl's hand, unthreaded the longish stitches the girl had been making, and sewed up one side with the tighter, smaller stitches.

"It would take a tree full of spruce sap to make those long stitches you make hold rice!"

The girl ducked her head and applied herself more diligently. Moon Song smiled because she knew that her grandmother was showing off a little now that she was feeling well enough to be outside working alongside the other women. Moon Song promised herself that whatever it took, whatever she had to do, her grandmother would not go hungry this winter, nor would any of the other elders. They were too precious. Without them there to entertain the children with the old stories, teaching the old ways of living, keeping their language alive, she feared they would lose their identity and turn into nothing more than second-class whites.

Early one morning after school ended, Sky-pilot packed his few possessions and walked to the nearby Chippewa village. Moon Song's boy cousin, Little Gray Squirrel, was the first to welcome him to the village. Sky-pilot and the boy had walked many miles together, and Skypilot had purchased him some treats at the store after they returned. The sack of candy he had given the boy had been large enough to make the child's eyes grow wide, and he had enjoyed seeing Little Gray Squirrel's happiness.

Now, that sack of candy was paying off in another way. The child was ecstatic to see him, and yes, Skypilot had brought sweets with him. Soon the old grandmother came to speak to him, and then others who were curious.

"You come trade?" an elderly and digni-fied Chippewa man asked.

Skypilot thought about his answer. He decided to be utterly honest. The only thing he had to lose was his dignity — which he wasn't terribly interested in hanging on to anymore.

"I am in love with Moon Song, grand-daughter of Fallen Arrow. She lives with her grandmother on the reservation. She will not have me until I have spent many moons living in the Rockland area. While I wait, I want to learn how to be Chippewa."

His statement was met with grunts of derision and disbelief.

"I am willing to pay. The first thing I want to learn is how to build a wigwam." Then he produced a small bag of coins, nearly the last money he possessed.

The older man, whom he assumed was a chief, took the bag from him, spilled it out into his hand, said a few words in Chippewa to those standing around, and then he disappeared into his own abode.

The money must have done the trick. Two women and Little Gray Squirrel worked with him all day, cutting saplings, embedding them into the earth, bending them over, and creating a skeleton that they then showed him how to cover with mats, skins, and the ever-present birch bark.

As they worked, they chattered in their language. He asked them to slow down and teach him a word here and there of Chippewa. Little Gray Squirrel became his translator.

That night, instead of the familiar sounds and surroundings of his boardinghouse, he had a self-made shelter large enough for him to stretch out in, that might, if he were lucky, keep most of the rain out. Tomorrow he would work to make it more rain tight. He went to sleep practicing over and over the four Chippewa words he had learned that day.

wild rice — *manoomin*
meat — *wiiyaas*
eat — *wiisini*
hungry — *nimbakade*

Four words closer to Moon Song. She had learned his language. Now, he would learn hers.

Although he did not know it, reports of Sky-pilot's attempts filtered back to Moon Song, brought by her distant cousins who came to visit and tell her of his efforts.

Skypilot's "summer school" was one of the most entertaining things to happen for quite a while, and her cousins were convinced that the big white man was a little mad in the head for doing such a thing.

From what Moon Song could tell, in addition to being taught true woodcraft, he was being made fun of quite a lot, and they sometimes played sly tricks on him.

"We showed him how to steep aspen and balsam poplar root," Fish Who Leaps told her. "He was very careful to follow our instructions. He drank it every hour just like we told him."

"And what did he hope to accomplish by this?"

"He had an upset stomach last week, and we told him it would stop if he drank it."

"And how did it affect him?"

"Oh, it worked very well." Peals of laughter. "The white man who lives among us has not had a monthly flow since."

Moon Song could not help but laugh. The idea of the masculine Skypilot sitting at a campfire, sipping a brew meant solely for slowing down women's menses, really was quite funny. She just hoped that was the worst joke they played on him.

Eventually, as the days passed, the stories brought to her village became a little more respectful.

"He now knows one hundred Chippewa words," Hopping Cricket informed her a few weeks later. "And he is chopping wood with his sharp axe. He brings the firewood to the wigwams of two grandmothers who are no longer strong enough to gather wood for their fires."

This was a huge thing to do, and probably troubling to the tribe. Wood gathering was women's work, no matter how ancient the woman.

"What does he ask for in return?" Moon Song asked.

"He asks for nothing in return."

She kept wondering when he would grow tired of this. She kept expecting to be told that he had given up and gone back into town, into his comfortable boardinghouse. Instead, she saw the laughter slowly growing to respect, and eventually some envy began to creep into her girl relatives' voices.

He had mastered three hundred words. Now, four hundred.

The big white man had killed a fat deer and shared it with the tribe.

The big white man who was as strong as a bear had talked the town doctor into treating a little Chippewa girl's sore eyes after their own medicine failed.

Big White Bear, the name the elders had given Skypilot, had shot six pheasants and given two each to the old grandmothers.

Big White Bear had asked Frog Who Laughs how to make snowshoes for the winter, but Dancing Fawn had made him a pair as a gift. The gossip in the tribe was that Dancing Fawn, who had lost her husband twelve moons ago, was trying to show him what a good wife she would make.

This was not gossip Moon Song wanted to hear. In fact, it displeased her greatly. Dancing Fawn was young and attractive. Most men's heads would be turned by her. The fact that a full year had passed meant that she had grieved well and was ready to look for a new husband.

"Did he keep the snowshoe gift from Dancing Fawn?" she asked.

"No. He said he needed to learn how to do this. Dancing Fawn was disappointed and gave them to Loon Swimming instead."

His dedication to learning the culture of the woman he loved did not escape the notice of the braves of the village. Many began to pay more careful attention to her. She knew it was because they thought there must be something special about her to elicit such dedication from this former timberman.

Gifts began to appear for Fallen Arrow, who tried to talk her into becoming interested in one of the braves instead of Sky-pilot.

"No, Grandmother," Moon Song said.

Small toys were offered to little Standing Bear. Dolls made out of birch bark, or pine boughs to make dance in the water. One Chippewa brave carved a series of five ducks and made Standing Bear laugh by placing them into a small stream where they floated until he caught them again.

Moon Song thanked him on behalf of her son, but she was careful to show no interest in the brave himself, and he went away disappointed.

Even had she not cared so much for Sky-pilot, she would have been afraid to give her heart to one of the Chippewa men who were showing interest in her. She was, as Sky-pilot pointed out, a wealthy woman. No one knew about this inheritance yet — she had not even told her grandmother what the tin box truly contained — but her people were notorious for undervaluing land and selling it. How could she have any assurance that some Chippewa brave she might marry would not do the same with property that belonged to her?

Right or wrong, her father had sacrificed his life to build this inheritance for her, and she would not dishonor that sacrifice by selling it.

In her heart, she was cheering Skypilot on, hoping he would not give up. She hoped that he would continue to love her enough to learn to cherish her people.

Five hundred words, a cousin reported.

Six hundred.

He had put away his white man's clothes.

He now wore the buckskin of the braves. His hair had grown longer and had to be held back with strips of leather. He had asked permission to put off going back to the white man's school for another moon. He said he had not yet learned enough.

He had mastered the bow and arrow and had brought down a large buck with one he had made with his own hands.

The Chippewa children were starting to gather around him as he drew the words into his word-catching notebook. Even some of the older people were starting to sit around, and he was beginning to teach them how to read.

His amazing ability with his axe had helped provide nearly enough firewood to get the village through a hard winter. With that chore lightened, the women were able to spend more time gathering the hickory, walnuts, beechnuts, and rich butternuts that were falling now.

Seven hundred words. All of them written on a stack of paper that he pored over every afternoon. He had to rely on English less and less. The tribe was beginning to take him seriously. None of the women giggled anymore about the crazy white man who loved Moon Song. Instead, all were beginning to look at her with envious eyes.

24

Skypilot could no longer put off starting the school back up again. The beginning of October would be a late start back East, but this was the frontier.

He was in the church building, preparing a few lessons for the next day, when Harvey Turney walked in. Skypilot was glad to see the man. He had several things he wanted to talk to him about. Newer textbooks, for one thing. The possibility of filling some of the desks with a few of his little friends from the Chippewa village for another. Those children were learning so quickly, and they were teaching him quite a lot besides.

Harvey didn't beat around the bush. "I hear you've been spending part of the summer living with the Chippewa tribe outside of town."

"That's true."

"In a wigwam?"

"Yes. Why?"

"A lot of people in town aren't real happy about the idea of our schoolteacher choosing to live among a bunch of savages."

Was this the same man who had stood there spitting tobacco juice at a cat the first time he'd met him?

"I can't imagine why."

Harvey fidgeted with his pocket watch. "Because, well . . . you know."

Skypilot kept his face impassive. "No. I do not know."

"We do not think this is a proper activity for a man who will be guiding the minds of our children. If you are going to be our teacher, we insist that you start living like a proper white man."

"And who is this 'we'?" Skypilot asked.

Harvey Turney drew himself up to his full height. "Those of us who pay your salary."

Skypilot closed the notebook in which he had been making out lesson plans. "Good luck finding another teacher."

Harvey got flustered. "Now, look here, you know we'll have a hard time finding a teacher willing to come all the way up here, let alone one who can deal with these students."

Skypilot had learned a thing or two from the Chippewa. He stood impassively, watching this man bluster.

"I suppose you could stay with them awhile longer, but you'll need to be moving back into the boardinghouse before it gets cold. You can't possibly survive out there over the winter."

"They do," Skypilot said. "They survive."

"They live like dogs!" Harvey's voice rose.

Skypilot did not trust himself to speak. Instead, he picked up his notebook of Chippewa words and walked toward the door. He knew he had to leave before he knocked Turney senseless.

"Who's going to teach our children?" Harvey yelled after him.

"Don't worry," Skypilot said. "I'm not going to abandon the children. I'll be back on the job tomorrow."

Turney's eyes were angry, narrow slits — a man unused to being thwarted. "Not unless you start living like a civilized human being, you won't. We don't want Indian lovers teaching our kids."

"Why don't *you* try it yourself if you're so concerned," Skypilot said.

"I just might!" Harvey said. "In fact . . ." A calculating look came into his eyes. "I think I will."

"It's true then? The copper giving out, is it?" It was the only reason Skypilot could think of that would tempt Turney into step-

404

ping into the role of a teacher instead of a mine foreman.

"You're fired." Turney turned his back on him. "I'll be taking over starting today."

"Fired?" Skypilot could hardly believe his ears. He wondered if this had been in the back of Turney's mind when the man had come in here. He gave Harvey a long, hard look before he left. "You won't last a week."

As satisfactory as that parting shot was, Skypilot now had a problem. He had no job in a town where jobs were getting scarce. The only thing he could think of was the possibility of getting a job in the copper mine, which was still working, in spite of less and less copper being brought out.

He didn't want to go down into the mines, but on the other hand, he was broke. Choosing to live in a wigwam was one thing. Having to live there because he couldn't afford to live anywhere else was another.

He headed over to the copper mine to check into applying for work. As he approached the place, he saw what looked like a body wrapped in sheeting being carried out. Several weary-looking miners were walking beside it.

"What happened?" he asked.

"Poor man was coming up from the 120th fathom in a shaft he was helping to sink," one of the miners explained as both of them watched the others carrying the body up the hill. "When he got to the 110th fathom, his hand missed the top rung, and he fell backward to the bottom. Seventy-five feet he dropped. He hit his head something terrible. We had an awful time getting him out of there. He's still alive, but I don't think he'll make it the night. Got a wife and four children."

Skypilot noticed that the man had blood all over the front of his shirt. "You were one of the ones who got him out?"

"I was." The miner swiped a sleeve over his eyes. "They ask too much of a man, making him climb so far, hand over hand when he's already dead-dog tired. And those rungs slick as grease most days from the damp. One slip. Just one. It's all it takes. And him a miner since he was only a boy."

Before Skypilot could say another word, the miner walked on toward the sad procession.

Skypilot looked at the mining office and then back at the group of men toting their broken friend back to his home.

If he had a wife and children to feed, he would go into the mines if it was the only way to take care of them. But with only himself to take care of, he would find something else, or do without. After watching that procession, living on venison in a wigwam all winter didn't seem like a bad option.

Moon Song and Standing Bear were deep in the woods, competing with squirrels to see who could gather the most acorns for the winter. Standing Bear at twelve months was able to walk quite well for his age. He was bright enough to be a lot of help at this task. Together they were making a game of gathering acorns and heaping them into a basket.

When they finished, she would cut the nut meat out of the acorn and then he would enjoy playing in the stream, helping her rinse the poison bitterness out of the acorns. Once all that was left was the sweet goodness of the seed from which the great oaks grew, she would dry it and pound it into flour to thicken stews or mix with corn cakes.

Suddenly, she saw one of the older boys race past. His eyes were wide with pure terror.

"Hanging Leaf!" she shouted in Chippewa. "Why do you run?"

He halted and looked back at her, panting.

"They have come."

"Who has come?" They had no sworn enemies anymore, and they and the neighboring whites got along well enough as long as they stayed on their reservation and didn't try to encroach on land the whites now considered theirs.

"Government people."

This was puzzling. They waited sometimes too long for the government workers to show up with the annuities that they had been promised, but that only meant having to wait in long lines. Government people meant that food, guns, ammunition, blankets, and sometimes money were going to be distributed. Her people did not run away from gifts.

"Why are you afraid?"

"They have come to take us."

"Take who? Where?" Nothing he was saying made sense.

His breathing had grown steady enough that he was able to speak without panting. "They say they have built schools that will help Indian children learn to live in the white man's world."

"What kind of schools?"

"I overheard two of them talking to each other as I hid behind our cabin," Hanging Leaf said. "One said she could not wait to clean us up and cut off our braids."

Oh my! The reason behind his terror became clear to her. It was one thing to wear white man's clothing. Many of the men and women had various articles of clothing they wore because a color appealed to them or because they were fascinated with brass buttons or simply needed covering for warmth.

But it was another thing to have hair like a white man.

An Indian boy or man who had short hair was considered a coward, and he would be ridiculed mercilessly by the others for it.

No doubt the government workers thought they would just be tidying the boy up. They probably had no idea they would be destroying his reputation as a man. Perhaps a few words from someone who had lived in the white world and yet understood the Chippewa culture would help.

But would they truly take the children away? She had not known the schools were ready yet. When she'd heard about them, she thought this time would only come several years from now.

"Stay here. Rest and hide. I will go try to talk some sense into these people."

She was not expecting the chaos she saw as she drew near to the village.

Children were crying and clinging to their mothers, who were looking as wild-eyed as Hanging Leaf. The braves had gone on a hunt, and the older boys like Hanging Leaf had all disappeared. Their chief, an elderly man with only a few words of English at his command, was trying to talk to three bored-looking white people. Two men and one woman.

"You go. Talk." Fallen Arrow grabbed little Standing Bear out of her arms and shoved her toward the chief and government people. "Get this stopped."

Moon Song did not need her grandmother's urging. She could tell that something bad was happening and hoped that her fluency in English could serve her people.

"Can I help you, Uncle?" she asked in Chippewa to their frustrated chief.

"I think they have come for the children," he said. "I cannot tell. They use words I cannot understand."

Moon Song turned to the white people. "Please forgive the confusion in my village. Our chief has few English words. He, and others, think that you have come to steal our children."

The man who seemed to be the leader snorted in contempt. "We aren't coming to steal anything. We merely want to take some of the children away to help give them a better life. We have a beautiful new boarding school built at great expense to house a certain amount of Indian children. We have teachers who will not only teach them how to speak English but also teach them how to be productive citizens with manual skills that will help them make a living. They will be fed, clothed, and educated. We are not stealing children, we are helping them."

Moon Song's heart plummeted. The rumors she had heard were true.

"Where will the children sleep? With their parents?" She hoped she was misunderstanding what he was saying. She hoped this was simply yet another day school. Some churches had been known to set up a day school for Indian children, but they got to go home overnight.

"No," he said. "That's the whole point. We want these children to learn English as their first language, not as their second. We want to teach them how to be self-sufficient and not have to rely on the government for handouts anymore. It is the government's intention to turn them into productive citizens."

She saw him glance around at the village with disgust. One mother sat in front of her cabin, within hearing distance of the conversation, nervously pulling lice out of her three-year-old daughter's long hair. The child's face was dirty, as was the mother's.

What the government worker didn't realize was that it was hard keeping little hands and faces perfectly clean all the time when one lived close to the earth and cooked over open fires.

"Where is this school?" she asked.

"Oh, it is over in Pennsylvania." A woman in a dress that looked elaborate and expensive broke into the conversation. Moon Song figured she was one of those do-gooder women Delia had warned her about. Someone with too much time on their hands, Delia had called them. Always meddling in someone else's life.

"The children will get a lovely train ride there." The do-gooder woman dabbed at her nose with a lacy handkerchief. "It will be quite educational."

"How often will they come home?"

Do-gooder woman had the grace to look a little embarrassed, and dabbed at her nose again. "Well, the train ride will be rather expensive. Probably not until they graduate." Her voice took on the enthusiasm of a true visionary. "But they will bring home wonderful skills that can help lift your people out of the poverty into which they've allowed themselves to sink."

Moon Song thought of the caches of food that she and her friends had made from the abundance of their limited forest. She had not felt particularly impoverished as she'd helped harvest and preserve the food that they'd grown.

"Give us time to think, please?" she asked the woman.

The woman's face took on an imperious expression. "Oh no. I don't think you understand. This is not an option. It is a government mandate. We are to extract one child from every family here to educate for the betterment of that family."

This went so far beyond cutting a boy's braids that the audacity of it took her breath away. What they were proposing would destroy their families and their tribe. So far, only the do-gooder woman and one man had spoken. The other government man had remained silent. She took his measure now. He was more muscular than the man who had spoken with her, and she saw that he was carrying two guns on him. He was there to enforce this new law with weapons if necessary.

If they tried to take the children right now, there would be bloodshed because the mothers would put up a fight. She was afraid that the life of a Chippewa mother would have little weight compared against filling a government-mandated quota.

"What are they saying?" the old chief asked.

"I will explain when they are gone, Uncle," she replied. "Please trust me for now."

He nodded, folded his arms, and waited.

"I have lived with whites," she said. "They treated me well. I know children need learning. My child is still small. When he is older, I will make sure he learns much from white man's books and ways."

She watched the three white people visibly relax. They thought she was on their side, which is exactly what she intended.

"If you take the children away now, many mothers will not understand the great good the government is trying to do for them. They will fight you, and bad feelings will come. Give me time to convince them why this school is a good thing. Give us time to make food and clothing for children's long journey."

"I'll give you two days," the man said.

"Pardon?"

"I'll give you two days to get the mothers convinced and the children ready. We'll be back on the morning of the third day. I expect one child from each family to be packed, dressed, and ready. If they are not, we will take the quota of children by force."

"It will take much talk to convince my people. I will need two weeks, not two days."

"Two days. Take it or leave it."

Moon Song's hand itched to reach into her boot, remove the knife, and make this arrogant dog beg for his life. Instead, she meekly nodded and agreed to his request. He had no idea how quickly she would act once he left.

The do-gooder woman, for whatever reason, felt it necessary to reach out and shake her hand. This was not a pleasant experience. Not only was the do-gooder woman's hand small and limp, it was also moist. Moon Song surreptitiously wiped her palm on the side of her skirt the minute the woman turned away.

As they left, she overheard the do-gooder woman say to the man who had talked, "But what if they aren't here when we come back?"

"Where else would they go?" His laughter was seasoned with derision.

If you only knew, Moon Song thought. If you only knew where we will go.

The minute the white people left, everyone gathered around her. Many had caught a word here or there and understood the gist of what was happening, but they wanted details.

After she had quickly explained what needed to happen, she sent the young women who were fleetest of foot to gather in the braves who were out hunting. Then she singled out Hanging Leaf, who had slunk back into the village with the other older boys.

"Choose one other boy from the village," she said. "Someone who is as fast as you. Run to the town of Rockland. Find the man there that our Chippewa cousins know as Big White Bear. His other name is Skypilot."

"And what do we tell him?" Hanging Leaf asked.

"Tell him that we need him here."

"What if he doesn't want to come?"

"Tell him that our village is in trouble and that Moon Song is calling for him." She felt a measure of pride in front of her village as she said, "You might have trouble keeping up with him on the journey back. That is how fast he will come to me."

"Boozhoo," Skypilot said the minute he saw Moon Song. She was quickly rolling up rush mats and tying them with twine. *"Aanii."*

She glanced up, smiled, and said in English, "Greetings and hello to you too! *Ani-ish na?*"

"I am fine, thank you for asking," he said. *"Gi zah gin."*

He had just told her that he loved her in Chippewa. It was one phrase he'd practiced over and over. Now, he saw the words sparkling in her eyes as well, but they did not come out her mouth.

"We have big work, Skypilot," she said. "You love me? Help me make my people disappear before we lose our children. I'm moving my village to the Huron Mountains, to my father's land. The government dogs will be surprised to find our village gone when they come back."

"The boys told me what has happened. I agree that these boarding schools are a bad idea, but are your people with you on this plan to move to your land? The Huron Mountains are many days' journey away."

"It is our only hope. They will come with me."

"I fear for the children in my tribe as well," he said.

"Your tribe?" She glanced at him, surprised.

It surprised him too, even as he spoke, that he had said the words "my tribe" as naturally as if he were truly a part of the people with whom he had been living.

Moon Song smiled. "You care about them."

"I do. They were kind to me and taught me much."

"Those who want to come with us will be welcome, although they will have to prepare themselves quickly. I will send one of our fastest braves back to them. In the meantime, you can help me prepare for the journey."

"Just show me what to do."

It struck him how wise the Lord's timing was sometimes when it least seemed like it. Being fired from his teaching job by Harvey Turney had infuriated him — but it had given him the freedom to leave the instant Moon Song needed him. Turney would not be as good of a teacher as Skypilot, but the white students needed his help less than the Chippewa children right now.

The other men of the tribe did not seem particularly surprised to see him there. He found out later that day that practically every move he had made the past two months had been discussed throughout the various groups of Chippewa.

Frankly, he did not think his life merited such interest.

As soon as those relatives from the other

tribe who wanted to accompany them arrived, the procession to the Hurons began. Moon Song's plan was simple. They walked into the forest with only what they could pack on their backs. The older people took turns riding Moon Song's mule when they tired. Sometimes the good mule held two or three small children, allowing their mothers a rest from the labor of carrying them.

Moon Song was loaded down like a mule herself, as were all the young women. The young men, however, carried only their weapons. This behavior had gone on for centuries and made some sense to Skypilot now. The men were there to protect and hunt, not to be drudges who carried the heavy loads. A warrior would fight to defend his woman, but he would not lighten her load. That was the way it had always been.

In this way, they made their way toward the Huron Mountains. Toward the land Moon Song's father had given her.

25

It was an early, unexpected snowstorm that slowed them down. A blizzard. Two days into their walk east across Upper Michigan from the western shores of Superior to the Huron Mountains, the snow had come. It was too soon for winter, but strange things sometimes happened this far north. Blizzards came, unexpectedly and deadly, sometimes in the fall. He was shocked, but the others were not.

The blizzard could not have come at a worse time. The tribe had several elderly and young ones to care for and at least another four days' walk. They needed shelter. A sturdy longhouse that could house the whole tribe would have been ideal, but there was no time to stop and build one — not with government people possibly on their heels.

There had been a time in his life when he would not have believed that Moon Song's tribe would need to run from the government. Now, however, he'd heard enough from the old ones in the tribe to know that it truly was better to run and hide than try to fight an elected leadership that viewed Indians as children who did not know what was good for them.

It bothered him that if the quota was not filled by Moon Song's tribe, it would be filled with another, but he could not protect all the Chippewa — only this tribe and those who had come from the one outside the Minnesota Mine. Keeping those two tribes safe and alive would be a great enough challenge.

They spent that first night in an old-growth pine forest that Skypilot scanned with a timberman's eyes and knew someday would probably delight some owner of a lumber camp. In the meantime, the tribe sheltered the best it could in the cold and damp.

It was during that night when they were all so cold and wet that Moon Song began to cough.

The snow did not let up. It snowed all day and all night for three days. There was a great deal of discussion among members of the tribe over what to do. If they stayed there, it might be spring before they dug out again. On the other hand, no one had ever seen it snow this much in October. It was a freak thing. It would stop. They would go on.

What if it didn't, others argued. What if it had settled in early to stay? The giant pines could hold back, to some extent, one or two light snowfalls. But they could not withstand steadily falling snow like they were getting right now. It was not unusual to get twenty-five to thirty feet of snow per winter in this area, and here they were, with no tipis, no wigwams, no longhouses, and only the food they could carry on their backs. Some of the men were debating the wisdom of having left.

Moon Song's generous offer to share her land was starting to look like a foolish idea compared to what they had left behind on the reservation. At least on the reservation, they could continue to stay alive, even if a few of the children had to go to a government school.

Moon Song could hear the mumbling, but it was as though from far away. She had developed a fever, and she found it hard to concentrate. Her cough was deepening. She ached all over. Visions of the white woman with her lacy handkerchief dabbing at her red-rimmed nose wove their way through her feverish thoughts, along with the feel of shaking the woman's moist hand.

She was terribly sick, and she knew it. Too sick to fight her tribe about which direction to go. They would have to decide if they wanted to go back to what they knew or forward several days' journey to a land none of them had seen and that existed solely on a paper that only Skypilot could read.

She didn't blame them, but she pitied the children and their mothers when finally more than half the tribe elected to go back and face the consequences rather than gamble on pushing on to the land she had wanted to share with them.

The old chief of her own tribe was torn. He would not command them; that was not the way their people worked out decisions. But she knew he was saddened at the idea of abandoning their plan. He had once been a great warrior and still had a warrior's heart, but sometimes it was hard to have a warrior's heart in an old man's body.

"I will only slow you down," he said. "I do not think I will see another winter. I will go back to my cabin in Ontonagon and there live or die. I have no children left to fight for. It is the young men's battle."

Many of the people left with him, turning

back to Ontonogan, back to what they knew.

By the time the chief made that decision, Moon Song was very ill.

"I can take you back, Moon Song," Skypilot said. "The government won't take little Standing Bear. Not yet. He's too young."

"No."

"We're much closer to the reservation than we are your father's property."

"No."

Fallen Arrow was bathing her face with snow, trying to keep down her fever. Standing Bear had been wrapped back into the cradle board and was not happy about it. He had begun to whimper for his mother, but Moon Song could not rouse herself to care for him.

Skypilot wondered if she had pneumonia, otherwise known as "the old man's friend" because it was a relatively quick and painless way for the elderly to die. Unfortunately, even though Moon Song was far from elderly, he knew that like the rest of her people, she had a weakness to the white man's diseases. A simple case of childhood measles could take her life.

"I want to leave now," Moon Song insisted.

"No, sweetheart." He'd rigged a canopy

of pine boughs over her to keep the snow out of her face. "Rest. Get well."

"I want to go now," she said. "I want to see my father's gift before I die. I want to know my people are safe."

"We need to turn back, Moon Song. Like some of the others have done. You're too sick to continue."

"I want to go on."

"Moon Song, please," Skypilot said. "Don't do this. Don't sacrifice yourself just to keep a handful of children from going to government schools. They'll be all right. We'll fight back in some other way. After you are well again."

"No. Children should not be taken from parents."

"Moon Song . . ."

"No!" Her feverish eyes blazed up at him. "If I perish, I perish!"

It was then that he knew he had permanently lost his argument. If Moon Song was quoting the book of Esther at him, a book he had read to her and Isabella after their steamboat exploded, there was no use trying to reason with her. Perhaps it was her own experience of being raised without a father or having been taken from her mother that steeled her resolve. Whatever it was, the woman was determined not to turn back, and he did not have the right or the heart to make her.

If Skypilot had thought that his trek with Moon Song and Isabella had been harsh, it was nothing compared to the next few desperate days. Moon Song was no longer able to carry Standing Bear. That became his job. Strangely enough, with Moon Song too sick to walk, Fallen Arrow grew stronger and stronger. He began to see why Moon Song had held her grandmother in such reverence. The old woman became as one made of granite as they pushed forward. Her love for her granddaughter was too great to allow her to show weakness now.

Fighting Sparrow's grandson and grand-daughter were both of school age, and she chose to push forward with them. Hanging Leaf's family came along too. Snowbird's only child was young enough to be carried on her back, and that young woman trudged forward as well, her husband at her side.

And it continued to snow.

Others with school-age children followed them, believing in Moon Song's promise that there would be a land that no one could take away from them.

From time to time, they stopped long enough to eat pemmican and rest. Little Standing Bear was old enough to eat the pemmican now. Skypilot and the other men scratched around in the snow long enough to find grass and weeds upon which the mule could forage. He did not have words big enough to express his gratitude to the Lord for having given him the desire to purchase this strong animal.

Moon Song continued to live, in spite of what sounded to him like her lungs filling up. Sometimes she coughed until she retched, and still she hung on. He began to wonder if she was conscious at all.

Finally, Fallen Arrow began to fade. The old woman who had been so valiantly trying to walk without faltering fell and lay without moving. She had given all she had and could walk no more. Moon Song did what few other women would have had the will to do. As ill as she was, she pulled herself off of the mule and made her grandmother climb on. Then for mile after mile, she walked beside the mule, one arm around its neck, the other around Skypilot's waist, nothing but sheer grit fueling her as she put one foot in front of the other.

He was certain that when she could no longer walk, she would crawl, so great was her desire to get her people to the land her father had promised her.

Finally, the time came when even her

great heart could not make her legs hold her any longer, and she collapsed. He was a strong man, but with one-year-old Standing Bear strapped to his back, it was a great struggle to carry her — and yet, carry her he did, and they trudged on.

He was surprised when Snowbird's husband made him stop long enough to lift Standing Bear's cradle board from his shoulders and put it on his own. This was highly unusual behavior for a Chippewa brave. Not once had Skypilot seen an Indian man carrying a cradle board, but he was grateful. Another brave then helped secure an unconscious Moon Song onto his back. With her weight distributed more evenly, he trudged on many more miles, steadying Fallen Arrow upon the mule, thankful to the men of her tribe for helping him.

He was grateful that she lay so close against his back. He could feel her breathing, and knew that at least for now she was still alive. He could not imagine surviving her death, but he kept putting one foot in front of the other, knowing that if she died, at least he had done everything within his ability and strength to take her to the land her father had saved for her.

"Hold on, sweetheart," he repeated over and over. "Hold on. We'll be there soon."

As he walked, he prayed harder than he had ever prayed before in his life. He prayed that she would survive, and that when they arrived, there would be some sort of shelter where he could care for her. To come into the promised land of the Huron Mountains with his girl deathly ill and find only more wilderness was too awful to consider.

And then, as far as he could calculate, they were there. He knew a small bit of surveying, and he knew how to read a deed and could judge distances. They crested a hill and he could see Lake Superior spread out before them.

"Look, sweetheart," he said, pointing at the giant expanse of water. "It's your lake. We're here. I think we're on your father's land."

Moon Song roused from her stupor. He could feel her lifting her head, looking out over the lake, and in a voice so soft it was barely a whisper, she said, "Oh, it is so beautiful!"

He untied the ropes that secured her to him, squatted, and allowed her to slip to the ground. He was so drained, he could think of little else except letting go and simply falling to the ground beside her. He was so exhausted that the idea of cradling her in his arms until they died together seemed the only thing left to do. Living without her was unimaginable.

It was then that he heard a gunshot, and a piece of bark flew off a tree near his head.

26

He was nearly too tired to care. If someone wanted to shoot him, so be it. His feet were half frozen anyway. Moon Song was not going to survive unless they got her shelter and a doctor.

The others barely twitched at the repeat of the rifle. They merely stood, like cattle. Dumb from exhaustion and cold. They had pushed so hard for so long. A trip that should have taken three or four days had turned into an eight-day trial of endurance and hardship and near starvation.

Now someone was shooting at them. The only weapon Skypilot carried was his axe, and it was strapped to the mule. He forced himself to try to reach for it.

"Stop!" a voice said.

Skypilot stopped.

A strange sight emerged from the woods — a man with wild hair and beard, dressed in ragged buckskin and rabbit fur badly sewn into a rough cape.

"I've been following you," the man said, keeping his rifle trained on Skypilot. "You're trespassing."

"I apologize," Skypilot said. "I thought we were in the right place."

"You're a white man. Why are you walking around with this band of Chippewa?"

"Trying to help them."

"Looks like you've been doing a poor job of it."

"True." Skypilot staggered but managed to right himself. "We meant no harm."

"What's wrong with that Indian girl?" The man motioned at her with his gun.

"She's sick. I think it's pneumonia."

"Are you her husband?"

"Not yet," Skypilot said. "Probably not ever unless we can get her into some sort of shelter. Either shoot me and be done with it or help me get her under a roof somewhere. Don't keep us standing here. These people have been through enough."

The man lowered the rifle and jerked his head to the east.

"I got a cabin over there a ways. You and her and the old woman can stay with me. Those people over there can make whatever use they can from the barn."

His spirits lifted slightly. "We're grateful

432

for whatever help you can give us."

The barn, when they got to it, was tight, well built, filled with hay, and compared to where they had been, downright cozy with the body heat of several farm animals. The rest of the tribe fell into the barn and sat there in a daze. The wild-looking man seemed troubled.

"I'll come out later and tend to them. Let's get the girl and the old woman inside."

It took every last bit of strength he had, but he lifted Moon Song, who was unconscious now, into his arms and carried her into the man's home.

The log cabin, when they entered it, was more spacious than he'd expected. It was not a one-room affair but had two bedrooms, one to each side, plus a loft.

"In here," the wild man said. "She can have my bed."

Skypilot gently laid her on the man's rope bed, and then he sat down on the floor at her side.

Fallen Arrow had collapsed onto a thick rug that was in front of the fireplace. It was humbling to Skypilot how completely at this stranger's mercy they were. He wished he'd been better at reading Moon Song's property title, but perhaps this was the Lord taking care of them. Instead of finding their way to Moon Song's land, they had found this man who might actually save their lives.

The first thing the man did was set a huge kettle of water to boiling on the fireplace, out of which he made cups of tea sweetened with real sugar. Skypilot sat with his back against Moon Song's bed, sipping the tea, trying to get his strength back while the man walked back and forth looking out at the weather.

They had barely made it here in time. The wind picked up once again and began to whistle around the corners of the cabin. The man appeared to make a decision. He left and came back from the barn with the rest of the tribe.

"It was getting too cold out there," the man said.

The people said little. Instead, they huddled around the pot while he poured more cups of tea. Although his cups were limited and they had to share, no one seemed to mind.

After everyone had warmed up with the hot liquid, the man added more water to the pot and then poured several pounds of beans into it along with some cut-up fatback and set it back to boiling.

"Kisinaa," Moon Song said through chattering teeth.

"She says she's cold," Skypilot explained. "Although I don't know how she could be. With that fire going, even I'm starting to sweat."

The man placed the palm of his hand on her forehead, and in so doing, brushed the tangled hair out of her face.

Skypilot heard a strangled gasp as the man got a full look at her face. He didn't understand. Moon Song was beautiful, but not to the point of making a man gasp in surprise.

"Dear God," the man said as though uttering a prayer. "Who have you brought to my door?"

"Her name is Moon Song." Skypilot said.

"Of course it is." The wild man's comment made no sense to Skypilot, but then nothing made a whole lot of sense right now.

He knew more about curing a fever than Skypilot did. He brought in snow from the outside, rolled it in oilcloth, and placed it under her neck and shoulders and beneath her arms and behind her knees. This he changed every few minutes until the fever cooled enough that he was able to bring a special drink to her.

"What is that?" Skypilot asked.

"The inner bark of the willow," the man said. "It's good for fevers and headaches."

"Where did you learn that?"

"From an old friend."

Suddenly Skypilot realized that in his haze of fatigue, he'd lost track of little Standing Bear. "Where is the baby?"

"One of the other Indian mothers is feeding him."

The man's answers were short and to the point but not unkind. As Skypilot watched him dribbling the willow bark water into Moon Song's mouth, he realized that he did not have to be strong for her any longer. He dragged himself off into a corner and fell into an exhausted sleep.

He slept deep and hard and when he awoke, it was to quiet laughter and the liquid sound of the Chippewa language. He stood up and saw that Moon Song was still unconscious but her teeth were no longer chattering. He walked over, felt her head, and found it cool to the touch. He almost panicked, thinking she had died, until he saw that she was breathing regularly. Then he opened the door and walked out to where the others were crowded together, eating beans out of a pot.

"I saved you some," Snowbird said in Chippewa as she handed him a bowl of beans with a large piece of fatback in the middle of it.

He realized he was ravenous, and downed

it in a few gulps. Then he saw what the laughter was all about. Standing Bear was doing a little stomp and dance step for the group.

"Where is Fallen Arrow?" he asked.

Snowbird nodded toward the fireplace. "She ate well and is now sleeping again. I think she will regain her strength."

"Where is the stranger who saved us?"

"He and my husband went out to tend to the livestock."

"Moon Song's fever has broken," he said. "She sleeps without coughing."

"Ah, that is what the white stranger said." She turned her attention back toward the enjoyment of watching Moon Song's son revel in all the attention.

The cabin was very crowded, and it was growing very warm. Even though it was still snowing, he stepped outside to breathe the fresh air.

"Do you love her?" He heard the wild man's voice behind him. It was a strange question to come from the lips of a virtual stranger, but then again, it had been a strange journey.

Startled, he turned around and realized that once again he was staring down the muzzle of the man's rifle.

"I'm getting very tired of this," Skypilot

said wearily. "Either kill me or put that thing away."

"Do you love her?" the man once again asked.

"Life would be a whole lot less complicated if I didn't, but yes, I love her. I love her more than my own life. Who *are* you anyway?"

"I'm the caretaker of this place," the man said.

"Then who's the owner?"

"From what I can tell," the man said, "it's that girl lying in there." He shook his head. "She sure does look like her mother."

Skypilot got cold chills down his back. "How do you know her mother?"

"Because I'm the one who killed her."

To Skypilot's utter astonishment, the man dropped his gun in the snow, fell to his knees, and covered his face.

27

"How's Moon Song?" Skypilot asked when he went back inside, with the rifle over his arm, unloaded and the ammunition safely in his pocket.

Fallen Arrow had awakened. "She's up and asking for you."

"I think there's someone here she needs to meet."

"Who?" Fallen Arrow asked. "There is no one here except us."

Skypilot did not answer. Instead he opened the bedroom door to Moon Song's room, where she lay curled up beside Standing Bear. She was conscious and was stroking the baby's face.

"How are you feeling?" he asked while the wild man stood beside him.

"Not well, but much better," she said. "I will try to get up soon. We cannot stay here forever."

"I don't know about that," Skypilot said.

"I think we probably could if we wanted to."

She sat up and looked at the two men. "What do you mean?"

"I was not wrong in my calculations after all," Skypilot said. "We're on your land. Right in the middle of it as a matter of fact."

"But why is he here?" she asked. "Are you a squatter? It is all right, if you are. You helped save my life. I will be happy to let you stay and share my father's land."

"No, it's your property and your cabin. I've just been the caretaker until you came."

"I don't understand," she said. "My father's letter said nothing about a caretaker or a cabin."

The man looked at Skypilot.

"Don't look at me," Skypilot said. "You tell her."

"My name is Benjamin Webster," the man said. "I'm your father."

Her eyes widened. "That can't be true. My father is dead."

"I thought I was dying when I wrote that letter," he said. "The doctors insisted that my problem was inoperable and irreversible. They suggested I get my affairs in order and then make myself comfortable and await death. I followed their orders exactly. Except for one thing. They expected me to go to my home in Boston to await death. Instead, I decided that if I had to die, I would prefer to do it where I could see my beloved lake and trees, the place where I'd been the happiest in my life. I bought a tent and a ticket on a steamboat and a little food. I climbed to the top of this mountain where I could see forever out into the lake, and I waited to die.

"I waited a very long time. One morning I decided that if I was going to die anyway, I might as well accomplish something while I was waiting. And so I walked to Marquette, bought some tools, and decided that I would start building a cabin for you so that you would have some shelter when you came. I built this cabin where it could be seen for miles; that way you could find it. I didn't expect to be able to do much, maybe fell a few trees, drag a few rocks over for the foundation. Except something strange happened. The more I worked, the stronger I felt. I was twenty when you were born. I just turned forty. I'm not young, but not so terribly old. Before long, I began to feel nearly as strong as I had when I was twenty and living here.

"It's the oddest thing. I don't know what happened. All I know is I'm still here. I can't explain it, and I certainly didn't mean to lie to you, but two weeks to live turned into two months, and now it's been nearly eighteen months and I never felt so strong and healthy in my life."

The man was standing at the foot of the bed as he told her all this. As he finished, he simply shrugged, and then became silent as he stared at the floor, apparently waiting for her to decide how she was going to react.

"Come here," she said.

The man walked over to her.

"Give me your hand."

He gave her his hand.

And then she did one of the sweetest things Skypilot had ever seen. She opened her father's hand, placed a kiss in the middle of it, and closed it back up. "Will you hold it tight forever?"

He watched as her father, with tears streaming down his face, got down on his knees, reached for her hand, lifted it palm up, placed a kiss in it, and closed it into a fist. "I held it tight, my little one, forever and ever, just like I promised the last time I saw you. I held it so tight it gave me life."

Skypilot could hardly bear it, the thought of his beloved Moon Song remembering the parting gesture of her father after all these years.

As Moon Song and her father embraced,

he remembered the first time he'd seen her — a young Indian girl with a baby. She had barely registered with him until he was hurt and she chose to take care of him. Who could ever have guessed all that had gone on in her life before he met her? How many other stories were waiting just outside this door?

It was not his place to watch this reunion. It was a holy thing and not for his eyes. He turned, left the room, and closed the door softly behind him.

28

The weather turned fine again, and as the wind from the lake swept over the woods, the trees shook off the snow like a retriever shaking off water. Moon Song's tribe did what it had done for centuries. They built a small village, foraged for food, explored their new land, and played with their children.

It took several weeks for Moon Song to regain her health. During this time, she and her father discussed their two lifetimes away from one another and spent much time talking together. Ben, as he liked to be called, enjoyed the miracle of getting to know his daughter and little grandson, while Skypilot worked with the Chippewas as they erected sturdy wigwams to get their tribe through the true winter that would come soon.

Fallen Arrow, who had hated long and hard this man who had innocently been at the root of her daughter's death, accepted the truth of his faithful heart, and although she could not forgive him completely, she tolerated him well enough when she saw the joy her granddaughter took in having her father once again in her life.

It was too late for the tribe to forage and preserve all the food they would need to get through the winter, so Skypilot and Ben made several trips to Marquette with the mule and two of Ben's horses to purchase and bring back provisions. Ben was generous with his remaining funds, and Skypilot felt content that this was one winter when the elders would not have to go hungry so that the children could eat.

He was also content with watching Moon Song grow strong and helping the tribe prepare itself for winter. He did not press for marriage or try to spend much time alone with her. He sensed that she needed time to absorb all that had happened, and he derived great pleasure in watching her and her father's relationship grow and heal. Having finally found himself in Fallen Arrow's good graces, he set about learning as much as possible from her about the Chippewa culture.

Fallen Arrow was a walking encyclopedia of their beliefs, their legends, and their medicines. Memorizing had always come easy for him, and the things Fallen Arrow was teaching him were important, so he applied himself to remember as many things as possible. When she was gone, he knew that many of the old ways would die with her unless he could preserve them. On one of his trips to Marquette, he purchased paper and ink and began to commit her teachings not only to memory but to paper. The more he learned, the more he found himself admiring the Chippewa people.

With so much to build and do, it was the end of November before Skypilot and Moon Song found themselves truly alone again. Moon Song had gone out to set some rabbit snares. When she did not return by nightfall, he grew concerned and went looking for her.

He found her sitting on a rock overlooking the great lake. She looked especially beautiful bathed in the light of the full moon.

"So, did you get all your snares set?" he asked as he sat down beside her.

"I did." She did not seem startled by his sudden presence. Instead, she leaned comfortably against him, and he put his arm around her waist. "Tomorrow I will see if I caught anything. You were worried about me?"

"A little," he admitted. "But I also missed you and wanted an excuse to come find you. This feels nice."

"I was planning to come in soon." She snuggled closer. "I was growing cold, but now you are my campfire."

"What were you thinking about, sitting out here all alone?"

"I was enjoying the sight of the full moon on the water, and I was thinking about my father."

"Which moon is this, by the way?" he asked.

"This is what the Chippewa call the Freezing Moon."

"That's appropriate. I saw a skiff of ice on the stream behind your father's cabin this morning." He paused. "What were you thinking about him?"

"He is a good man, I think. Much like you."

"Thank you." It felt so good holding her. He was grateful for this small bit of privacy. "I'm glad you feel that way."

She turned to look at him and her eyes were troubled. "My father has very strong beliefs from the Bible. Much like yours."

"I know. We've talked at some length on our trips to Marquette," he said. "He told me that he became a man of faith by trying

447

to become the exact opposite of his father."

"He would like for me to share that faith." Moon Song's voice grew small. "But I cannot."

His heart nearly stopped. He had known about Ben's discussions with Moon Song and had backed off, thinking it was her father's place to teach her.

"Why?"

"I can believe the old stories like the one you read me on our journey, about Noah and the flood and Queen Esther. I do not have any trouble at all believing in a God who is a Creator of the world. The God you speak of sounds a great deal like our Gitche Manido — the Creator of everything. I can even admire the wise teachings of the man called Jesus."

"But?"

"But we have had many wise Chippewa teachers too." She laid her hand gently over his. "I know it would please both you and my father if I could believe that this Jesus you worship is the Son of the Great Creator, but I cannot. I'm so sorry. I just cannot."

This was so blunt, Skypilot felt his world crumble. He would love her forever, but the words in the Bible about not being unequally yoked to an unbeliever had been bothering him ever since he had fallen in

448

love with her.

He'd hoped if he prayed hard enough and lived a good enough example before her, God would change her heart and convict her of the rightness of the message of salvation that Christ had given them. He'd hoped that her father's teachings would sway her, but it had not.

He knew she would marry him if he asked. His own steadfast love added to her father's faithfulness had erased the doubts she had toward all white men. If he asked her to marry him now, he was certain she would say yes.

The problem was . . . his faith had defined who he was for most of his life. If he did not believe in the resurrection of Christ, he would be a very different man. If he married Moon Song, they would become one, not only in body but in mind and spirit. Could he marry a woman who believed his Jesus was no better than one of the Chippewa wise men?

His head told him no. His heart told him yes. His common sense told him that it would be an uphill struggle.

Dear Lord, what can I say? What can I do? How can I give this woman up after coming so far with her?

He stared silently at the reflection of the

moon on the water. A heavy cloud passed between them and the moon, and they were thrown into darkness — a darkness that matched his spirit. A Scripture came into his mind but it was one he'd not contemplated for many years.

"You are so quiet," Moon Song said. "What are you thinking?"

"I was thinking about a Scripture from the Gospel of Luke about a great darkness."

Moon Song leaned her head back against his chest. "Tell me."

" 'And it was about the sixth hour,' " he quoted. " 'And there was a darkness over all the earth until the ninth hour. And the sun was darkened, and the veil of the temple was rent in the midst.' "

"What do those words mean?"

"Luke is describing the crucifixion of Jesus. The people were watching him die. Some were happy, and some — like his friends and family — were grieving. The Bible says there was a great darkness that came over all the earth in the middle of the day and lasted for about three hours."

"I have seen that happen," Moon Song said. "When the moon blots out the sun."

"My people call it a solar eclipse," Sky-pilot said. "The moon gets between the sun and the earth and it gets very dark. But that isn't what happened the day Jesus died."

"How do you know?"

"Because he was crucified during the Jewish celebration of the Passover, which was one of their major feast days."

He thought back to his seminary training.

"The Jewish Passover was always held on the fourteenth of Nisan, the middle day of the moon cycle, the day on which a full moon — like the one we're seeing now — would be visible in the evening sky."

"The covered suns that I've seen never happen when there is a full moon in the sky," Moon Song said. "Grandmother taught me this the last time we had a great darkness during the day."

"That's because when a moon is full, it is about half a million miles out of place for it to blot out the sun. It's on the opposite side of the earth."

"Then the day your Jesus died, it was impossible for the moon to get between the earth and the sun?"

"Yes. There had to be another reason for there to be such a great darkness for three hours."

Moon Song grew agitated and turned to face him again. "How can you know for sure any of this happened?"

It had been a long time since Skypilot had

reason to be grateful for the education he'd gotten, but he was grateful for it now.

"Actually, there was a Roman historian named Thallus who lived at the same time of Jesus. He wrote about the crucifixion of Christ too. Except he was not a Christian, so he tried to explain the three-hour darkness away by saying it was caused by a solar eclipse."

"But he was wrong?"

"Yes. Thallus was wrong. I believe the darkness had to be miraculous."

"And you believe this Jesus died and came back to life?"

"I do. There were too many people who saw him in the flesh afterward. Not one of them ever took back their story that he rose from the dead, not even those who were tortured to death. The gospel stories are signed in their blood."

"Skypilot?" Moon Song's voice was thoughtful.

"Yes."

"Can you prove that Jesus is more than a story, that he truly is the Son of God and not just a trickster like our stories about Gitche Manido's son, Nanabozho?"

Skypilot thought about that question for a long time before he answered. "No, Moon Song. I wish I could prove it, but I can't."

His arm tightened around her waist. "I'll tell you one thing, though — I'm betting my life on it."

"I must think about this," she said.

Another passage came unbidden to his lips as the dark cloud scudded away, leaving the full moon shining brightly once again.

" 'The heavens declare the glory of God,' " he quoted. "And the firmament sheweth his handiwork.' "

Moon Song looked up into the sky. "I have been told that the moon was full the night I was born, the night my grandmother sang to me."

Skypilot could not help but hope that the song of the moon — the song of God's miraculous firmament — might reach her tonight and enable her to feel the reality of Christ's love and sacrifice.

He suddenly realized that he had been a selfish man. He had hoped that Moon Song would become a Christian so that he would feel free to marry her, but there was so much more at stake than that. This precious girl who had been through so much, deserved to feel not just the assurance of her earthly father's love, she deserved to feel the depth of God's eternal love for her as well.

His own love, although strong, was small

compared to that.

He had sadly underestimated Moon Song's brilliant mind and tenacious spirit. The woman gave him no peace for months. With his help, she achieved a mastery of the written word, which she then applied to reading the Bible her father had left behind for her in that tin box. Sometimes it felt to Skypilot like she was peppering him with more questions than any mortal man could handle. It took every bit of knowledge he had to keep up with her.

Some of the questions made him uncomfortable because they challenged things he had been taught by others and had accepted without question. Unlike him and her father, as Ben pointed out, she was not reading the Bible through stained-glass windows. Everything was new to her. Skypilot found some of his own beliefs drifting into new ways of seeing, and after deciding that this was a good thing, he began to relax and enjoy the spiritual adventure that Moon Song was taking him on. His admiration for her grew daily.

God was faithful. There came a day the following July when Skypilot waded into the waters of Lake Superior with Moon Song. With a heart bursting with love and gratitude, he baptized his bride-to-be into the body of Christ. Two weeks later, they were married standing on the crest of the mountain in front of the cabin her father had built.

They had sent word to Father Slovic to come marry them, and although Skypilot knew that most Catholic priests would not have done so without a certain amount of catechism, Slovic was a law unto himself in these parts, and he had evidently decided to leave well enough alone.

Skypilot had no doubt, nor did Moon Song's father, that the prognosis of the doctors that he had only weeks to live when he came here had been correct, but evidently the Lord had other plans for him. Or perhaps he recovered because he'd been able to let go of some of the hatred he'd carried for so long.

Her father had not killed her mother, but he'd blamed himself for it to the point that he felt like he was completely responsible. Over the winter, Skypilot and Moon Song helped him realize that he'd been a victim of his father almost as much as she. They never did learn who had been responsible for her mother's murder. They decided that for everyone's sake, it was something that needed to be left alone. It was a rough land they lived in. After sixteen years there was a good chance that whoever had taken money to kill Moon Song's mother was no longer alive.

One thing they all had grown to realize was that hatred could do terrible things to the person who did the hating, and they determined to start a fresh life together.

Father Slovic's home was not terribly far from Moon Song's land, and he had brought along a rather surprising wedding guest.

"Isabella!" Skypilot exclaimed.

It took him a minute to recognize her. She was wearing men's britches and hiking boots. She carried a rucksack of some sort, which he found out later was filled with artist supplies.

She looked rested, happy, at peace.

"I came to sketch your wedding, Skypilot," she said. "It's the least I can do after all you and Moon Song did for me."

"Are you feeling, ah . . ." He wasn't sure how to politely ask if she felt any desire to take little Standing Bear and run.

"I have my own children now." She laughed softly and gave him a hug. "I won't be trying to borrow Moon Song's baby ever again. I promise."

Her own children? It had been less than a

year since they had last seen her. He glanced at Slovic, hoping for clarification.

"Her husband had created a small family with an Indian woman before he met Isabella. He abandoned them. Isabella did not. The mother was having a terrible struggle raising them before she succumbed to diphtheria. One of the men at the fort contacted me, and I contacted Isabella, who stepped in."

"Where are they?" Skypilot asked.

"Royally entertaining Mrs. Veachy, unless I miss my guess," Isabella said. "They are little scamps and I love them to pieces. Do you want to see their pictures?"

"Pictures? I would love to."

From her rucksack, she produced a small booklet that she had filled with sketches. As she named and pointed out each of the three children, he could hear the pride and joy in her voice.

"I'm so happy for you, Isabella."

"I'm not happy that their mother is no longer here," Isabella said. "But I am happy that I can do the Lord's work in providing for and loving them."

"Where do the four of you live?" he asked.

"Not far from Father Slovic and Mrs. Veachy," Isabella said. "I support myself by drawing detailed pictures of the various tribes that Father Slovic introduces me to. I sell them to one of his friends, an art collector, who has taken a shine to my drawings and says he's creating the greatest collection of authentic images of Indian life in North America."

"Do you enjoy this work?" Skypilot asked.

"More than you can ever know," Isabella said. "Truly, Skypilot. I know I lost my mind for a while, but I'm all right now. I'll always miss my little one, but the ache no longer makes me wild with pain. Now I have my other little ones to think of. I know it was a strange gift that my husband left me, and I realize that he was not a good man, but sometimes the Lord can make something good out of something bad. The children are innocent of wrongdoing, and so am I. There is no reason on earth I should not enjoy being a mother to them. Now, where is your lovely bride, and where is the marriage ceremony going to be? I want to set up my easel."

The marriage ceremony was simple and brief. Almost a letdown compared to the hours and hours Moon Song spent on preparing a proper bridal dress for herself. It was quite beautiful, perhaps the most beautiful she had ever seen. The beadwork was exquisite. The nearly white doeskin as soft as butter. She and her grandmother worked on it for weeks. The headdress alone was a work of art.

It was worth every bead and every pricked finger to see the look on Skypilot's face when she walked toward him and Slovic. She saw his quick intake of breath, and his eyes widen with appreciation as she approached. As for herself, she had to blink away the tears that kept threatening to spill she was so happy.

So many miles they had walked together, so many obstacles they had overcome to find themselves at this point. She had tried to keep herself from loving this man, but in the end, her love for him had been the one thing she could not overcome. They were meant to be together, and no one or nothing but death itself would ever be able to tear them apart.

She knew this to be true because Skypilot had promised her, and he was one man who did not lie.

The service the Jesuit read was not in her language, nor Skypilot's, nor even in the bit of French she knew. It was a language, as far as she could tell, unique to the priest and that mattered little. She knew she was pledging her heart to Skypilot and he was pledging his life to her, and that was all that mattered.

As the priest pronounced them husband and wife, Moon Song felt a profound feeling of security wash over her. It was done. She was married to a man named Skypilot who, appropriately enough, had helped her navigate the sky, giving her a glimpse of a hope bigger and better than anything she had imagined — a God who was no trickster like Nanabozho but who had come to earth and conquered death solely because of his love for her and the rest of humanity.

She was, at this moment, the happiest woman on the face of the earth. The oil painting that Isabella left behind, propped upon the mantel to dry, was an astonishing portrait of a woman who had seldom seen an image of herself. She was truly beautiful, and Skypilot . . . oh the love that was in his face for her and in hers for him.

Isabella laughed when she exclaimed over that fact. "Ah," Isabella had said, "I saw that look in his eyes from the beginning, even when you were wet and bedraggled and half frozen."

A few days after the wedding, Moon Song realized that she was seeing less and less of her father. He seemed to be always in need of something from Marquette. Skypilot informed her that from what he could tell, Ben Webster had become quite smitten with Isabella's house full of children, her easel, and her easy smile.

Moon Song decided that she could live with that. Even if it meant having Isabella as a stepmother someday. Her father deserved a second chance at life. He had certainly given up enough of his own to create a second chance for her.

EPILOGUE

Three years after Moon Song and Skypilot's marriage, the government workers found the small tribal village on top of the mountain and insisted they were to take a quota of the Chippewa children to the boarding school for Indians in Mt. Pleasant, Michigan.

Standing Bear was not yet of school age, but still, for a moment, Moon Song again felt the fear of having her child taken away from her. That was, until her husband informed them that the children of the village were already under his tutelage along with three other teachers.

He introduced himself as an instructor of English and theology. He introduced his mother-in-law, the now famous Isabella Webster, as artist-in-residence who was teaching the children the fundamentals of drawing and painting. He introduced Fallen Arrow as a teacher of natural biology, herbalism, and native culture.

Moon Song's father, Benjamin Webster, Skypilot quietly introduced as an excellent mathematics instructor as well as a trained attorney-at-law who would, if necessary, take the matter all the way to the Supreme Court if they laid one finger on the children of their village. Then he informed them that they were on private property but were welcome to tour the excellent school facilities whenever they wished.

The government workers took note of the sturdy buildings, warmly dressed, well-fed children, and hawk-like eyes of the attorney, and they never came back.

Theirs was a prosperous tribe, but they kept their prosperity a closely guarded secret.

Moon Song's father, although a foolish young man at one time, had turned out to be rather excellent at judging land and minerals. Something he neglected to tell his father.

After the government workers left, she and little Standing Bear each took a flat tin pan with a curved lip and walked a mile from their village until they came to a small stream.

Standing Bear dug several handfuls of the black sand and placed it into his pan. Then he swirled the water around and around. This was a favorite form of play to him, and to her while the older children were at school.

"Am I doing it right, Mother?" he asked.

"Tip it a little more, son," she said. "Let just a bit of the soil wash away each time."

"I found one!" He triumphantly held up a small, rough pebble that shone in the sunlight.

"Yes, you did." She put the tiny pebble into a small pouch that she kept tied to her waist. Then she went back to washing the black sand out of her own pan. It was pleasant work when the weather was fine. Frequently she brought a small picnic and they stayed all day.

No. Her father was no fool. He had chosen his land wisely and very, very quietly. He had not purchased land near the mountains of copper that marched up the western side of the Keweenaw Peninsula. Nor had he chosen land near the mines of Iron Mountain.

Instead, he'd chosen the relatively unnoticed land of the Huron Mountains.

"Mother," Standing Bear said, "I found another pretty yellow rock for your collection."

"Very pretty, little one." She took the

small, shiny nugget from his hand. It was not big enough to be worth a lot, but then, they didn't need a lot. Her people had always lived simply.

Soon, there would be enough for her father to make another quiet, discreet trip on a train, carrying her pouch with him, and monies would be deposited into a private account, and then he would come home and they would go back to living the way they had chosen to live.

They had all learned a great deal. The best lesson of all was that gold, real gold, true gold, was found only within the hearts of those who loved.

AUTHOR'S NOTE

Many years ago, the mother of a friend showed me an old photo of her great-great-grandmother who was full-blooded Cherokee. I was fascinated and wanted to know more, but she knew little about her. I gathered that there had been some shame in having a native mother and grandmother and that in her later years, the native woman had been kept hidden.

Her name was Moon Song.

That name has haunted me for years. Such a beautiful, hopeful name to give a baby girl.

When a Native American was needed as a minor character in my first book of the Michigan historical series, *The Measure of Katie Calloway,* I asked for permission from the family to use Moon Song's name. Little did I know that her story would eventually take over an entire book.

I had one idea in mind for her story, but

my Moon Song character had another. Moon Song had some things to tell me, and I listened. The more I researched, the more the book changed from the simple, sweet love story I had planned of Moon Song and Skypilot traveling north together to her home. Things cried out to be included that I had not known when I began her story.

The forced boarding schools were a dark time in our country's history and ended, to my shock, within my own lifetime. "Kill the Indian, Save the Child" was a famous rallying call.

The scene of Moon Song's father hiring men to hold her mother back as he boarded the ship with their child happened in real life. White fathers did wrest their children away from native mothers. "Country marriages" between white men and native women were common and had little to no legal weight. One real-life heroine I discovered in my research was a white "legal" wife who insisted on supporting her husband's native "country wife" and his children long after his death. I enjoyed redeeming Isabella by giving her that choice.

Other heroes in my eyes were those many white men who honored their "country marriages" and stayed the course, living out their lives where their native wives would be accepted and happy.

Reading about the slow dissolution in the 1700s and 1800s of the Native Americans' ability to support themselves because of their increasing dependence on foreign goods, and their eventual dependence on government subsidies, was extremely disturbing and forced me to draw a parallel with our society's similar modern-day dependence.

One bright spot in my research was my discovery of a Jesuit priest named Father Baraga, otherwise known as the "Snowshoe Priest," who traveled hundreds of miles each winter throughout the Upper Peninsula. He was a welcome guest in every wigwam, longhouse, or cabin. He was revered by Native Americans and whites alike and died the year my story begins. Father Slovic is a thinly disguised representation of the man I imagined Father Baraga to be.

Although I personally entered the depths of an 1800s-era Keweenaw copper mine, I did not, in the end, have the heart to force Skypilot to work down there, although that had been my initial intent. I thought his time would be better spent trying to take control of an unruly, divided classroom of American, Cornish, and Irish children.

Steamships did blow up, catch fire, collide

with one another, and sink at an alarming rate on the Great Lakes. Skypilot, Moon Song, and Isabella's plight at Painted Rocks Lakeshore is based on a story I heard while sailing along that coast, of a man and woman being the only survivors in that area after a similar accident.

Also, even though there have never been any truly productive gold mines in Michigan (the Ropers Mine did produce for a short while, and there are rumors of others opening in the future), I was surprised to learn that there have been at least two purported discoveries of gold mines in the Huron Mountains that have been lost and never again found. I like to think that Moon Song and her little boy had a wonderful life playing in the streams of the Huron Mountains, panning for gold, quietly surface-mining one of those lost discoveries.